Legal Eagles vs. Deadly Testimony

"Hung Jury" *by Jack Ritchie*
The term "hung jury" takes on a chilling new meaning when a bumbling, but brilliant detective uncovers the shocking truth behind the suspicious suicides of three members of a jury who let a killer go. . . .

"The Decision" *by Joe L. Hensley*
The fate of a woman accused of poisoning her husband and child is in the hands of a highly regarded judge, but the memories hidden in the recesses of his mind may sway his verdict more than any evidence can. . . .

"A Matter of Conscience" *by Gary Alexander*
A dedicated public defender is told to go through the motions when he gets the case of a boy accused of murdering his parents, but he's ready to risk his own future to fight for a troubled child's life. . . .

"The Lie Detector" *by James McKimmey*
The murder of a famous movie director leads to the arrest of his beautiful, young sixth wife for the crime. Her renowned attorney is losing her case until his assistant dreams up an ingenious defense . . . and maybe the real killer's identity.

AND TEN MORE CASES OF
MURDER ON TRIAL

MYSTERY ANTHOLOGIES

☐ **MURDER ON TRIAL** *13 Courtroom Mysteries By the Masters of Detection.* Attorney and clients, judges and prosecutors, witnesses and victims all meet in this perfect locale for outstanding mystery fiction. Now, subpoenaed from the pages of *Alfred Hitchcock's Mystery Magazine and Ellery Queen Mystery Magazine*—with the sole motive of entertaining you—are tales brimming with courtroom drama.
(177215—$4.99)

☐ **ROYAL CRIMES, New Tales of Blue-Bloody Murder, by Robert Barnard, Sharyn McCrumb, H. R. F. Keating, Peter Lovesey, Edward Hoch and 10 others. Edited by Maxim Jakubowski and Martin H. Greenberg.** From necromancy in the reign of Richard II to amorous pussyfooting by recent prime ministers, heavy indeed is the head that wears the crown, especially when trying to figure out whodunit . . . in fifteen brand new stories of murder most royal.
(181115—$4.99)

☐ **MURDER FOR MOTHER by Ruth Rendell, Barbara Collins, Billie Sue Mosiman, Bill Crider, J. Madison Davis, Wendy Hornsby, and twelve more.** These eighteen works of short fiction celebrate Mother's Day with a gift of great entertainment . . . a story collection that every mystery-loving mama won't want to miss.
(180364—$4.99)

☐ **MURDER FOR FATHER 20 Mystery Stories by Ruth Rendell, Ed Gorman, Barbara Collins, and 7 More Contemporary Writers of Detective Fiction.** Here are proud papas committing crimes, solving cases, or being role models for dark deeds of retribution, revenge, and of course, murder.
(180682—$4.99)

*Prices slightly higher in Canada

MURDER ON TRIAL

Courtroom Mysteries
from *Ellery Queen's
Mystery Magazine* and
*Alfred Hitchcock's
Mystery Magazine*

EDITED BY

Cynthia Manson

A SIGNET BOOK

Contents

Introduction

Murder on Trial is a collection of stories from *Alfred Hitchcock's Mystery Magazine* and *Ellery Queen's Mystery Magazine* in which most of the action takes place in a courtroom but justice does not always prevail. Over the years, mystery readers have been fascinated with the American judicial system. Readers like to uncover the ways in which lawyers attempt to manipulate the system to their clients' advantage and to discover how the courts protect the innocent and the guilty. This book offers a wide variety of stories that portray prosecutors, defenders, judges, jurors, witnesses, and the accused in many different guises.

For example, in Henry Slesar's "Hanged for a Sheep" the main character is an attorney who cleverly influences his client for self-serving reasons. Outside the courtroom, we see people take the law into their own hands so justice will be served, demonstrated in "P." by Robert Twohy and "The Lie Detector" by James McKimmey. Witnesses are used by attorneys to manufacture evidence that will affect the jury's final ruling, as is skillfully illustrated in "The Auteur Theory" by Jon L. Breen and "Witness for the Defense" by Helen Nielsen. At the other end of the spectrum, a lawyer is conned by his clients in "The Affair of the Reluctant Witness" by Erle Stanley Gardner, and a judge and jury are misled by a character witness in "Money Talks" by Cornell Woolrich.

Enjoy this entertaining collection of courtroom mysteries in which the legal system is viewed from every angle and the line between the innocent and the guilty takes on new shades of gray.

—Cynthia Manson

Witness for the Defense

Helen Nielsen

The woman in the hall sat alone on a backless wooden bench, her cotton-gloved fingers laced over a large pouch bag, her sensibly shod feet set flat on the marble floor, her ramrod-straight back stressing the seams of a heavy tweed ulster purchased before the added weight of middle-age, and her Viking-grim face staring ahead at the soiled plaster wall with eyes that saw nothing—and remembered much. Her name was Martha Lindholm, and she was the sole witness—with the exception of three psychiatrists—for the defense of Larry Payne.

Larry Payne was a murderer. He was twenty-three years old, handsome in a weak, boyish way, and only partially aware of what was happening to him. It had been a complicated trial, so full of legal ramifications that the once sensation-hungry spectators gradually lost interest, and the press, represented by three locals and one correspondent from San Francisco, had to tax their imaginations to make readable copy for the daily editions.

Now the trial was almost over. The double doors leading to the courtroom of Superior Court Judge Dwight Davis were closed; behind them an empty chamber awaited the return of a jury which would decide if Larry Payne were to live or die. The jury had filed out at four P.M. It was now ten minutes past midnight.

Except for the woman on the bench, the hall was empty. All was silent outside the press room where four newsmen and one female observer from the Department of Sociology at the local university lingered over a stale game of draw poker.

The female sociologist raked in the pot.

"Beginner's luck," Mark Christy growled.

"The superiority of science over the seat of the pants," she said crisply. "The coming age, Mr. Christy. You romantics will soon be obsolete."

Her name was Lisa Wyman. She was about twenty-eight and would have been pretty, Mark Christy conceded grudgingly, if she hadn't been so scientific. He rubbed a handful of fingers through his unromantically thinning hair and shoved back his chair.

"Wounded?" Lisa asked.

"Weary," Mark said.

He came to his feet and walked across the room to a filing cabinet that stood near the hall doorway. On it was a thermos of coffee. He picked up a paper cup and glanced at the wall clock.

Morrie Hamlin of the *Herald* had sharp eyes. "You lose again," he said. "It's after midnight and still no verdict. You said it would take only two hours."

"I said," Mark answered acidly, "that no twelve sane adults would waste more than two hours before finding Payne guilty."

"The voice of retribution," Lisa intoned, "and after all those weeks of professional testimony!"

The other men in the poker game were Sam Jorgens, editor of a county weekly, and young Ed Combs on his first assignment since graduation.

"Please, teacher," Sam asked, "what did all that technical jargon mean? Poor Larry didn't have all the love and kisses and bright sunlight he needed when he was a little boy. Well, who did?"

"Dr. Wyman's right," Ed Combs insisted. "Payne's a sick man."

Mark Christy held the paper cup under the spigot of the thermos and filled it to the brim. "I'd be sick too," he said, "if I'd stuck a knife in a prison guard. Larry-boy can't be such a martyred saint or he wouldn't be in a place where they have guards."

"Payne was sent up on a charge of statutory rape," Combs reminded. "You know what that means."

"He didn't get a life sentence for statutory rape. He tried the knife at least once before he killed that guard."

Sam Jorgens was a philosopher. "Lincoln's doctor's dog," he observed. "I've got ten dollars that says Jay Bellamy gets an acquittal for Payne—not because of the head-shrinkers, but because of the corn he pitched to the jury." Sam's voice dropped mockingly. "Larry's parents abandoned him—he was left with a maiden aunt—somebody killed his little dog—"

"A dog he loved deeply," Lisa Wyman interrupted. "A child has to love."

"And he couldn't love Old Stone Face," Combs added. "Who could? Can you imagine what would happen if a man came near her?"

There was still a tinge of adolescent arrogance in Ed Combs's laughter. Mark Christy stood in the doorway with the cup of coffee in his hand. His eyes found the hall and the woman on the bench sitting exactly as she'd been sitting these many hours.

"She's still out there," Mark said softly.

"Knitting?" Lisa asked.

"Knitting? Why?"

"Madame La Farge knitted."

Ed Combs tittered appreciatively.

"I don't think that's fair," Mark said. "She did come all the way from Dallas to testify for Payne." He turned away from the hall and looked back over his shoulder. Lisa Wyman was dealing another hand.

"I have two children," she said. "If they were in trouble, I'd fight for them—and I mean *fight*! But that woman out there has no emotion at all—not a drop."

"If that's true—if she doesn't care what happens to Payne—what is she waiting for?" Mark demanded.

"The payoff," Combs said. "She got stuck with an unwanted kid twenty years ago—"

"I asked Dr. Wyman!"

There was enough late-hour irritation in Mark's voice to cause a momentary freeze. Then Sam Jorgens grinned.

"You didn't lose that much, Mark," he scolded. "Come on, pick up your hand and we'll give you a chance to break even."

Mark ignored the invitation.

"Why is she waiting?" he challenged Lisa Wyman again.

"Mr. Combs may be right," Lisa said, "although I'm inclined to think it's an expression of guilt. She has to punish herself for her failure to be a woman."

"Couldn't she be waiting out of love for Payne?"

"You heard her testify. Did she speak one loving word? Did she show one sign of compassion?"

There was no answer. Lisa completed arranging the cards in her hand, then looked up. Mark Christy was gone.

The woman on the bench didn't notice him at first, but the cup of coffee Mark held out to her gave off a tantalizing aroma. She turned toward him inquiringly.

"I thought you might be able to use this," he said. "Be careful—it's hot."

Her reflexes were slow. She stared at the cup for a few seconds, then unlaced her fingers and accepted it with one gloved hand. There was something very proper about the way she took the cup that reminded Mark of his own manners.

"I'm sorry," he said. "Do you take cream?"

The question might have been one of deep philosophical significance. "No," she answered soberly, "I don't. I haven't taken cream since before the war. For a long time there wasn't any—just canned milk—and I don't like canned milk."

She closed both hands around the cup and drank slowly. Mark watched her—fascinated by the one mystery remaining in a headline-exhausted case. Did she think of the war because it was at that time Larry Payne was placed in her care? She would have been in her early thirties—an old maid by the standards of a small Texas community. By her own choice, surely— she was a plain woman but not homely.

"It must have been tough," Mark mused, "stuck with a child nobody wanted."

She lowered the cup and looked sharply at him.

"You're one of those reporters, aren't you?" she asked.

Mark grinned. "Don't hold that against me. I have to earn a living."

But the confidence he'd hoped to foster was destroyed. She was now uncomfortable. She shifted her position nervously, and one foot scraped against an object on the floor. Mark looked down. It was a shabby suitcase.

"It's mine," she said quickly. "Checkout time at the hotel was two P.M., but when the jury went out at four I made them let me go without paying for another night."

Mark Christy scowled. There wasn't a hotel room in town expensive enough to justify so long a vigil on that hard bench—unless Lisa Wyman's analysis was correct.

"Look at her hands clutching that purse," Lisa had said. "Look at her tight mouth. She's miserly about everything—especially love!"

That was said the day Martha Lindholm took the stand, exactly two weeks after the trial had begun . . .

Sutton County was a ranching and winery area. The old courthouse at Sierra Vista dated back to a time when the State capital was at Monterey, and the superhighway that snubbed the city at the overpass was only a stage-coach trail to the booming settlement of San Francisco.

Many outward changes had come to Sierra Vista—a

new front on the Vallejo Hotel, parking meters in the business district, and a fruitful crop of television antennas stretching from Mexican town to the new Rancho Cresta subdivision. But inward changes came slowly. It was three days before Jay Bellamy got a jury that gave him any confidence. Larry Payne was a convicted rapist and a killer. To the ranchers and housewives and merchants of Sutton County these were the ugliest crimes in the human repertory of evil.

Bellamy was a young man—quick, alert, his hair worn in a close crew-cut. He was the scientific half of the law firm of Bellamy & Raines, appointed by the state to defend Larry Payne. Lew Raines was gentler—he brought a "bedside manner" to the courtroom. Women jurors were selected with an eye to Lew's talents.

"But there's no emotional side to our case," Lew complained. "The emotion will be on the other side. All Hastings has to do is unbutton his coat and show his galluses."

Fred Hastings, the District Attorney of Sutton County, was a rancher. He wore a big hat to the courtroom and placed it conspicuously on the table beside his brief case. There was something steady and unchanging and dependable about that hat—it inspired confidence in nervous jury candidates.

"Do you believe in the death penalty?" Hastings asked.

The prospective juror was a small rancher. He held his own big hat tightly in sun-browned hands. After sober thought, he answered, "Yes, sir. I do."

"And do you understand that—because the defendant is already serving a life term for a felony offense—that a verdict of guilty calls for a mandatory death sentence?"

Quietly, "Yes, sir."

"Candidate acceptable for the prosecution."

Jay Bellamy approached the stand. There was no familiarity when he posed his single question.

"What is your opinion of psychiatry?"

The hat twisted slowly in the rancher's hand.

"I don't know as I'm an expert . . ."

"None of us is," Jay responded. "I merely want to know if you will honor the statements of qualified psychiatrists who will testify for the defendant in this trial."

A year ago it would have been stifling-hot in the room, with only the sweep of the old ceiling fans to cool the court. But a year ago the county budget had provided for air conditioning. Perspiration now came from nervous tension.

"Well, sir, I have a son the same age as Larry Payne. He's stationed at Canaveral and he's expected to obey orders even at the cost of his own life. I don't go along with coddling murderers."

Tersely Jay said, "The candidate is unacceptable to the defense."

Even when the jury was finally completed, Jay Bellamy had misgivings. People liked a simple world with simple definitions. In 1843, fifteen English judges had defined legal insanity in what was known as the M'Naghten Rules. Roughly, they declared a person not criminally responsible for an offense if at the time the act was committed he was mentally unsound so as to lack knowledge that his act was wrong. In the light of modern psychiatry the law was obsolete—but that light had yet to reach the statute books.

"We aren't fighting Hastings," Lew Raines predicted ominously. "We're up against a hundred and twenty years of Anglo-American legal mythology. Look at the faces of those jurors, Jay. I tell you, change the plea to self-defense before it's too late."

"Payne stabbed the prison guard in the back," Bellamy answered. "*In the back,* Lew. We have no plea but insanity."

"But it won't sell!" Raines insisted. "Think of Payne's record. For a conviction of statutory rape he was sent to San Quentin. For possession of a knife he was given an automatic life term. Now he's charged with a murder that never would have happened had he received proper treatment in the beginning. Legally we're not in the Twentieth Century, Jay. Legally we're in the Dark Ages!"

Bellamy picked up his brief case and moved toward the door.

"I'm familiar with Payne's background," he said quietly, "but the plea is still 'Not Guilty by Reason of Insanity.' "

"Hastings will throw the M'Naghten Rulings at you."

Jay smiled wryly. "I expect he will, and then we'll find out."

"Find out?"

"If this is really the Twentieth Century—or the Dark Ages."

Larry Payne's face mirrored an innate innocence—as if the sordid crimes charged against him had been committed by a sleepwalker. He was brought handcuffed into the courtroom, then his hands were freed, and he was allowed to sit between his two attorneys. He smiled shyly for the press photographers. Mark Christy watched from the press row.

"How do you like that for a killer?" Mark said. "He looks more like an honor student from Sierra Vista High."

"It's the release," Lisa Wyman explained. "He's killed. He's had his release."

"That's great!" Morrie Hamlin growled. "All they have to do is turn him loose and he can go on using his knife for therapy."

Morrie's viewpoint was the wall of resistance Jay Bellamy had to break down. Their client's record was ugly—one of increasing violence without any sign of reformation . . . Methodically, Hastings laid out the mechanics of the crime before the jury.

The first witness was Carlos Ventura, Larry Payne's cellmate.

"Tell the court in your own words," Hastings said, "exactly what happened the day the prison guard, Warren, was killed."

Carlos Ventura looked out over the courtroom with bland, non-committal eyes. Only when his glance rested on Payne was there a flicker of contempt.

"Well, there was this trouble about a knife missing from the kitchen. Warren came to the cell to search Payne's bed."

"How did Payne react?"

Carlos Ventura's mouth formed a hard smile. To be a prisoner called to testify in court was to be nothing; but nothing was better than Larry Payne.

"Like he was scared," he said. "Warren knew it. You always know when a guy's scared."

"And then what happened?" Hastings asked.

"Warren told Payne to face the wall while he searched the bed. Payne turned around—then all of a sudden he whirled and made a dive for the mattress. That was it."

"What was it?"

"The way it happened—fast. Payne grabbed the knife and shoved it in Warren's back."

"Did Payne say anything? Did he give any warning that he intended to stab Warren?"

"He didn't make a sound. He dived for the knife and let Warren have it in the back."

Raines leaned forward, listening. Bellamy watched Payne for a reaction; but there was none—the prisoner's attention was elsewhere. A fly buzzed lazily above Judge Davis' head and then lighted, unnoticed, on his collar. It seemed highly amusing that a dignified judge should wear a fly on his collar. Larry Payne smiled. A flashbulb winked nearby. The morning editions would carry the photo with a descriptive caption like *Payne leers as cellmate tells how he stabbed prison guard*.

Anticipating Bellamy, Hastings put a psychiatrist for

the state on the stand. Dr. Lodge testified that Larry Payne had been given exhaustive tests after the murder. The psychiatrist, a slight, intense man, stated firmly that he had found the defendant coherent, responsive, and fully aware of the nature of his act.

"And therefore responsible under the law?" Hastings pressed.

"As I interpret the law, yes," Lodge answered, "I found the defendant sane."

Raines was almost beyond restraint. He leaned across the defense table and tugged at Bellamy's sleeve.

"That's impossible," he protested. "We have the analyses of Toler, Britt, and Stauffeur!"

Bellamy calmed him with a gesture. He rose and came forward to cross-examine.

"Dr. Lodge, at the time you examined the defendant, had he received prior treatment of any kind?"

Lodge hesitated. "I'm not sure I know what you mean."

"Had he been under the care of a medical doctor?"

"I don't know that I can answer that question."

"But I can," Bellamy said quickly. "Immediately after knifing Warren, the defendant was taken to the prison infirmary where he was treated for hysteria. He was later transferred to the county jail—under sedation. There—still under sedation—he was questioned by the District Attorney. What I'm trying to establish is simply this: was Larry Payne under sedation at the time of *your* examination?"

"Yes," Lodge admitted. "He was."

"And you have never examined him at any time when he was *not* under sedation?"

"No, sir. I have not."

The admission was a telling blow—but there was no way of knowing how it registered with the jury—all juries are unpredictable. At the close of the day's session Bellamy reminisced while packing his brief case.

"I once defended a car thief," he recalled, "who was

caught in the act, chased by the police and wounded five times in a running gun battle. The jury found him Not Guilty."

"You've made your point," Raines admitted grimly, "but I think we missed something with Ventura—" Raines didn't finish his statement. He looked up to see Hastings in the aisle, and reticence wasn't one of Lew Raines's noticeable traits.

"How does it feel to ask for the life of a man so mentally ill he doesn't know what's going on?" Lew demanded.

Hastings smiled wryly. "I stopped feeling years ago," he said. "Now I just take the oath of office and try to do my job. If you can convince the jury that Larry Payne didn't know right from wrong when he killed Warren, you'll have done your job."

"Is that your criterion for sanity?" Bellamy demanded.

"It's the law's criterion," Hastings replied quietly.

"An obsolete law," Raines protested. "The M'Naghten Rulings were made over a hundred years ago—prior to Freud, prior to studies in compulsive behavior, prior to—"

"—prior to the existence of the drug that kept Payne rational while he confessed the murder," Bellamy added, "and you know that as well as we do."

For a moment Hastings met Ballamy's direct stare.

"Is that what you're trying to do—use Payne as a *cause célèbre* to get a new definition of insanity in this state?"

"What we're trying to do," Bellamy answered, "is to defend a client the state has charged us to defend. If, in doing so, we can help science force the lock on an antiquated mental dungeon and let in a little light, we're all the winners."

But dungeons, even with rusty locks, are not easy to open. Three of the finest psychiatrists available had found Payne insane. John Britt, young and explosive, likened him to a martyr—as much a victim of society as Jean Valjean.

"Who stole bread because he was hungry," Hastings commented.

"There are different kinds of hunger," Britt commented in reply.

"Are you suggesting that a man has a right to take love by force, Mr. Britt?" Hastings thundered.

"No, sir. I'm stating that a *child* in a man's body—*a mentally retarded child*—attempted to satiate his hunger by force. At that point Larry Payne needed psychiatric help—not a sentence to San Quentin where he would go on repeating a destructive pattern."

The second defense witness was Aaron Toler, older and more poised. In academic language he explained the nature of Payne's problem. Payne was a challenge—a human guinea pig who, if spared, might help science unlock secrets of the mind.

"Or who might kill again?" Hastings suggested.

No one could answer that question negatively. By the time the third psychiatrist, Stauffeur, took the stand most of the spectators, foreseeing the outcome, had left.

Raines whispered earnestly to Bellamy. "We're not getting through. Stauffeur sounds like a public accountant. The jury has to *feel* that Payne is insane."

"What do you want to do?"

"Recall Ventura to the stand. There's something missing in his story. I'm sure of it."

It was the last day of the second week of the trial. Something had gone wrong with the air conditioning and the fans were no longer connected. Carlos Ventura's face was bearded with perspiration as Raines approached the witness stand holding the death knife. Murder needed a trigger, and under pressure Ventura broke.

"All right," he admitted, "Warren called Payne a name before the kid went for the knife."

"What was the name?" Raines demanded.

For the first time Larry became aware of the proceedings. His eyes were fixed on Ventura.

"A name for what Payne is," Ventura said. " 'You stand with your face to the wall,' Warren told him. 'Don't you move a muscle, you—' " and Ventura mouthed a shocking word.

Payne was on his feet. "Don't you call me that!" he screamed. "Don't you call me that again!"

He lunged forward, clawing at Ventura. A woman juror screamed. The bailiff and a uniformed officer sprang forward, but not before Larry Payne, the mild-mannered boy who smiled shyly at cameramen, had become an enraged animal. Still shouting, he was dragged from the courtroom as Judge Davis ordered a recess.

As the courtroom cleared, Bellamy turned on his partner.

"You overdid it, Lew!" he stormed. "You left nothing to the imagination."

"I proved that Payne was goaded into the attack," Raines insisted.

"Yes—but you also proved he's capable of killing— and that's what the jury will remember! Payne did need *that* kind of image. If only we had someone who liked him—just one person who could take the stand and make Larry Payne sound like a human being instead of a case history."

Jay Bellamy didn't believe in luck—or in magic. The sweat on his face was his luck, and the knowledge in his mind was his magic. But there were times when a natural sequence of events seemed the work of Providence.

The courtroom was now empty—the doors left open for ventilation. Moving toward the doors, Bellamy paused—intrigued by what he saw in the corridor. The woman would have been conspicuous anywhere on such a day. In spite of the heat, she wore a heavy tweed coat, a hat, and gloves. In addition to a large, unstylish handbag, she carried a cheap suitcase and a folded newspaper at which she kept glancing.

At the entrance to the courtroom she stopped.

"Is this," she asked timidly, "where Larry Payne is being tried?"

"It is," Bellamy answered, "but court has adjourned for the day."

The woman frowned, unsure of herself.

"Who did you want to see?" Raines asked.

"A lawyer—" She consulted the folded newspaper again. She was obviously near-sighted, but she didn't wear glasses. "—named Jay Bellamy. His name's printed here in the paper. I've come all the way from Texas to tell him the truth about Larry Payne."

Bellamy sighed.

Her name was Martha Lindholm. She was called as a surprise witness for the defense. Larry Payne was in court again—subdued and apparently oblivious to the furore he had caused. As the woman passed him, his face brightened with recognition. Starting up from his chair, he cried, "Aunt Martha!"

Martha Lindholm halted. She seemed under a great strain. Those close to her could see the muscles of her jaw tighten before she turned her head to give Larry Payne a cold stare and then move on. Bewildered, Payne sank back in his chair. He looked like a small boy who had been slapped and didn't know why.

From the stand Martha Lindholm's voice was firm and without a trace of emotion. Bellamy led her into the past to the day an unwanted child was placed in her care.

"I had no place for him," she said bluntly, "and no time. I worked as a practical nurse for five dollars a day. It wasn't easy to feed an extra mouth."

"How old was the boy when he first came to you?" Bellamy asked.

"He was five. Not old enough to work for his keep

or even help around the place. Just old enough to want."

"Want?" Bellamy echoed.

"Things he couldn't have—a wagon, a bicycle, a puppy. I told him we couldn't afford to feed a puppy, but he got one anyway. It wasn't my fault that— "

She stopped abruptly, embarrassed.

"Your fault?" Bellamy repeated. "What wasn't your fault?"

"It died," she said. "One day I heard Larry screaming in the yard. I ran outside and found him holding the dead puppy in his arms."

"What happened to the dog?"

Angrily she retorted, "How do I know? It was dead, that's all! After that Larry hardly ever spoke to me."

The air conditioning was still out of order. There was an undercurrent of irritation in the courtroom— silent but easily sensed. Martha Lindholm's gloved fingers worked nervously at the catch of her bag, and relentlessly Bellamy continued to gouge out the past.

"As the boy grew older was he difficult to manage?"

"Very difficult," she answered. "I had to work nights a lot. I paid eighty dollars to have a high fence built around the property and I always locked it when I went out. But Larry found a way to get over it."

"Then the boy was left alone nights. At what age was that?"

"Off and on until he was fifteen." Quickly she added, "But he was safe enough. Sometimes the storms frightened him, but he wasn't hurt. Then, when Larry was fifteen, he got into trouble. He took some money."

In the press section, Lisa Wyman leaned toward Mark Christy. "Stealing," she whispered. "The classic symptom of the love-starved child. Look at her hands clutching that purse. Look at her tight mouth . . ."

From the witness stand Martha Lindholm's voice droned on

". . . twenty dollars," she said. "I told the Sheriff the boy was getting too much for me to handle. Maybe twenty dollars doesn't sound like much, but it was a lot to me."

In a surprised voice Bellamy asked, "The money was yours, Miss Lindholm? *You* preferred the charges?"

"It was my household money!" she said angrily. "Larry squandered it taking a lot of strangers to the circus. Not people he knew, mind you. Not friends. Just strangers he picked up in the street. When the Sheriff asked why he did that, Larry said he wanted somebody to like him."

All through her testimony Larry Payne looked bored. His gaze wandered to the jury box. A middle-aged woman with lonely eyes was staring at him in a strange way. He smiled at her and she looked down quickly, fussed with her purse, and took out a handkerchief. She patted her perspiring face nervously.

A complaining whine came into Martha Lindholm's voice. "I never understood Larry," she continued. "I gave him a good home, treated him like my own right up to the day he ran off. But he never appreciated anything I gave him. What do you do with a boy like that? What *can* you do?"

The jury deliberated Martha Lindholm's questions until twelve forty and then the foreman, having solemnly tabulated the last ballot, informed the guard outside the jury room that a verdict had been reached.

Judge Davis was notified, Larry Payne was brought up from a lower-floor cell, and the weary survivors of the long vigil reassembled in the courtroom to hear the quiet announcement that Larry Payne—by reason of insanity—was Not Guilty.

Minutes later the manacled prisoner was escorted back to his cell. A few steps from the doorway he paused and looked pleadingly at Martha Lindholm. She lowered her eyes, and Payne, shoulders sagging, moved on.

Mark Christy watched intently. Why had she not

faced Larry Payne? Vengeance? Guilt? Remorse? Now that the trial was over, the woman could permit herself to show some emotion.

Mark felt he had to know why she waited. He lingered in the emptying courtroom as Bellamy and Raines greeted her.

"Miss Lindholm," Bellamy said cordially. "I'm so glad you stayed on. I called your hotel and was told you had checked out."

"It was eight dollars a day," she explained. Timidly she then added, "You promised to give me bus fare back to Texas."

"Bus fare?" Raines echoed. "After what happened here tonight? Why don't you take a plane?"

"There's no need for that," she said. "Do you have the money with you? I've been waiting a long time."

Mark Christy now had his answer. He turned away disgustedly. If he hurried, he could catch Lisa Wyman and the rest of the pressroom group at the corner bar and celebrate a victory for the Age of Science. The thinning of his hair, he decided, wasn't coming any too soon. He was losing touch with reality. He had almost believed there could be such a thing as an unselfish motive.

In the courtroom Jay Bellamy finished counting out the bus fare and placed it in Martha Lindholm's hand.

"I'm sorry for what I had to do," he said. "I didn't know any other way to make the jury sympathetic to Larry—except by turning you into a heartless ogre."

There was both sadness and warmth in Martha Lindholm's eyes.

"It doesn't matter what people think of me," she said, "just so the boy finally gets help. I told you the day I came, he's been sick in the mind for a long time. But in that little town . . . in those days . . . nobody knew what to do with him. And nobody cared."

"Except you, Miss Lindholm."

"I did what I could, but there was a devil inside

Larry that made him do terrible things. I saw it the first time on the day he killed the puppy he loved so much."

Martha Lindholm folded the bus money and put it in her purse. The catch snapped loudly in the empty courtroom.

"And he did kill him, Mr. Bellamy," she added, "even if you wouldn't let me tell that part of the story from the witness stand."

Your Word Against Mine

by John F. Suter

Defending counsel Roberts looked up from his notes as Assistant Prosecuting Attorney Sutherland got to his feet.

The ceiling fixtures in Intermediate Court cast a yellow light over the dark walnut courtroom. The tall windows were gray blanks as the last of winter dissolved in slow, monotonous March rain. The tiled corridors outside were sharp with carbolic smell, but in the overheated room a heavy odor of damp wool mingled with a bitter whiff of wet overshoes and umbrellas.

The spectators' benches were packed.

Roberts, watching his small, bald, ferret-faced opponent gather himself for his closing remarks, found the day and the situation in league against him. *You can't snoop out all the surprises. But what to do about the one they pull out of the hat, as in this case? What to do?* He knew that he must expect Sutherland to hit it hard. It had to be hit back. *Can I make it come through?* A sneeze at the rear of the courtroom reminded him of the cold he was developing, another weight to be added to the pressure on his brain.

Be sharp, Roberts, be sharp. Sutherland's already used one or two of your own tricks against you.

The defense lawyer looked at the child, hoping to surprise the malice that must be there, that must show itself, if only once—hoping that the jury would see it, too, when it did show. But her face was placid and innocent. He looked at her father. That craggy, ashescolored face was no graven image. Anger and hatred ebbed and surged there, giving way to satisfaction as the prosecutor prepared to unmask the devil before the jury.

Roberts ignored the jury. He would get to them all too soon. He glanced at his client, Arthur Bradshaw, instead. Bradshaw—like his antagonist, the little girl—was utterly serene. His banner of prematurely white hair was smoothly brushed. His pink skin was unmarked save for the crow's-feet of humor at his blue eyes. All his lines were finely cut—face, hands, and even the bones of his legs and ankles, as Roberts knew. Bradshaw personified dignity. The thing at issue was the integrity behind the dignity.

And Roberts looked at himself. *It's all very well for Sutherland. He can be a machine if he likes. Strip another man to his bare bones, and if you've never had to open your own heart you won't mind it. My trouble is that I have too much heart. Wouldn't Bradshaw be better off if I didn't have an eleven-year-old girl myself?* He thought back to the clear, windy day at the beginning. Both he and Sutherland had indicated to Judge Weaver that no sequestering of witnesses was requested. The jury was impaneled and ready to listen, and it was time for opening remarks. His mind's ear again heard Sutherland's dry, dusty voice addressing the twelve attentive jurors . . .

"Ladies and gentlemen of the jury [Sutherland had said that first day of the trial], we are here to try a man accused of contributing to the delinquency of a minor. This is a case which I am most distressed to prosecute, because I am aware of the regard with which this community has held the defendant, Arthur Bradshaw."

Attempting to trump my ace already, Roberts had thought.

Sutherland had rubbed his bald head in affected embarrassment. "But in this life we cannot always do the things we should like to do. I am sure that my opponent, Mr. Roberts, would like it better if our positions were reversed because, as some of you may know, while I am unmarried he is a father. His natural inclination in this case must be to prosecute, not defend.

"I feel a great responsibility in this case. A responsibility to Virginia May Tucker—to her parents—to everyone in our community. For this could be a crime against any child in town, not just Virginia May Tucker. The defense counsel's child, for instance. Or *your* child." He threw one arm out in Bradshaw's direction, but did not mention him by name. "So I want you, friends, not to look upon me as a prosecutor in this case, but as a defender—a defender of the things we all cherish most: our homes, our families, our children. Think to yourselves, ladies and gentlemen: Have you ever regarded the Prosecuting Attorney's office as your defender?"

Sutherland had paused to wipe the sweat delicately from his palms. "Now, I do not wish you ladies and gentlemen of the jury to imagine that I intend to introduce evidence to show that Arthur Bradshaw is the man who has been trying to lure other little girls into his car—the man the police have hunted for months.

(*No, damn you,* Roberts had said to himself, *but you can play on their prejudices. Who hasn't read about that animal?* Then he had remembered his own Bessie and the constant worry that she might not heed his and June's warnings.)

"The evidence we shall introduce is concerned only with the question: Did Arthur Bradshaw make advances to the Tucker child, or did he not? You must consider this, and this alone. If you are satisfied that he did—and we shall attempt to prove that he did—then you must find him guilty as charged.

"We shall attempt to show—"

After a time Roberts had been on his feet himself, facing the jury for his own opening. He knew exactly how he had looked standing there—six feet two, broad-shouldered, high-cheekboned, one lock of black hair falling boyishly over his left eyebrow—a picture of the

clean young defender of the wronged. A picture Roberts
had tried to preserve across the years.

But he always forgot this picture when he began to
speak. It never failed to surprise him, when he spoke to
a jury, that these people were no more than his own
neighbors. The owlish banker, Martin—foreman of the
jury—was like Joe Hazleton, the insurance man who
lived across the street. The pleasant-faced brunette in
the second row could be a sister of the soda fountain
girl in the neighborhood drug store. The stocky man
sitting beside her could double for the meatcutter in the
supermarket. These were just people, bent on seeking
an answer as best they knew how. And he had spoken
to them as people, not as an audience. *If I'm to save or
break a man by talking, I can't be a performer, I must
be a communicant. I must communicate with these
twelve people.*

"I must confess to you, ladies and gentlemen, that in
his opening speech Mr. Sutherland has given us all
something to think about—especially me. And he has
shown me that I ought to look at this case not only as
an attorney, but as a father. For, as Mr. Sutherland
has said, in so many words: What if this were *your*
child? That is a terrible question to have to answer.

"Ladies and gentlemen, terrible as that question is, I
must ask you to try to answer one equally terrible:
What if you stood in Arthur Bradshaw's place?"

He had paused a moment, to let it sink in. *That's one
for our foreman to think about.*

"By that question, ladies and gentlemen, I do not
mean the familiar one: What if I were sitting there, on
trial for murder—or some other crime? The question,
rather, is: What if it were I, about to see my whole life
wrecked, my good name torn to shreds, by someone's
false testimony? For, ladies and gentlemen, is it not
more terrible to strip a man of everything he is, and
then let him live, than to take his life?

"I shall attempt to show, beyond question, that my
client's life is as unblemished as you can expect any

average man's to be—probably more. Such a man is inevitably the target of people who cannot tolerate the good among us, who must continually look for flaws in them. It is a tribute to Arthur Bradshaw that I have had dozens of offers from persons who want to testify for him. I could fill this courtroom with such character witnesses. If a time should ever come when I were on trial, I should be proud to have so many plead to speak in my behalf. Some of these people will tell you their stories later . . ."

Roberts leaned across the table toward Bradshaw.

"Look again. Do you see anyone here who might have a grudge against you?"

Bradshaw said calmly, "But I have never given anyone cause to have a grudge."

The lawyer reddened. "That's not the point! People bear grudges whether you've give them reason or not. All they need is imagination. And the more well-known you are, the more they imagine. Someone like that might have used the Tuckers to set you up. Now, will you at least try to help me? Will you please look?"

Bradshaw scanned the courtroom.

"I don't see anyone who might fit your description."

Roberts leaned closer and spoke in an intense undertone. "One thing Sutherland might do is to have someone swear that you've tried this sort of thing before. If you saw anybody here who might say that, it would help me to have some background on him."

"I don't see anyone."

Roberts thought: *So, if it comes, it'll catch me flat-footed. Well—*

The voice cut through their conversation: "Will Virginia May Tucker come to the stand?"

As the child rose and made her way to the stand, Roberts stared in surprise. *The first witness? No warm-up, no preliminary witnesses?* He hardly heard them getting the child to affirm the truth of her testimony. *Is Sutherland hitting for the deepest impression*

*by putting the child first? Or does it mean that he has
no supporting witnesses—as Bradshaw said?*

The child should make a good impression . . .

There was nothing falsely angelic about her features;
they were only a little better than plain. Her light
brown hair, which would later be mouse-colored,
tended to be straight, but no false crimps had been put
into it. Carefully placed barrettes caused it to fall
softly, just far enough back from the face to create an
image of placidness and honesty. Her blue print dress
was faded and mended; but it was clean, and the nee-
dlework was neat.

The prosecutor spoke gently. Roberts said to himself: *He sounds like an old uncle played by a ham actor.* But juries weren't drama critics. It was always
effective.

"Now, Virginia May, tell these ladies and gentlemen,
how old are you?"

"Eleven." The childish voice was faint.

"I'm afraid not many of us heard you, honey. Try to
talk a little louder."

"I'm eleven years old. Last June."

"And you live with your mother and daddy, do
you?"

"That's right."

"And go to Sunday School?"

"Yessir, at St. John's. Nearly every Sunday, except
sometimes when the weather's bad."

The prosecutor reached into his pocket and pulled
out a small book.

"Do you recognize this, Virginia May?"

"Yessir. That's my New Testament. I got it for not
missing Sunday School a single time for six months."

Roberts rose and addressed the judge. "Your Honor,
this is a pleasant interlude, I am sure, but I hardly think
that we are here to find out how well the child knows
her catechism. I suggest that this testimony be stricken
and such questioning be left to her Sunday School
teacher."

Sutherland smiled ironically. "Your Honor, I think it unfair to assume that the defendant has a character, while this little girl has none." He turned to the jury, held out the Bible, shrugged, and smiled again. Roberts fought to keep from reddening at the pantomime criticism: *What manner of adversary is antagonistic to a child's religion?*

Judge Weaver, a very short, very hairy, very gray man, glanced from beneath shaggy brows at both attorneys. "You have a point, Mr. Sutherland. The testimony may stand. However, I suggest you get on with your case."

Sutherland nodded and turned to the child. "What grade are you in at school, Virginia May?"

"Fifth. Miss Kincaid."

"Have your schoolteachers ever tried to teach you right from wrong?"

"Yessir. All of them. Miss Temple, in the fourth grade, was *always* going on about how we ought to do this and ought not to do that."

The prosecutor rubbed the side of his face, then the top of his head, a picture of discomfort. "Now, Virginia May, I want you to tell these people exactly what happened on October 8th. Don't be afraid. Just speak out."

The child folded her hands in her lap and began speaking to the judge. "I was—"

Judge Weaver interrupted her, speaking quietly. "You must not turn to me, my dear. Those people over there won't be able to hear you. Speak to them."

She turned to the jury. "I was downtown that day, and I guess I got interested in looking in the dime store too long. All at once I saw by the clock at Moore's Jewelry that I'd better be getting home. So I went to the bus stop and was waiting there. I guess a bus had gone just before that, because I was the first one there."

Sutherland interrupted tenderly. "You were standing there alone, honey?"

"Yessir. By myself. Well, I wasn't there very long when this car drove up and stopped. It was a blue car, all nice and shiny and clean. I guess it wasn't new, but it did look nice. The man in it leaned over and opened the door and called to me. He said: I'm *going east, little girl, and I'll give you a ride if you want.*"

"And you got in with him right away?"

"No, sir, not right away. I'd been told not to. I knew it was wrong, but I thought about being late. And I'd always thought that bad men were dirty and ugly. He wasn't. His car was pretty, and he looked nice. So then I got in."

"And then what happened, Virginia May?"

"We started off. He asked me my name and how old I was and things about school. He told me that I was a nice little girl. He asked me where I lived. He acted real friendly. Then, when we got to Plum Street—that's about five blocks from home—he started asking me if I wouldn't like to have a box of candy, all for myself. He said he had one there in that little place in the front of the car. He opened the little door and showed me. I said, well, maybe I would. Then he said was I in a hurry to get home. I said, yes, I was. He said oh my mother wouldn't mind, let's go for a ride, say out to Media Park. I said no, I had to get home. He kept coaxing, and next thing I knew we were going right past the street where I live. I told him about it, but he didn't seem to hear. When I said it again, and he didn't stop, I got scared. I reached over and turned that key there on the dashboard and pulled the key out and threw it on the floor. The motor quit and he had to stop the car to reach down for the key. I jumped out of the car real quick and ran home. It was about four blocks back by that time. My Mom and Dad were there and I looked scared, I guess, so they got out of me what had happened. Dad got awful mad, and he found out who it was after I gave him the license number of the car. And that's all."

Prosecutor Sutherland pulled at his nose. "Would

you know the man who gave you the ride if you were to see him again?"

"Yessir," She stood up and pointed at Arthur Bradshaw. "That's him."

Bradshaw shook his head and smiled ruefully to Roberts.

"Poor child," he murmured. "To misuse her this way, so young."

Roberts did not reply. He was listening intently.

Sutherland spoke to the child again. "Virginia May, what fraction of a pound is one ounce?"

She puzzled, worrying her lower lip with her teeth. "One-eighth?"

He smiled gently. "No, it's one-sixteenth."

"Oh."

He leaned toward her. "Now, honey, another man wants to ask you some questions." He nodded to Roberts. "Your witness."

Roberts approached the stand almost gingerly. *This could blow up in my face any minute,* he thought. He looked at the unsmiling, slightly apprehensive little face. *She could be my own little Bessie. No, not Bessie. Think of her as Joan, the two faced one from the next block, the liar and trouble-maker, the one who runs back and forth with the she-said-this-about-you tales.*

"Virginia May, I am glad to find that you are so good about going to Sunday School. Do you know how God looks upon people who don't tell the truth?"

"Yessir. They're sinners. He punishes them."

"You don't want to be a sinner, do you?"

"No, sir."

"Then we don't need to worry about anything you tell me."

The child looked at him skeptically. "No—sir."

"Have you any brothers or sisters, Virginia May?"

"I have a brother that's older and a brother and sister that're younger."

"Four children in your family, then?"

"Yessir."

"What does your daddy do?"

"I'm not sure—"

"What is his work?"

The prosecutor jumped to his feet. "Your Honor, I object! There is a deliberate attempt here to create prejudice against a man who is less fortunate than others!"

Roberts turned to the judge with surprise stamped on his face. "Your Honor, such reasoning had not crossed my mind. I should be the first to affirm the thesis that all men are equal in a court of law. If Mr. Sutherland had listened to my opening, he would now realize that this is the very point I want to make in this trial. My present object is different. May I proceed?"

"You may proceed."

Roberts addressed the girl again. "I'll ask you again, Virginia May, what is your daddy's work?"

"He's a foreman on the night shift at the Iron Works."

"What time does he go to work?"

"Three in the afternoon."

"Do you see much of him?"

"Mostly just on Saturdays and Sundays. He's usually asleep when I go to school, and he's gone when I get home."

Roberts half turned to the jury and said only, "I see." He paused.

Then he said, "Virginia May, what day of the week was October 8th?"

She hesitated. "Why—it was a Thursday, wasn't it?"

Roberts stepped quickly to the table where he had been sitting and picked up a calendar he had spread out there. He returned and showed it to the child. "Thursday is right."

He turned and showed the calendar to the jury, giving them time to look it over. Then he rolled it up swiftly.

"Thursday, October 8th. Is that a school holiday?"

She made no answer. He leaned closer.

"Virginia May, was there a holiday that day?"

She looked at Judge Weaver. He nodded sternly. "You must answer, child."

A small voice: "No, sir."

Not asking her to repeat, Roberts said, full-voiced, "You say it was not a holiday. Why were you downtown, then? Why weren't you in school?"

Her hands twisted. "Mom asked me to go down to buy some things for her."

"Oh, your mother asked you. I see. That would make it all right."

"Yes—sir."

"Your daddy wouldn't have any reason to be angry, then, if you came home when you were supposed to be in school? Not if your mother had asked you to go shopping downtown."

"No, sir. I guess not."

"By the way—you weren't carrying any packages when you got into Mr. Bradshaw's car, were you?"

"No, sir," she said quickly. "I couldn't find what my mother wanted."

"All right, Virginia May, I won't ask any more questions. That's all."

He turned and walked away.

Bradshaw whispered to him, "I'm glad you weren't too hard on the poor little thing."

Roberts frowned. "She's a chronic liar. And her lying can ruin you. I'd like to shake her until her teeth rattle."

"I still feel that you should have let me discuss this thing with the child and her parents. It might never have come to this. That little one will remember this all the rest of her life."

Roberts leaned close to Bradshaw and spoke earnestly. "Right. I *want* her to remember it. If she's not headed off now, there's no telling. . . Look! You never had any kids. Sure, you've worked with boys for years, but you see only the good side of them. Kids can be the worst liars on earth. But we have to be careful to handle this one just right. If she goes to pieces in front of the jury—"

Prosecutor Sutherland's dusty voice said, "Will Alfred Tucker take the stand, please."

Roberts settled back and studied the child's father as he took the oath. Short, burly, with mouse-colored hair shot with gray and a seamed skin robbed of color by a lifetime of sunless foundry work, Tucker faced the court defiantly.

The prosecutor leaned toward him.

"Your full name, please."

"Alfred Charles Tucker."

Sutherland glanced at the jury. "Ever mistaken for Alfred J. Tucker?"

Tucker snorted. "The head of the bus company? Are you kidding?"

"What is your occupation?"

"Just like my kid said—foreman at Moore Iron Works."

"What are your hours there, Mr. Tucker?"

"Three to eleven—the night shift."

"That doesn't give you much time with your children, does it, Mr. Tucker?"

"No. Hardly any."

"But in spite of that, you think your children ought to be brought up properly. Is that correct?"

"That's right! I'll have none of my kids hoppin' from one gutter to another. If they're not brought up right, it'll be no fault of me and Sade."

"By the way, Mr. Tucker, your wife isn't here to testify because she's so upset by what happened that she's in bed under a doctor's care? Is that correct?"

"Yes."

"Now, Mr. Tucker, you've heard Mr. Roberts suggest that you pay very little attention to your children. Is that true?"

Tucker's face darkened. "That's a lie! Sure I'm not around much because of my hours at the Works, but when I'm home it's the kids first and other things second."

Sutherland coughed. "I'm sure of that, Mr. Tucker. Now, suppose you tell us what happened at your home on October 8th."

Virginia May's father frowned. "It was about 2:30 in the afternoon. I was getting ready to leave for work. I'd just picked up my lunch box when the front door bangs open and Ginnie comes running in, all out of breath. It's not time for her to be out of school, and she doesn't look so good, so I ask her what's wrong. She tells me about this guy giving her a lift and trying to pull some funny stuff on her. This makes me see red, and I'm all for going to look up this guy, but she says he drove off in a hurry. And, anyway, she remembers his license number. So I tell the cops and give 'em the number. So after a while they ask the kid to identify this guy and his car, and that's it. That's him, all right."

Sutherland glanced at the jury. "Did you ever know Mr. Arthur Bradshaw? Ever work for him?"

"Never laid eyes on him before in my life. Read in the papers about him from time to time, but hardly enough to remember."

"Anyone in your family, or your wife's family, ever know him before?"

"No, sir. Not a one."

Roberts got to his feet. "Objection. Such matters would be pure hearsay on the part of the witness."

"Sustained."

Sutherland smiled. "Very well. But you *did* have Arthur Bradshaw's auto license number."

"That's right. The kid gave it to me. That's the way the cops found him."

Sutherland smiled again. "Your witness, Mr. Roberts."

Roberts opened with a calm he did not feel. "You're a foreman at the Iron Works, I believe you said, Mr. Tucker?"

Tucker's animosity was ill-concealed. *You say I*

don't take care of my own kid! You're on the side of this Bradshaw! We'll see!

His answer was a growl. "I am."

"You work eight hours as a rule, exclusive of overtime?"

"That's right."

"Heavy work?"

"It's a man's work and then some."

"Takes lots of sleep?"

"It does that. I don't usually roll in before midnight, and it's 10-11 next morning before I'm up."

"What time did you get up on October 8th?"

"I don't remember for sure. About 10 or 11, like I said."

"Did you see Virginia May before afternoon?"

"No, not till about 2:30."

Roberts became almost apologetic. "Mr. Sutherland implied that I cast doubt on your responsibility as a father—that I thought you paid little attention to your children. He misconstrued the questions I asked your little girl. I realize that you only have limited time to give your children, and I think this jury should realize it. That *is* right, isn't it, that you have only limited time?"

Some of the antagonism left Tucker's face. The harsh lines relaxed.

"Yes, sir. Like I told him, I do the best I can in the time I've got."

"But, of course, Mr. Tucker, in the very little time you do have at home, you let the children know their father's around?"

"That I do. They'd run all over their mother if I didn't make 'em toe the mark."

"You're strict with them, then?"

"I am. I'm not ashamed of it. Those kids'll be brought up right."

"In what way are you strict, Mr. Tucker? How do you discipline your children when you feel they need disciplining?"

"I tan their hides good. A taste of the belt works best of anything I know."

Roberts nodded gratefully, and the last trace of Tucker's antagonism vanished. "By the way, Mr. Tucker. Your daughter Virginia May said she wasn't in school the day all this happened because her mother asked her to go downtown. That's so, of course? Her mother did ask her?"

"I guess she did, if Ginnie says so."

"Oh, I see, you haven't checked that with Mrs. Tucker," Roberts said worriedly. "I see . . . Mr. Tucker, what if Ginnie *hadn't* been asked to go downtown that day? By your wife, I mean?"

Tucker glowered. "You mean what if she'd cut school? Why, I'd have blistered her—" He stopped suddenly.

Roberts turned away. "That's all."

He sat down and glanced thoughtfully over his notes. A glimmering of Sutherland's still-to-come attack was beginning to appear. *Can I head him off? Or neutralize it if I can't head him off?*

Roberts was still turning the matter over when Sutherland said, "We intend to call no more witnesses, Your Honor."

Roberts stared in disbelief, unable to fathom Sutherland's motive. But it would help, it would help. It gave his own planned opening move a legitimate excuse.

"Your Honor," he said, rising, "the defense is unprepared for such a brief presentation by Mr. Sutherland, I must confess. If Your Honor please, I should like a fifteen-minute recess to confer with our witnesses."

Judge Weaver bobbed his gray head. "Court will take a fifteen-minute recess."

After the recess seven witnesses in succession took the stand and testified to Bradshaw's high character. Some had known him since boyhood. They said that Arthur Bradshaw was a wealthy man of fine family who had devoted most of his life to youth work; that he had built the city's playground program nearly single-handed; that he had been a leading vestryman of his church for 26 years; that he had held office after office in charity and civic drives, all without compensation; that he had been on the board of directors of the YMCA; that although he had no children, he had been happily married for almost 30 years; that he was never known to drink; that he had never been charged with anything more serious than a ticket for overtime parking.

The prosecution found no loopholes. The witnesses were unimpeachable.

Roberts was about to call his eighth witness when Judge Weaver leaned over the bench.

"Mr. Roberts, how many character witnesses do you have?"

"Twenty-two, Your Honor."

"I shall ask that the fact be noted. However, I think it unnecessary that the jury hear them all. I shall limit you to one more witness of this type, as I am permitted by law. I am sure you understand."

"Yes, Your Honor."

"You may proceed."

The eighth witness hammered home the spiritual side of Bradshaw's character. This one, Bradshaw's pastor, one of the city's most prominent clergymen, likewise could not be shaken by Sutherland's respectful probing.

The judge glanced at the clock. "Gentlemen, the hour is getting late. Court will recess until 10 o'clock tomorrow morning."

Roberts had begun the next day's session by calling a schoolteacher, Anna Temple, to the stand. She was an excellent witness, with a firmness of manner and tone that overlay the appearance of innocence her small size, round face, and wide eyes gave her. Her hair was a pale red—not a deep enough shade to warn off the unwary.

Roberts was matter-of-fact. "Miss Temple, what is your occupation?"

"Schoolteacher."

"At which school?"

"Walnut Street."

"What grade do you teach?"

"Fourth."

"Have you ever had Virginia May Tucker as a pupil?"

"Ginnie Tucker was in my room last year."

"What sort of student would you say Virginia May was?"

"What I would call average." Miss Temple glanced at Sutherland, who was rising from his chair, and her green eyes flashed. "By that I mean that she was neither very dull nor very bright. She was like so many of the rest of us." And the prosecutor sat down again, choosing to smile.

Roberts smiled, too. Then he went on: "How would you characterize her ability to learn, Miss Temple? Did she memorize readily?"

The answer was emphatic and precise. "She did *not* memorize readily, Mr. Roberts. Virginia May had to work for the things she learned."

Roberts' next question was more a plea for advice. "Miss Temple, would you say that Virginia May Tucker was a well-adjusted child?"

"Not altogether."

"Why do you say that?"

"Oh—for instance—she often made a fuss about some possession of hers being 'missing.' She would tell me this not in private, but before the whole class. *Someone took my ruler.* Or, *My box of crayons is gone, and somebody's got it. Somebody, somebody*—you know? So we'd stop class and look. Invariably the missing object would be found in her own desk."

"Have you any idea why she did this, Miss Temple?"

Sutherland's quick "Object!" was suppressed by the

teacher's equally quick, "I'll leave that to a psychologist, Mr. Roberts."

Judge Weaver looked at Sutherland. "Does the Prosecution still object?"

Sutherland waved handsomely. "We withdraw the objection, Your Honor." He had suddenly decided not to tangle with the red-haired Miss Temple.

Roberts asked carefully, "How was Virginia May's attendance record, Miss Temple?"

"Very poor during the year I had her. One more absence without a legitimate excuse, and she would not have been promoted."

"These were mostly willful absences, not for illness or other permissible reasons?"

"That is correct."

"What reasons did she give you for these willful absences?"

"She made up fanciful stories and stuck to them."

Still carefully, Roberts asked, "You mean Virginia May lied to you when she did wrong, and stuck to her lies?"

"About her absences, yes."

Roberts said gently, "She lied to you, and stuck to her lies. That's all, thank you, Miss Temple." He looked at Sutherland. "Your witness."

Sutherland's cross-examination was obvious. Lying was a common trait in children, Miss Temple admitted. So was rebellion at confinement in schools. Yes, even the finest children rebelled and lied sometimes. Yes, otherwise, Ginnie Tucker was a well-behaved child. Yes, Miss Temple had taught other children who were far bigger headaches. And so on.

Roberts merely said: "I now call Ethel Kincaid."

Ethel Kincaid was another teacher, but tall and bony with iron-gray hair and quick, black eyes.

"What grade do you teach, Miss Kincaid?"

"Fifth."

"Which School?"

"Walnut Street."

"Do you know Virginia May Tucker?"

"She's one of my pupils."

"Tell us what you know of her."

"Well, I've been sitting back there listening to Anna Temple. I see no need to add to or change anything she's said. Of course, I haven't had the child in my room for more than a few months, so perhaps I'm being unfair."

"But, in general, you confirm Miss Temple's testimony?"

"Yes. Of course the absences—maybe it's too early to tell. But there does seem to be a trend—a definite trend already."

Roberts glanced aside. The child's face was expressionless; her father's was mottled in anger.

"Now, Miss Kincaid, please tell me what you remember about October 8th and what Virginia May did on that day."

The teacher's features drew together in concentration. "It was a beautiful day, as I recall—real Indian summer. I remember the leaves on the maple by the schoolroom window were beginning to fall, and the class seemed far more interested in watching them than paying attention to me. The Tucker child had come in that morning acting very listless. It was particularly hard to keep her attention. Late in the morning I noticed that she had her head pillowed on her arm. She said she felt sick, and I sent her to the school nurse. The nurse reported that the child had no temperature, but of course was to be excused if she said she was not feeling well. I wrote a note to Mrs. Tucker and sent Virginia May home."

"This was about what time, Miss Kincaid?"

"It was around 11."

"And that was all you saw of Virginia May that day?"

"That's correct."

"And she was back in school next day?"

"Yes—and quite a different young lady," said Miss

Kincaid dryly. "As chipper as you please. Completely recovered."

Roberts turned to the jury, raised a knowing eyebrow, and smiled. "Your witness," he said to Sutherland.

Sutherland approached the stand, looking thoughtful.

"Miss Kincaid, Miss Temple has testified that in her class last year Virginia May was just an average student. What she learned was by experience, not by memorizing. Is that your impression, also?"

"Substantially, yes."

"Now, Miss Kincaid, you said that on the day in question this child appeared to be ill, so ill that she had put her arm on her desk and pillowed her head on that arm?"

She answered calmly, "That is correct."

"You also said that you sent the child home. You mentioned no one's accompanying her. Are we to infer that she went alone?"

Miss Kincaid drew herself up. "She insisted on it. Begged us not to call her mother, as her mother might be frightened. Since there was no sign of anything seriously wrong with her, and she lives very near the school, I allowed her to go home alone."

Sutherland threw up his hands. "What kind of teachers do we have who let a sick child make her way along the public streets *alone*?" He walked away. "That's all."

As Miss Kincaid retired to her seat, face flushed, Roberts arose. "I shall ask Arthur Bradshaw to take the stand."

The buzz in the spectators' section had not yet subsided when Bradshaw, a striking figure, was sworn and sat down. The light gleamed on his fine white hair.

"Mr. Bradshaw," said Roberts quietly, "please tell us what happened on October 8th."

Bradshaw spoke in a clear, controlled voice.

"Certainly. I assume you want details bearing only on this—incident. I was downtown that day, buying two footballs at the Sports Center. The city playground touch-football league was just getting under way, and replacements for two old footballs were needed. I bought them and was starting to take them out to Jack Shields, our activities director, when I saw the Tucker child standing on the corner. She looked rather woebegone—worried-looking, I thought. I hate to see a child unhappy, so I stopped and offered her a lift. She accepted. We talked of a few general things. When we reached a point about four blocks from where she lives—as I now know—she asked me to let her out. I did. Why she got out there, I don't know. That evening the police came to question me, and the next thing I knew I was charged with this—this offense."

"Mr. Bradshaw, let's get this clear: You say that *you* stopped the car to let the child out?"

"Yes. As soon as she asked. But, as I say, I have no idea why. At the time, I assumed she lived near where she asked me to let her out."

"Is it true that you offered her candy?"

Bradshaw smiled. "Oh, yes I always carry a box or two in the glove compartment. I've never met a boy or girl who doesn't like candy. She took some, too."

Virginia May jumped to her feet.

"That's not true! That's a big lie, and he knows it! I didn't even touch his old candy!"

Judge Weaver rapped sharply, and Alfred Tucker pulled his child back to her seat. The judge looked at Tucker and spoke evenly: "Sir, your child's testimony has been heard. Please restrain her. I will not have this sort of thing in my court!"

"Yes, Your Honor." Tucker's expression wavered between embarrassment and indignation. He muttered fiercely to Virginia May, who shrank back defiantly.

Roberts nodded to Bradshaw. "Please continue, Mr. Bradshaw."

"Why, that's all there is," said Bradshaw, spreading his hands slightly. "The incident was so trivial that I almost forgot it. If the officers had not come to my home so soon afterward with a warrant—on this ridiculous charge—I would not have remembered it at all."

Roberts gestured to Sutherland. "Mr. Sutherland"

Sutherland walked slowly around Bradshaw, looking him up and down. Time ticked by as he looked. Finally, he spoke, "Mr. Bradshaw, your witnesses would have us believe that you're a living saint. You'll pardon my curiosity. I've never seen a saint in the flesh, and I want to remember you. Answer me this question: Even assuming that you've led the blameless life they say you have, have you never heard that men can change in their ways? In their later years?"

In his seat, counsel for the defense closed his eyes. *Here it comes.*

Bradshaw replied courteously. "I certainly make no claim to being anything but human, sir. I have heard of what you say, yes. As far as it would apply to me, it is untrue."

Sutherland leaned close to him, "Can you prove that?"

Roberts was on his feet. "Objection. Your Honor, Mr. Bradshaw is not required to prove the truth or falsity of such a gratuitous allegation."

"Sustained!" The judge was not young, either.

Sutherland said suddenly, "What's the license number of your car, Bradshaw?"

"23309—no, 233084J."

Sutherland smiled. "Not easy to remember, is it?"

Bradshaw reddened slightly. "Not under circumstances such as these."

Sutherland turned toward the jury. *"Virginia May remembered it!"*

Defending counsel Roberts looked up from his notes as Assistant Prosecuting Attorney Sutherland got to his feet and turned to the jury to make his summation.

Roberts jerked his thoughts back from the past with an effort. Days of this, and now it was approaching the climax.

He looked at Bradshaw's face, hoping to find in its calm a release from his own worries. But the serenity and confidence he saw there only caused him to reflect, *Doesn't he realize? Is it real—or only pose? In a few minutes from now, Sutherland can . . .*

Sutherland began, "Ladies and gentlemen of the jury, you may wonder why the prosecution has made its case so very simple. The answer is that it *is* a simple case. That being so, why should I complicate it for you?

"We have here a situation in which there are no direct witnesses for either side. We have only the testimony of an innocent little girl on the one hand, and a grown man who has lived the best part of his life on the other. No other person, adult or child, was present. No person saw Virginia May get into Bradshaw's car, no person saw her get out—or, at least, no one has come forward so to testify.

"You have listened to a great many witnesses giving Arthur Bradshaw, a wealthy and prominent man, glowing character references. You have heard attempts to darken the character of the young victim, to make her out a chronic liar, and worse—a shameful heaping of insult on injury! All this adds up to a *complete* attempt on the part of the defense to make a case. You may ask yourself *why*? The People's case is simple and direct. We have complete faith in the integrity of this child, and her good, hard-working parents, without a great parade of witnesses. And so, I think, have you."

Sutherland pursued his original attack along several variations of this theme of simplicity, with flanking references to the iniquity of middle-aged men who prey on the young. It was clear that he was depending on the brevity of his speech and the innocence of childhood to carry the day.

Then the moment came that Roberts had been dreading.

"I want to call your attention to one further fact," said Sutherland. "You will recall that this man Bradshaw was traced by the police because little Virginia May remembered his auto license number. You will recall that this was no simple number—Bradshaw himself had trouble remembering it! Ah, but perhaps this child is a mathematical genius, a prodigy with figures? Hardly! When I asked her what fraction of a pound one ounce is, you heard her answer, 'One-eighth.' Besides, both of her teachers have said—witnesses for the defense, mind you!—that Virginia May is a poor memorizer. *What better proof of her story can anyone ask than that she remembered a complicated license number?"*

With that, the prosecutor sat down.

Now that he had actually heard it said, Roberts felt relieved. The die was cast. The question was: Whose version would the jury believe—Sutherland's or his?

He faced the jury, his expression as grave as he could make it. "Ladies and gentlemen, I repeat what I said in my opening: In these times there are far too many assaults on the integrity of blameless men who have a lifetime of good works behind them. This is the thing which faces us here. I will say no more about Mr. Bradshaw's character. You saw the caliber of people who testified to it; you heard what they had to say about him. Let us get down to cases.

"Mr. Sutherland has accurately stated that we have no witness to what took place in Mr. Bradshaw's car on October 8th. But we have had ample testimony as to some significant other events of that day. You have heard the child's teacher give sworn testimony that she sent Virginia May Tucker home because of an allegation of illness that was not borne out by the school nurse's examination. You have heard Alfred Tucker, her own father, testify that Virginia May did not arrive home until 2:30 in the afternoon—although she was sent home from school at 11 in the morning. But the child says her mother asked her to go downtown to do some shopping. Did Mrs. Tucker send a sick child downtown shopping? Obviously not. Then it must have been Virginia May's own idea to go downtown. But if she was not feeling well, why didn't she go straight home? I don't have to point out to you, ladies and gentlemen, the almost embarrassing contradictions in this child's testimony.

"You have heard both of Virginia May's most recent teachers testify as to her unreliable character—her lying; her record of unexcused absences. You have also heard Alfred Tucker admit that he deals out violent punishment to his children when they do wrong. Do you begin to see the truth?

"Is it not clear that Virginia May Tucker deliberately faked illness that day, and without her family's knowledge went downtown to window-shop or go to an early movie, after which she drove home through Arthur Bradshaw's kindness—and then realized she was getting home too early, that her father had not yet left for work and would want to know why she was home before school let out? Wasn't she counting on the long slow bus ride, with frequent stops, to get her home after her father had left? Didn't the speedier ride in Arthur Bradshaw's car destroy this plan of hers? *Don't you see that Virginia May invented this fairy tale about Mr. Bradshaw to divert attention from her own misconduct and to avoid punishment by the father she feared?*"

He scowled long and hard at all twelve of them. "Ladies and gentlemen of the jury, Mr. Sutherland has made much of the fact that this child, a poor memorizer, remembered a complicated auto license number. I ask you to think: *Isn't it far more likely that she made a special effort to remember that number just so her story would sound more convincing to her father?*"

Roberts paused, then said with weary repugnance, "Perhaps she also sought to gain attention as children just entering adolescence sometimes do, by the device of accusing an adult man of wrongdoing. An unpleasant thought; but, ladies and gentlemen, the defense did not make this case unpleasant."

Roberts thrust the clean, sharp lines of his face forward. "I tell you, ladies and gentlemen, I am a father of a child—a girl—the same age as this one. Had I not been convinced of Arthur Bradshaw's utter innocence, I would never have undertaken his defense."

The jury deliberated the rest of the day. Someone took Virginia May out of the courtroom, and she did not return. Her father sat stiff in his chair, doggedly seeing it through. Sutherland spent much of his time in conversation with the bailiff near one of the windows. The judge was busy going through a mound of papers. Bradshaw methodically read a packet of letters he had brought with him.

Roberts occupied his time organizing an army of notes he had made for an auto theft case which was pending. Concentration was intermittently difficult. At one point, the jury requested a transcript of the evidence. *What do they want to know? Aren't they convinced the child has lied? Or did I slip up somewhere?* He glanced at Bradshaw, calmly reading business letters. *He's the one who should be wondering. Does he still think it can't happen?*

The day wore on. Finally, it was clear that the jury would have to be locked up for the night.

Bradshaw leaned over and whispered to Roberts, "What do you think?"

Roberts shrugged. "I try not to." He stood up. "Not very successfully, I'm afraid."

The morning was sunny. The courtroom was jammed. At 10:25 A.M. the jury filed back into the jury box.

Judge Weaver leaned across the bench, his hands clasped. He addressed Martin, the foreman.

"Have you reached a verdict?"

Martin's owlish face assumed a look of exhausted pique.

"No, Your Honor, we have not."

The judge considered. "Mr. Martin, do you think that by further discussion the jury can arrive at a verdict?"

"We do not, Your Honor."

"How are you divided?"

Martin looked in Bradshaw's direction. "We stand eight to four for acquittal. This has not changed for nine hours. We were up all night."

Judge Weaver pursed his lips and nodded. Then he leaned back. "Very well. The jury is dismissed from this case. . . . The others—please report back here at the usual time tomorrow morning."

The courtroom was quiet. There was no sound of either gratification or sympathy.

The spectators drifted away in knots of twos and threes. Alfred Tucker, in a glowering group of friends and relatives, muttered with Sutherland. A number of Bradshaw's friends came up to express regrets and leave.

Roberts sat there alone at the table, packing papers into his brief case. He looked ten years older this morning—far more worn than he had looked the night before. His hands were trembling a little.

"What's next?" It was Bradshaw, bending over him anxiously.

Roberts looked away. "They'll ask for a new trial."

"But I thought you couldn't try a man twice!"

Roberts glanced up briefly, then back at his brief case. "There was no verdict, Mr. Bradshaw."

"You think that next time—?"

Roberts laid the brief case down and buckled it shut. Then he rose and looked directly into Bradshaw's eyes. "There won't be any next time—for me, I mean."

Bradshaw frowned. "You're quitting? You don't think you can beat them?"

Roberts said slowly, "The best thing you can do right now—and I should have insisted on it before I took the case—is to see a psychiatrist."

Bradshaw's face went bloodless suddenly.

Roberts said, "Four people on that jury didn't believe the kid lied about you—even though they may well have believed that she lied about other things.

"Well, Bradshaw, they were right. I didn't see it till I got home last night.

"Bradshaw, both you and the girl made it clear that you didn't let her out near her home. She said she had to make you stop. You said you stopped where she asked. But it wasn't *near her home*. All right. Maybe somebody on the jury thought of it. I thought of it—too late—and that's why I don't want to go on with this. I'm a father, remember. Next time, Sutherland will think of it.

"Bradshaw, if that child wanted to avoid being punished by her father, it wasn't necessary for her to lie about you. She wasn't that close to her home. *She could have stayed away from her block until she was sure her father had gone to work.*"

Money Talks

by Cornell Woolrich

The detective caught Al after about a three-block run. That is, it would have been a three-block run if it had been properly sectioned off into blocks. In that case he wouldn't have caught him at all, for the detective was a good deal heavier, had a sizable paunch to push ahead of him, and Al was running for his life. Or at least his freedom, a possible ten-to-twenty years of it, and that can make a man really run.

But there were no separate blocks—it was a straightaway, an ocean pier, as a matter of fact. Al was scaled in, couldn't get off on either side. Along the first stretch, if he jumped over the rail to the sand below he'd stand out like a black dot on a white die-cube—the beach was that bright under a seven-eighths moon. And with Al down there, the detective could have used a gun on him—there were no bathers around any more. Farther out, if he jumped over the rail, he had a choice between getting away dead-drowned or being rescued with a handcuff. He couldn't swim a splash.

It was a cul-de-sac, and a beauty. The detective couldn't have done better if he'd blueprinted the whole thing ahead of time.

So he caught him.

His hand came down on Al like a ton of bricks and they both staggered to a stop. For a minute they were both too winded to say anything. They just stood there breathing a gale between them. But the detective wasn't too bushed to shift his hold from Al's shoulder, which wasn't too secure a place, to a double lock at the back of the coat collar and the cuff of one sleeve.

By this time people had formed a ring around them, the two of them posing in a tableau, in what was obviously a still life of a just-enacted arrest. Neither one of them cared about that—the detective because it was part of his profession to make arrests in public, Al because he was caught now, stuck, on the wrong side of the law, and these people couldn't help him. He knew they couldn't, and also he knew they wouldn't even if they could.

Al managed to speak first. "What's it for, copper? I'm not out of bounds down here."

"You're out of bounds any place you lift a bundle of dough."

Al's voice shrilled to a squeak. "For Pete's sake, I didn't do no such thing!"

"Then wha'd you run for?"

"I have a record, and you know it. I don't stand a prayer."

"You gave yourself away by running this time. D'you bust out running every time a patrolman starts over to check on you?"

"Not when I see them just walking towards me. But you were already running after me when I turned and looked. I just lost my head, is all."

"You lost your immunity, is all," the detective told him. "C'mon back and we'll take it up with her."

They started back along the pier, trailing a cloud of buzzing spectators like a wedge-shaped swarm of bees coming to a point behind a pair of leaders. Al was too experienced an arrestee to waste his breath making any further pleas. If they were going to listen at all, they'd listen from the original stopping position. Once they started moving you off with them, the time for listening was over. Al knew that as well as he knew his own name.

The concessionnaire was a very large woman. Large-size women seem to make better concessionnaires—

they stand out more against their usually garish backgrounds. She was blonde to the point of silveriness, shrewdly made up to take a few years off at the top, and tough as a 25-cent steak. Her pitch was a refreshment stand—hamburgers, frozen custard, soft drinks, hot dogs—*So fresh they bite you*, one little sign said.

She scowled angrily at Al as the detective brought him to a halt up against her counter.

"Got him, did you?" she said.

"Got me for what?" Al rasped. "What're you talking about, lady?"

"I'm talking about the day's receipts, wise guy. Is it on him?" she demanded of the detective.

"That's what we're coming to right now. Wait'll I get a little help here."

A boardwalk patrolman joined them and took over Al's bodily custody, freeing the detective for the search. A second policeman came up and moved the close-packed crowd back. It required a stiff-arming of chests and a shoving between shoulder blades to get them to budge at all. It was like kneading dough, because as the policeman pushed them away in one place, they closed in again in another. Many climbed up on the boardwalk railing to get a better look.

The detective went through Al's pockets as though his hands were a pair of miniature vacuum cleaners. He deposited everything on the concession counter. Al's worldly goods did not amount to much. Monetarily they consisted of seven quarters, four dimes, three nickels, four pennies, and two subway tokens, all from the right-hand trouser pocket. He carried no billfold.

The detective then searched Al in places where there were no pockets. He ran probing fingers along the hem of his coat, up and down the linings of his sleeves (from the outside), felt along his ribs, and across the chest below his undershirt. He even made Al unlace his shoes and step out of them briefly, then get back into them again.

"What 'dje do with it?" he demanded finally.

"I never took it to begin with," Al insisted.

The detective turned to the woman. "Did you *see* him grab it?"

"I didn't really catch him in the act, no—"

"Then wadaya accusing me for?" Al protested hotly before she could even finish.

"Because who else could it have been? You were at my stand just the minute before."

"Any other customers besides him?"

"Only a man and his two kids. But they had already left."

"A man taking his youngsters on an outing doesn't go in for lifting," said the detective with good psychological insight, "if only because he can't make a getaway. How much did it come to?"

"Two seventy-five."

"You mean two hundred and seventy-five dollars?"

"That's what I'm talking about," she said crisply. "Y'don't think I'd blow my stack like this over two bucks, do you?"

One of the boardwalk patrolman whistled. "You make that much in one day? I'd better change jobs with you, lady."

"Don't forget this is a three-day take—it's a holiday week-end."

"What I can't figure," said the second beach cop, "is how could he take it out of the till without your spotting him, when the cash register's over there on the opposite side, over by you."

"He didn't take it out of the till, I did," said the woman testily, as though angry at her own carelessness. "I've been in this business twenty years and I never pulled a boner like that before in my life. But there's a first time for everything, they say. See, I just finished stacking it to take home. I was due to go off, and my husband was coming on in another quarter hour or so. I don't like to leave so much money in the drawer until we close down—we stay open until one in the morning, and it gets kind of lonely along here at that hour. So I snapped a rubber band around the bills. I had the drawer out, and I put the dough down for just a second, like this. I had a batch of franks on and they started to smoke up. So I took a step over to flip them, then took a step back. It was gone, and he was gone. Add it up for yourself."

"Well, it's not on him now," the detective had to admit. "I've been all over him with a fine-tooth comb."

"Look," said the woman sharply, giving the cash drawer a quick ride out, then in again. "There's my proof. You never yet saw a cash register drawer with only a few singles and some silver in it, did you? Where's all my fives and tens? You know we break plenty of them during the day."

"I'm not doubting you, lady. I'm only saying—"

"Well, he ditched it on the run, then."

"Did you see him throw anything away?" one of the boardwalk police asked Al's original captor.

"No, I was watching for that. I kept my eyes on his hands the whole time. He never moved them. All he moved was his feet."

The two of them retraced the course of the flight, searching for the bundle every step of the way, while the third one remained at the stand, holding onto Al. They were still empty-handed when they came back.

"Of course it's gone," assented the woman, annoyed. "Somebody picked it up by now. How long do you think it's going to lie there, anyway?"

"Nope, he never threw it," the detective insisted. He gave Al a vicious shaking up. "Wha'd you do with it?"

"To do something with anything, you got to have it first," Al protested, through teeth that would have rattled if they hadn't been his own.

"That's great," said the woman bitterly. "George all the way. So whether you pull him in or not, I'm still out the dough. I stand here all day on my feet, and all I've got to show for it is a lot of salt air."

"You're covered, ain't you, lady?" said one of the patrolmen knowingly.

"My insurance ain't paying me back dollar for dollar," she snapped at him.

"Well, in *you* come," the detective told Al grimly, "whether we've found it or not."

Al trotted along beside him but with his head slightly bowed, as if to say, This is my kind of luck.

Al's wife's sister was married to Joe Timmons, a doctor more or less. Al had never been able to figure out whether this made them brother-in-law or not. But anyway Joe was Rose's brother-in-law. There could be no argument about that, and since the two of them, he and Al, got along fairly well, Al was willing to let it go at that.

Actually, Joe was a genuine enough doctor. He had attended Medical School and received his degree, but too much tinkering with bottles, of the kind that did not contain medicine, had given his status an aspect that was cloudy if not downright shady.

He was the sort of doctor who, at an earlier stage of medical progress, would have had a dingy office two flights up in some old tenement; in today's world Joe had a dingy office just one flight up in a remodeled tenement, and kept three small ads of questionable ethics running in the far-back reaches of a number of spongy-papered magazines.

Joe Timmons came to see Al in his place of detention, and Al was so downcast, so preoccupied with his own troubles, that he didn't even realize the visit was purely voluntary.

"Hullo, Joe, they get you too?" Al said dolefully without even looking up.

"What's the matter with you?" said Joe impatiently.

"What're you crying for?" Al had glanced up and seen Joe's tear-smogged eyes. "I've took it before, I'll have to take it again, that's all."

"Stop it, will you?" said Joe, more irritable than ever. "You know this is the ragweed season for me."

"Oh," said Al, remembering.

"Something's got to be done about you," Joe pronounced without further ado. "We were talking it over last night around the table, the three of us, over some cans of beer. Now if you go away this time you're going to be away a long time, and you know it, Al. Rose is going to just naturally pine away—she's really gone on you and no fooling. If Rose is unhappy, then Flo gets depressed. And if Flo gets depressed, then I have a miserable home life myself. So it's a losing game all around. Anyway, I promised the two girls I'd see what I could do for you."

"Since when are you a lawyer?" asked Al dejectedly.

"A lawyer ain't going to do you any good, Al. This is going to be three times and out for you. You're on parole and it's mandatory, it's on the books."

"But if they never found the money on me to this day, how can they make it stick?"

"That don't help much, it's still open and shut. The woman claims the money was taken. It's her word against yours. You've got a record, she hasn't. You were standing right there a minute before the money disappeared. You ran like hell. It's all stacked against you, Al. The natural supposition is going to be that you threw it away, even if the copper admits he didn't see you. They can't prove that you took it, but that ain't good enough for you. It's got to be proved that you *couldn't* have taken it."

He thought for a while.

"How much was on you when they nabbed you?"

"About seven or eight quarters, and a few nickels and pennies."

"How come no paper money?"

"I busted my last couple of bucks just before that at a shooting gallery. Then I remembered it wouldn't look too good if I was spotted practising at a place like that, even though I've never carried a live weapon in my life. So I drifted on my way with all this unused change still in my pocket."

Joe cogitated. "Something could be made out of that. We can't afford to throw anything away, no matter how little it is."

"So what can you make out of it?" said the realistic Al. "Only that I was low in cash. And they'll say that's all the more reason why I took the money."

Joe sneezed stingingly at this point.

"Somebody been sending roses to somebody in here?" he demanded indignantly. He raised his handkerchief toward his nose. "You may go up for ten, twenty years but at least you ain't got my allergy," he remarked wistfully.

"Thanks," said Al morosely.

Joe's handkerchief was still upended, without having reached his nose. It stayed there.

"I've got it!" he said. "I've got your out!"

He never did blow his nose.

"Now we'll make a deal, first of all. How much was it and where'd you put it?"

"Oh, no, you don't!" said Al firmly. "That's what they've been trying to get out of me the whole time. Wouldn't that be great, if I turned around now and—"

"But Al, I'm family," protested Joe, shocked. "I'm not a cop or a stoolie. Look, I'm sticking my neck out for you. You can't expect a favor even from a relative without making it worth his while. That's the way the world is." He waited a moment; while Al remained stubbornly silent. Then Joe said, "All right, then. Let's put it this way. How much do they *claim* you took?"

"The jane tabbed it at two seventy-five. I had no time to count it myself," said Al incautiously.

"Then here's how it goes," expounded Joe. "Two hundred to me, for getting you off, and you keep the seventy-five."

Al gouged the heels of his hands into his eye sockets. "Splitting it right down the middle, is what I call it," he intoned somberly.

Joe stood up, affronted, and made as if to leave. Then he turned his head and addressed Al over one shoulder. "Which is better," he said, "to have seventy-five smackers you can call your own, free and clear, out in the fresh air and sunshine, or to *know* where there's two hundred and seventy-five waiting—with a six-foot-thick concrete wall in between? You figure it out."

Al did, and finally gave in, with a resigned, upward flip of the hand. "It's the best I can do," he admitted glumly. "I haven't had any other offers today."

Joe reseated himself and leaned forward confidentially. "All right, where is it?" he said. "And keep it low."

Al dropped his voice. Now that the deal was made, he seemed relieved to get it off his chest. "It's still right there on the counter—" he began.

In spite of his recent injunction, Joe's own voice rose almost to a yelp of outrage. "Come on, who're you trying to kid?"

"Will you listen to me, or don't you want to hear?"

Joe wanted to hear.

"She has three big glass tanks there. One's a pale color—that's the pineapple. One's medium color—that's the orange. One is almost black—that's the grape. It's in that—the grape. The lids are chromium, but they're liftable. I tipped it up and shot it in there."

Joe squeezed his eyes tight. "And you expect it to still be in there?" he groaned.

"Sure, it's still in there. Not only that, I bet it'll be in there all the rest of the week. I cased the stand for nearly an hour, from a boardwalk bench opposite. I kept score. For every five customers for orange, there's only three for pineapple and only one for grape. It moves slow. I don't know why she stocks the stuff. Those tanks last. The next two days were slow days—Tuesday and Wednesday after the holiday weekend. And it was raining, to top it off. You know what that does to business on a boardwalk."

"It's paper, it'll be floating at the top."

"So what? She draws the stuff off from a spigot at

the bottom. Something makes them bubble, I couldn't figure what. That alone would keep it from settling to the bottom."

Joe digested all this for a while. "I've got it," he said at last, giving a fingersnap. "A fishhook. Or better still, a bent safety pin."

"Sure," said Al. "Make like you're lighting a cigarette, set fire to the whole book of matches at once. She can't prove it wasn't an accident. Throw it away from you, like anyone would—but so it lands on the floor *inside* the stand, over the other way to distract her attention. She'll be busy bending over and stamping it out. Then just tip the lid like I did."

"As soon as I have it, I'll go to work on you," Joe promised. He got up to leave. "I'll let you know," he said.

He came back to see Al only once more after that. He didn't stay long and he didn't say much—just three words.

"I got it."

Al saluted with two fingers from the edge of his eyebrow, and Joe gave him a knowing bat of the eyelashes as he turned and went out again.

Al's hearing was held in the judge's chambers. There was no jury trial since Al's previous and uncompleted sentence still hung over him like an axe, ready to fall and hit him in the back of the neck if the judge so decided. If Al was found guilty, X number of years resumed right where they had left off, plus; if found not guilty, Al was out on parole again.

The judge was a benevolent-looking man, the clerk was unbiased, but the arresting officer was neither. Also present were the concessionnaire, Al's wife Rose, and a physician who had treated the accused and wished to give expert testimony bearing on the matter at hand.

The concessionnaire having restated her complaint, the arresting officer having given an account of the accused's flight from the scene before he even knew what he was charged with, the physician now stepped forward and asked the judge's permission to submit certain medical facts which he felt to be of great importance to the case. The judge granted permission.

The expert witness identified himself as Dr. Joseph Randolph Timmons, and he presented a figure of such impeccable distinction, with his scholarly eyeglasses, dignified bearing, and air of professional erudition, that alongside him both the clerk of the court and the arresting officer appeared shoddy, rundown, and of little account.

Dr. Timmons asked only a single preliminary question of the arresting officer.

"When you caught up with the accused man, did he stand quietly, or did he fidget and wriggle around a good deal while you were holding him?"

"He stood perfectly still, never moved a hair," said the detective after a moment's thought.

Dr. Timmons then proceeded: "I am not here to vouch for my patient's character or honesty. I know nothing whatever about that. If I'd heard he was being accused of taking jewelry, silverware, furs, anything of that sort, I would not have come forward. But hearing what the charge was in this case, I felt it was my duty as a physician to bring certain facts to light.

"The patient first came to me in May of this year, complaining of an intermittent rash and itching. It would come and go, but it was causing him great trouble. At nights, for instance, when he was at home in bed, it never seemed to bother him. It was only at certain times during the day that it would suddenly show up, then gradually die down again. Sometimes it came on three or four times during the course of a single day, then again only once or twice.

"He told me that whenever he left a barber shop he had it, and whenever he went to a motion-picture show. But when he went into a bar to have a glass of beer, he didn't have it. Yet when he went into the same bar and had a couple of ryes, he did have it.

"He never had it on buses, but once getting out of a taxi he had it. If he bought a single package of cigarettes he didn't have it, but if he bought a whole carton at a time he did have it, before he even began to smoke them. A mysterious and interesting case, you will admit.

"I have here a record of his visits, taken from my office appointment book. If your Honor would care to examine it."

" 'A. Bunker, Monday, ten A.M.—' " read the judge aloud, rapidly shuffling through a number of loose-leaf pages the doctor had handed him. " 'A. Bunker, Friday, three P.M.—' He seems to have visited you at the rate of twice a week."

"He did, your Honor, all through June, July, and the greater part of August. He told me right at the start he couldn't afford to come to see me that often, but since the case fascinated me, and the poor fellow was badly in need of help, I told him not to worry about it—to pay me whatever he could as we went along."

The judge cast an admiring glance at the man before him. "There should be more practitioners like you, Dr. Timmons."

"Not all of us are money grabbers," said the doctor modestly. "Well, to go on with this man's case history. A quick test showed that the condition was not dermatological. In lay language that means that it was not a skin infection. I hadn't thought it was because it came and went, instead of being constant. Therefore there was only one other thing it could be. It had to be an allergy.

"But just knowing it was an allergy wasn't enough. It had to be identified, isolated, its cause discovered, or the patient couldn't be helped. I tested him on a number of foods first, and got negative results. Then I tested him on fabrics, such as are worn on the body—

wool, cotton, dacron. Again negative. I even tested him on lint, such as is commonly found in the linings of most pockets. Nothing there either."

He broke off to ask, "I'm not being too technical for your Honor, am I?"

The judge was sitting engrossed, his hands supporting the sides of his face. He said, "I don't know when I've heard a more interesting exposition than the one you've been giving, Doctor. Go on, by all means. This is almost like a medical detective story!"

"These exhaustive tests," resumed the magnetic medic, "might have continued indefinitely, might still be going on today and for many months to come, if it hadn't been for one of those little accidental breaks which pop up when least expected and give an investigator a short cut to the answer. As I've said, I was lenient in collecting payment for the treatments. After several visits for which he'd paid me nothing, the patient one day said he'd like to make a small payment on account. I agreed, of course, and he handed me a five-dollar bill. I'd already noticed he was somewhat improved on that particular day. The ailment had not disappeared by any means, but it was in one of its occasional periods of remission.

"I thought it only fair to dash off a receipt for the fee. When I happened to look up a moment later, I was amazed to see what had occurred."

Like the good showman he was, the doctor paused artfully.

"But rather than describe it in dry words, I'm going to let you see for yourselves just what happened."

He turned to Al. "Please remove your jacket, Mr. Bunker."

Al complied, but with a somewhat apprehensive look on his face. He handed the jacket over to the doctor, who in turn handed it to the clerk, who draped it neatly over the edge of his table-top desk.

"Now, roll up the sleeves of your shirt," was the

doctor's next instruction. "As high as they'll go—all the way up to your shoulders."

Al again obeyed, but with more and more of a troubled expression, like someone who knows he is in for an uncomfortable experience. In this instance the doctor speeded up the process by helping him, in the course of which his own hands, unavoidably, glanced lightly upward along Al's forearms.

The doctor turned to the others.

"I want you to look at his hands and arms before we go any further. Hold out your arms, Mr. Bunker."

Al stiffly extended his arms straight out before him at chest level, in grotesque resemblance to a high-diver about to launch off into space. His arms were no different from other arms of the male variety—hairy on one side, smooth and heavily veined on the other, but otherwise unblemished.

"Now I'd like a piece of paper currency from one of you, if I may. An ordinary banknote. I'm asking you to furnish it, instead of using one of my own, so there can be no question of the genuineness of this test."

Like three men at a table when the waiter brings the check, each reacted according to his personal characteristics. The arresting officer made no move toward his pockets at all. The clerk, who was on small salary, managed to outfumble the judge, even in spite of the latter's encumbering robes. The majesty of the law produced a wallet that seemed to contain nothing less than bills in double digits.

"Will a ten be all right?" asked the judge.

"Quite all right," assured the doctor. "It isn't the denomination that's the chief factor."

He turned back to Al with the ten dollars.

"Now take this in your hands, Mr. Bunker."

Al drew back, like a child who is about to be given castor oil.

"Now come on," said the doctor with a touch of impatience. "I'm trying to help you, not harm you."

Al pinched one corner of the bill between his thumb

and forefinger, as though he were holding onto a fluttering moth by one wing.

"Don't just hold it between two fingers—put all your fingers on it at once," insisted the doctor. Then when Al had done so, the doctor urged, "Now pass it over into your other hand."

A few portentous seconds ticked by, as though the doctor were taking a pulse count.

"That'll do. You've held it long enough."

Al released it with a long-drawn sigh that could be heard throughout the judge's chamber.

There was a breathless wait.

For several moments nothing happened. Then Al dug his fingernails into the back of one hand and raked it. Then the other. Then the back of one arm. Then the inside. Angry red blotches, almost the size of strawberries, began to appear.

By now Al was almost like a sufferer from St. Vitus's Dance. His feet stood still, but up above he writhed as though he'd been bitten by five hundred mosquitoes. He couldn't get at all the places that needed scratching. He didn't have enough fingernails.

"This poor devil," said the doctor with dramatic effect, "is allergic to paper money. Whether it is something in the paper itself, or some dye in the ink used in the engraving, I can't say. But I can say this: he can no more touch paper money, his own or somebody else's, without having this happen to him, than I can fly out of that window.

"You will remember from the detective's own testimony that this man had only coins on him at the time he was arrested. That was the result of instructions I myself gave him—a prescription, as a matter of fact, as much as if I had given him pills or capsules. His wife breaks a dollar or two every day—bills, you understand—and hands him the change when he leaves the house. That way he can make whatever small purchases are required without falling into the lamentable condition you see him in now."

Al's forehead was a ripple of parallel ridges. He wasn't making believe either. No actor could have simulated the wish, the yearning, the compulsion to scratch that so obviously possessed Al.

"And finally," concluded the doctor, "I only wish to point out that *had* my patient actually taken the money he is accused of stealing, he could not have run as he did and then later stood perfectly still while being searched. He would have been squirming uncontrollably, scratching himself all over, as you see him doing right now. The arresting officer admitted nothing of the sort took place."

The judge cleared his throat.

"It seems fair enough to assume, in view of what we have all witnessed with our own eyes, that the money could not possibly have been taken by the accused. It must have been taken by some other, unknown person, who somehow made good his escape in the crowd."

He addressed Al in an almost fatherly manner.

"You can thank Dr. Timmons for getting you out of what might have been very serious trouble. But you brought all this on yourself, Albert. Next time, don't run from a parole officer when you see him coming towards you. These men are your friends, not your enemies. They are only trying to help you."

"Yes, sir," said Al meekly. He looked at his friend the detective, and his friend the detective looked at him. It was a most undecipherable look—as a cat looks at its friend, the mouse, and a mouse looks at its friend, the cat.

"Charges dismissed," said the judge, with self-satisfaction.

Outside Joe walked a few steps with Al, toward where Rose was waiting. Joe had one arm slung over Al's shoulder, giving him sound medical advice. "And from now on, see that you keep your hot little mitts off any stray money that happens to be floating around. This is a trick that will work only once."

"For Pete's sake, what'd you do to me?" Al demanded.

Joe murmured, "A solution of itching powder, mixed with something to delay the action a few minutes, so I'd have time for my spiel."

"How come it didn't get you?"

"Skin-colored plastic gloves. I soaked them in it. You can't tell unless you look close—they have the nails painted on, and I wore my ring on the outside. Dunk yourself in a hot tub when you get home," he added. "It ought to wear off in about half an hour."

Al and Rose went walking off arm in arm, like the devoted man and wife they were.

"Mr. Bunker!" an urgent voice suddenly called out behind them.

Rose nudged Al sharply. "Better turn around and see what he wants. It'll look funny if you don't."

"Ung-ung," said Al in a calamitous undertone. He turned slowly.

It was the clerk of the court, panting with an inscrutable look on his face—a look impossible to describe unless you actually saw it.

"Would you mind—his Honor—I'm glad I caught up with you—you forgot to return his Honor's ten dollars."

The Lie Detector

by James McKimmey

I had seemed to be living elatedly somewhere in outer space after I'd graduated from law school the previous summer, passed the California bar examination, and been lucky enough to become an assistant to F. Berton Blackmore, the renowned attorney. But ever since the murder of movie director Peter Hurley and the arrest of his beautiful young sixth wife for the crime, I'd been gradually coming back down to earth.

Now, seated in a courtroom in the Sierra Nevada Mountains, I realized that I was at last solidly reunited with terra firma. The trial was not yet over, but I knew quite certainly that F. Berton Blackmore would lose the contest if it continued the way it had been going. And reporters, photographers, and television cameras were waiting to announce the event to the world.

For years I'd viewed Blackmore as an absolute hero, despite his irascibility. I'd envied him his fame, his wealth, and the beautiful women in his life. I'd imagined him to be virtually invulnerable in a courtroom.

It was true that he was now cast in a different role from his usual one. Normally he defended clients in malpractice suits and this was, at fifty-eight, his first murder trial. Yet it was totally surprising to me that his effort to win it for his client was sliding rapidly downhill without ever having gotten started.

The ambitious young prosecutor, smelling blood, stood questioning the last of several witnesses he'd called, including a few who had only the remotest association with the murder. The judge, a lugubrious-looking middle-aged man, appeared to be half dozing.

And the gorgeous auburn-haired Celeste Hurley who was on trial for murder had the look of a fragile flower brutalized by an unexpected rainstorm.

The jury, in spite of wide differences in age, sex, experience, and intelligence, displayed one facial expression that said: Our minds are made up. End these foolish formalities so we can declare this cheap little bit-part actress guilty and go home.

F. Berton Blackmore sat beside me in mournful silence, wearing one of his expensive suits. His thick, silvery hair appeared casually arranged though obviously styled by San Francisco's best hairdresser. His round face with its thick rosebud lips had sagged into the look of a defeated hound dog.

It was as though I had suddenly realized, despite all evidence to the contrary, that the sun rose in the west.

But facts were facts, and the facts were these:

Peter Hurley had finished his last picture, which had been shot in Micronesia, and returned to the States to join Celeste, his wife of seven months. They had come to his spectacular vacation home on the south shore of Lake Tahoe. Two hours after their arrival, Hurley had been shot dead by a weapon yet to be found.

The shots had been heard by a carpenter working on a new house nearby. The carpenter had summoned the police. Hurley's young wife, the most obvious suspect since no one else had been found in or near the house, had been arrested.

Mrs. Hurley had then telephoned Blackmore. Peter Hurley and Blackmore had been close friends for a long time. Blackmore had taken the case—surely out of compassion rather than his usual astuteness, I now thought. (I had driven Blackmore in his limousine from San Francisco to Tahoe—acting as his chauffeur was part of my job, despite my legal education.)

Celeste Hurley had denied murdering her husband. She claimed that the carpenter, a handsome, muscular twenty-three-year-old named Fred Apple, had appeared abruptly in the living room shortly after their arrival and shot Hurley several times.

Our investigation had turned up no evidence of any relationship between the victim and the carpenter. Fred Apple had insisted upon his innocence. There appeared to be no motive for Apple to kill Hurley.

Moreover, Apple had volunteered to take a lie-detector test by stipulation, meaning that the results could be used in court. And the test indicated that Apple was telling the truth when he said he hadn't murdered Peter Hurley.

Celeste Hurley had also been willing to take the test on the same basis, but Blackmore had advised her against it—I suppose because of some reservation about the absolute reliability of lie detectors.

But after the prosecutor, in his opening statement, had established the widow's probable motive for killing her husband—while filming in Micronesia, Peter Hurley had carried on a blazing affair with the movie's female star—I was no longer certain about Blackmore's directions. Three prosecution witnesses who had worked with Hurley on location had sworn to the effect that he had been cheating on his current wife.

Although that rumor had never been mentioned to me prior to the trial, I was certain Celeste had known about it. Knowing glints of anger had appeared in her eyes during the testimony of those three witnesses. Consequently, I'd decided that F. Berton Blackmore, with his skill in extracting pertinent facts from his clients, had known as well. And I began to wonder if Blackmore had advised the lady against the lie-detector test because he thought she might actually be guilty. Even so, he might have taken the case certain that a small-town prosecutor would be no match for him. But the prosecutor had proven more than capable. And the tide was now running strongly against our client. I knew that the jury was going to declare Celeste Hurley guilty as charged if the tide didn't change, and quickly.

* * *

The prosecutor finished interrogating his last witness and Blackmore was given the opportunity to cross-examine. He declined, and the judge adjourned proceedings until ten the next morning.

I was driving Blackmore toward the hotel where he had taken a suite and I had a small room on a lower floor. I could see his face in the rearview mirror: grim, petulant, hurt, angered, resentful.

"What can I say, Mr. Blackmore?" I offered finally.

" 'What can I say?' " he mimicked, his voice charged with sarcasm. "If you had deliberately set out to find one singular phrase calculated to annoy me, Mr. Cheves, you could not have been more successful!" He had addressed me as Mr. Cheves from the beginning of our relationship, never as Sidney. But I'd always known that genius did not necessarily breed likability, and in spite of the difficulty of maintaining a civil, if not warm, personal relationship I hadn't lost my awe of him.

For years I'd dreamed of one day achieving a similar position in my life and career. I'd studied hard and tried to emulate him, purchasing a flamboyant wardrobe to the best of my buying power and investing myself in amateur theatrical productions in the hope of learning his dramatic flair.

Now I realized that instead of being concerned that the woman charged with the murder of her husband was well on her way to prison, I was regretting the fact that Blackmore was on the brink of losing his first case since he had achieved his reputation.

I dined alone in the hotel coffee shop, trying to think of some logical avenue that might lead us away from the path matters were now taking.

By dinner's end I had made up my mind.

But the next morning I was feeling a new pride and a refreshing excitement as I drove Blackmore to court. I had handed him a sheaf of papers, saying, "Please read these, sir. I did some investigating last night. These are the results as well as my ideas on how to proceed."

He didn't give any reaction until I'd parked beside the Hall of Justice and he got out of the car and faced me squarely in the bright sunlight.

"I have always had misgivings about you, Mr. Cheves," he said, "but one of them was not that you suffered from the delusion you are Sherlock Holmes. What have you been ingesting, sir, to have acquired such a preposterous idea?"

He stuffed my papers into his briefcase, turned, and pushed brusquely past the reporters to go inside.

Yet minutes after the trial resumed he was on his feet, requesting that the carpenter, Fred Apple, be recalled to the witness stand.

Apple, who had been detained in an outer room, came striding into court with the brisk authority of a man who was entirely sure of himself. He went to the witness box, sat down, and looked around with an engaging smile. He wore jeans and a neatly pressed blue workshirt.

I was at the defense table beside Celeste Hurley when Blackmore moved across the courtroom to Apple. She asked me in a timorous voice, "What's he doing?"

I shook my head, but I could feel my pulse beating more quickly. He'd read my papers after all.

"Mr. Apple," my employer intoned grandly, "you have testified previously that your complete and sole knowledge of the details of Peter Hurley's murder was that you heard shots fired in the house where he died— and nothing more."

"You got that one right," Apple agreed in his rather slight voice with the Texas drawl.

Blackmore began pacing majestically. Then he said, his voice reaching to the farthest corners of the courtroom, "You are not at all what you seem to be—are you, Mr. Apple?"

The members of the jury became more alert. The judge seemed to wake up. The bailiff sat erect. The prosecutor frowned.

Apple grinned genially. "Well, if I ain't what I seem to be, then I don't know as to what I am! But what I think I am is a poor little ol' boy from Weatherford, Texas."

"Really." That one word seemed to carry more portent than the thousands of words that had flowed in this room since the trial began. Blackmore was indeed a superb performer, which was probably why he and the late Peter Hurley had been such great friends. In many ways, they had really been in the same business.

"I've received reports on you, Mr. Apple," Blackmore went on. "It's hardly a secret that you've been frequenting Mary's Café and Tavern since you arrived here in late spring."

Apple shrugged. "I like Mary. Like her place. It's a lot like home."

"Home?" Mr. Blackmore said. His eyes rolled upward. He took a deep breath. "Home?"

"Weatherford, Texas. Sure enough."

Mr. Blackmore seemed to be smiling at some secret joke. "Do they serve the beer warm down in Weatherford, Mr. Apple?"

"It sure gets hot enough sometimes that it warms the beer, all right."

"And you *like* your beer warm, don't you, Mr. Apple? Not refrigerated. That's why Mary keeps a warm supply especially for you. Isn't that true, Mr. Apple?"

"Too-cold beer always kind of froze my taste buds," Apple said, his voice becoming stronger and more penetrating.

"But you do occasionally drink something besides beer?"

"I like something with more jolt in her now and again."

"Such as a gin and tonic?"

"Your Honor," the prosecutor said, standing, "this is going nowhere. There's no relevance."

The judge held up his hand. "Proceed, Mr. Blackmore."

"Thank you, Your Honor." He continued to examine Apple. "You also prefer your gin and tonic without ice, do you not?"

"Like I said," Apple replied, "too cold always kind of—"

"Freezes your taste buds," Blackmore finished. "You often eat at Mary's as well as drink there, don't you, Mr. Apple?"

"Sure do."

"What do you like to eat when you're at Mary's, Mr. Apple?"

"Well, them good old American hamburgers she serves are mighty tasty."

"Anything else?"

"Can't beat Mary's steaks! Big, juicy, good old American steaks you can cut with a fork."

"And what do you like to go along with these good old American hamburgers and good old American steaks, Mr. Apple?"

Apple's smile widened. "Big gang of them good old American chips."

"Ah, yes," Blackmore said. "Do you mean potato chips, Mr. Apple? Or would you possibly mean French-fried potatoes?"

"French fries is what I mean. I love taters done that way."

Blackmore began pacing again. Now every jury member was watching him with great concentration. I was feeling tremendous satisfaction. I'd found out about Mary and her place from other guests at Apple's rooming house, and I'd interviewed her at length. She'd responded easily and with eagerness. Mary was a real talker.

"What else do you do besides carpentry, Mr. Apple?" asked my employer.

"Ain't got a particle of talent for any other thing," he said.

A furtive smile again shaped Blackmore's rosebud lips. He started to speak again, then hesitated. He paced out a small circle, then finally asked, "When Mary was about to take a journey to San Francisco a few weeks ago, did you tell her to bust an ankle?" (Mary had told me she'd thought it surprisingly crude of a man so otherwise pleasant.)

Apple's eyes narrowed. "I don't know as I said any such."

Again the prosecutor got to his feet. "There's no sense to any of this, Your Honor! What is my colleague trying to prove?"

"I'll tell you what I'm trying to prove," Blackmore responded. "And that is that this man is not what he claims to be!"

"I'm just a carpenter from Weatherford, Texas," Apple drawled in protest. "And I got the papers to prove it!"

"Oh, yes, I'm sure you do," Blackmore said dryly. "And you *have* obviously learned carpentry well enough to gain employment. You have also been speaking with a good enough Texas drawl to convince most people. But you've also betrayed little giveaways along the way. You like your beer warm, your gin and tonic without ice. You refer to French-fried potatoes as chips. You're really an Englishman, aren't you, Mr. Apple? Or whatever your real name is?"

"Objection!" shouted the prosecutor.

"Overruled," said the judge.

"I'm just a good old boy from—"

"Then," Blackmore interrupted, "you told Mary to bust an ankle prior to taking a trip—no doubt an intended similitude for the phrase 'break a leg.' Meaning, of course, in the theatrical world, 'good luck.' You've used other show business phrases and words according to Mary—run of the play, poor study, props, and so forth. You're really an actor, aren't you, Mr.

Apple? A very good actor? Your portrayal—especially in view of the fact that you are actually English—of a poor old boy from Weatherford, Texas, is a *tour de force*. And because you *are* such a superlative actor, it's my belief that you were able to fool the lie detector. Isn't that true?"

"Objection! Objection!" called the prosecutor.

Blackmore had led the man to the gate and now he was going to lead him through, just as my script had indicated.

Blackmore moved toward the witness until he was squarely in front of Apple. They gazed at each other unwaveringly, then Blackmore said, "I imagine that when you took the lie-detector test, you securely imagined yourself to be another person—an innocent party. As a consequence, your blood pressure, pulse, respiration, and skin response—all measures recorded by the polygraph machine—responded as those of someone who was innocent of the crime. You are formidable, sir, to have done that. Now why not admit not only that you're British, but that you are one of the finest actors alive?"

My words, just as I'd typed them out late the night before—designed to exploit Apple's ego!

"And then," Blackmore said to the witness, "tell us why you—and not my client—murdered Peter Hurley!"

"I object!" the prosecutor protested.

"Will you sit down, Harry?" the judge told him.

"Please answer the question, Mr. Apple," Blackmore said.

"Not Apple," the man said, "Grimstone—Robin Grimstone, from London England. 'E 'ad it comin', gov'nor. I shot 'im through the 'ead."

There was a gasp from the jurors and spectators. I felt light-headed with triumph.

Grimstone then admitted that he was indeed one of the finest actors alive—if not the best. Adding that if

Peter Hurley had not turned him down for a part in his latest motion picture, the entire world would know it by now.

But Hurley, stupidly, hadn't given him that chance. So Grimstone had worked out a plan to murder Hurley and he carried it out, strengthening his plea of innocence by asking for the lie-detector test. Yes, he'd killed Peter Hurley, he stated without regret. He even told Blackmore where he'd hidden the murder weapon. It mattered not that he would go to prison, he said—he'd been there before, and no walls could hold him. He would escape again, and reappear in other faces, using other accents, to prove—finally and universally his true greatness as a thespian.

At the end of his confession, the judge ordered the bailiff to take Grimstone into custody, then asked the lawyers to meet him in his chambers. When that meeting had ended it was mutually agreed that the trial should be terminated. Celeste Hurley was free, and Robin Grimstone was jailed to await trial.

Blackmore and I were walking toward the doors, outside of which reporters, photographers, and television cameras were waiting. "We did it, didn't we, Mr. Blackmore?" I said with enthusiasm.

"We?" he asked.

"You and I—yes," I said, startled.

"I rather think it was my show, was it not?"

"But I did the investigation."

"Certainly. You're my assistant."

"On my own, I mean! I thought up the way to handle it—it was all in the papers I gave you."

"What papers?" he asked archly, carrying the briefcase that contained them. He adjusted his tie and moved a hand through his hair to make sure it appeared casually rumpled. "You're deliberately trying to annoy me again, aren't you, Mr. Cheves? I should try to avoid that in the future if I were you, or I think I shall have to let you go."

Then we were outside facing a lightning storm of

electronic flashes. As reporters and television cameras moved in on him I stepped to the edge of the crowd and listened in grim silence as F. Berton Blackmore responded to questions from the press. He never mentioned my name.

The limousine moved swiftly down the mountain on the return trip to San Francisco. The chauffeur I'd hired, white-haired with a neat white moustache and goatee, drove. I sat on his right with my left wrist heavily bandaged. Blackmore was in back as usual, with Celeste Hurley beside him. Once again she looked quite stunning.

I was beginning to understand more and more about F. Berton Blackmore. He had admitted to me that he hadn't represented Celeste for reasons of compassion, or even for the money. The reason he'd taken on what had seemed to be such a risky gamble was simply an interest in acquiring one of Peter Hurley's beautiful women—although now that he had her, he already seemed bored with the acquisition.

"I think," he said angrily to me, "that you displayed an extreme degree of foolishness by visiting Grimstone in his jail cell! Why did you?"

"I told you, sir, I wanted to congratulate him on his talent as an actor."

"But he's a murderer."

"Of course he is—but he's still a marvelous actor."

"And now he's escaped! How could he *possibly* have acquired the gun that enabled him to walk out of that jail and disappear?"

"*I* certainly didn't give it to him, sir!"

"Your attempt at humor is abominably shallow, Mr. Cheves!"

The police had, of course, questioned me about that. But why would the assistant of the attorney who had deduced the fact that Robin Grimstone was the real murderer of Peter Hurley wish to smuggle a small pistol—the kind one might carry while traveling—into Grimstone's cell and so allow him to escape?

"Then falling down in your room and breaking your wrist!" Blackmore said accusingly. "Clumsy, as well as foolish!"

"My feet simply went out from under me," I said. I looked at the bandaged wrist. It did look professionally done.

"So now I'm required to have a new driver!" Blackmore said petulantly. "Are you certain this man is qualified?"

The driver looked hurt and drove on as Blackmore continued to grumble. "It ruined everything, his escape—made it seem that my apprehending him was useless. Why didn't they search him properly? Small towns! I've always hated them."

I was feeling better now than I had since the trial ended.

"Bugs," said the driver, pointing to where an insect had just smashed into the glass in front of us. "Gettin' all over da windscreen."

"What did he say?" Blackmore said angrily from the back seat.

"He said bugs are getting all over the *windshield*!" I replied, looking back and smiling. The girl smiled at Blackmore and moved closer to him.

I leaned back and relaxed. I might not enjoy it, but I could use several more months as F. Berton Blackmore's assistant in order to study his courtroom manners at greater length. I had the intelligence and inventiveness—all I needed was the style. And, with the help of another expert drama coach, I was going to get it. Success would ensue, and beautiful women would follow.

Contentedly, I turned my attention to the driver, hoping that he'd have the sense to keep quiet when not required to speak and that the bloke wasn't absent-minded enough to suddenly start driving down the left side of the road instead of the right.

The Auteur Theory

by Jon L. Breen

Martin Boyle had just returned from the screening of a particularly inept skin flick when he received Vince Kowalski's call. Although he and the lawyer were old acquaintances, the initial polite small talk didn't fool him for a minute. The call had to be about their mutual friend Gary Whitwood, the movie director who would go on trial for murder in a few days.

"Look, Vince," Martin said, interrupting some idle pleasantry, "get to the point. How is Gary doing? I haven't talked to him in a week or two."

"Well, he's been pretty busy finishing up *Close of Darkness*—they just finished shooting today." Whitwood had been allowed to complete his latest film while on bail and awaiting trial.

"I don't know how he could concentrate on making a film. Well, how's the defense shaping up? How does it look?"

"Bad. They have a strong circumstantial case, Marty. Very strong. Gary says he didn't do it, and I believe him, but getting the jury to believe him is going to take some doing. They don't know Gary the way we do, and my job is to make them know him."

"Vince, if there's anything I can do to help, you know . . ."

"That's what you said before, Marty, and that's why I called. I think you *can* help. I'd like you to testify for the defense at Gary's trial. I have an idea that might help him. Frankly, I'm at the point where I'll try anything."

"Sure, Vince, I'll be glad to. But I don't have any evidence to offer, unless I'm some sort of character witness. Is that what you had in mind?"

"Yeah, sort of. Marty, I'd like to talk to you about it in some detail. Are you free this evening or do you have to go look at some turkey?"

"No, I've done my turkey-watching for the day. A thing called *Deep Navel*."

"Great title, but it sounds like a . . ."

"That's what it is, and the title's the best thing about it. *Onlooker* wants me to cover the whole movie scene from top to bottom, and I thought a skin flick might be sort of fun for a change. But most of the early scenes are in shadows, and when the skin finally appears you wish they'd go back in the shadows—you know what I mean?"

"No, I never go to that kind of picture. Look, Marty, is it O.K. if I drop in around eight? It shouldn't take long."

"Sure, Vince. I'll see you then."

Martin Boyle hung up the phone. The invitation to testify surprised him. Maybe Vince wanted to have a film critic appear for the defense because the man Gary Whitwood was accused of killing had been a film critic—Grover Blunt, found viciously knifed to death in his hotel room a couple of days after his review of Gary Whitwood's most recent picture had appeared in print. The review had been a scathing pan.

It was absurd to think a director would kill a critic over a bad review, but the weapon had been traced to Gary and he'd been seen in the hotel by several witnesses around the time of the murder. Gary claimed he had come to the hotel to see Blunt but had changed his mind and never gone to the critic's room.

Bad as it looked, Martin couldn't bring himself to believe that Gary had done it. Gary was a warm, understanding, low-key sort of guy, not a murderer. That time when he'd found out about Martin's affair with Judy, his wife, for example. The three of them had talked it out like civilized and sophisticated people, and their friendship hadn't been affected at all. Of course, ending the affair had been the only decent thing to do under the circumstances, and both Martin and Judy had looked elsewhere.

Yes, as he'd told Vince, Martin Boyle would do anything to help Gary Whitwood out of the jam he was in, and looked forward to the lawyer's visit to find out the plan of action.

It was a full month before Martin Boyle actually took the stand at the trial of Gary Whitwood. At that, the action was going along at a brisk pace for such a highly publicized murder case, and the defense was scheduled to wrap up a day or two after Martin's testimony. Things had gone about as expected, the prosecution presenting a strong circumstantial case, with Gary's testimony a simple denial. The defense had been unable to explain how Gary's carving knife came to be used in the crime.

Martin felt his hand shaking slightly as he took the oath, but he had a good actor's confidence he'd do all right once the questioning began.

"State your name, please, for the record," said Vince Kowalski pleasantly.

"Martin Boyle."

"And your occupation?"

"Film critic."

"Mr. Boyle, would you kindly tell the court and the jury something about your experience as a film critic— that is, what would qualify you to speak as an expert about film?"

Hendricks, the prosecutor, rose and said mildly, "Your Honor, I fail to see what bearing the witness's credentials as a movie critic can have on this case."

"Your Honor," Vince replied, "my client is a well known filmmaker. Mr. Boyle's view of his films has a bearing on my defense."

"Truly," Hendricks countered, "I fail to see what the

quality or lack of same of Mr. Whitwood's pictures can possibly have to do with his defense against a charge of homicide."

The judge said, "I wish to give the defense every latitude. I trust you can make the connection clear, Mr. Kowalski?"

"I hope to, Your Honor."

"Proceed."

"Mr. Boyle, you were about to tell us something about your qualifications."

"Well, I reviewed films for my university daily, then spent several years on a limited-circulation film journal called *Montage* and one year as movie reviewer for *Lady's Day,* my services there abruptly terminated because I didn't like *The Sound of Music* very much. I am currently film critic for *Onlooker* magazine. I have done books on the films of Lowell Sherman, Ford Beebe, René Clair, and H. Bruce Humberstone and contributed . . ."

"If it will help speed things along, Your Honor," Hendricks chimed in, "I am more than willing to stipulate Mr. Boyle's experience and astuteness as a critic. I, too, had my reservations about *The Sound of Music*—all those appalling children . . ."

Boyle caught a look of dismay on the face of one juror. Cracks like that wouldn't help the prosecution much. Perhaps the Assistant D.A. could be trapped into knocking Mary Tyler Moore.

"I think we may confine our discussion to the defendant's films, Mr. Hendricks," the judge said. "Proceed, Mr. Kowalski."

"Thank you, Your Honor, and thank *you,* Mr. Hendricks. Now, Mr. Boyle, are you familiar with the films directed by my client, Gary Whitwood?"

"Yes, I am."

"Do you believe, Mr. Boyle, in the auteur theory?"

"Sometimes. It depends."

"Would you explain to the court what the auteur theory is?"

"To put it briefly, the auteur theory holds that the director is the author of the film and that the total output of a given film director expresses certain continuing motifs and a consistent world view, just as the total output of a novelist does."

"And when does this theory not apply?"

"In situations where the director is a hired hand and does not have full control over his material, as was often the case in the major Hollywood studios."

"Do you believe my client Gary Whitwood has full control over his product?"

"As I understand it, he does."

"Objection, Your Honor," Hendricks said. "That is a conclusion of the witness. Though why I'm objecting on that ground I can't imagine since this whole line of questioning seems quite irrelevant to me."

"That's two objections, Mr. Hendricks," His Honor said. "To the first one, I say objection sustained and direct that the answer be stricken on grounds of incompetence. To the second implied objection, I say overruled, trusting that counsel for the defense will soon connect it up."

"Mr. Boyle, let me phrase my question another way. Do Mr. Whitwood's films express a certain consistent viewpoint?"

"Yes, I believe they do."

"And how would you characterize that viewpoint?"

"I would say, as a pacifist viewpoint. A belief in non-violence as a means to achieve desired goals."

"Would you say that this view is typical of most commercial filmmakers today?"

"Decidedly not. Whitwood has been swimming against the tide."

"In Mr. Whitwood's recent films, have you seen opportunities for violence?"

"Certainly. They have been crime films and have presented many opportunities for explicit violence."

"But always the opportunities have been avoided?"

"That is correct."

"And most of the other contemporary filmmakers dealing with similar crime themes would, in your view, have resorted to violence?"

"Yes."

"Why would a filmmaker desire to tone down violence in his films?"

"Objection, Your Honor. Is Mr. Boyle to be expected to read the minds of countless movie directors?"

"I belive Mr. Boyle's expertise as established should qualify him to answer without resort to telepathy. You may answer, Mr. Boyle."

"Well, to get a more favorable rating, perhaps—a G or a PG, say, instead of an R."

"And what were the ratings of Mr. Whitwood's last three pictures?"

"R."

"Meaning that unaccompanied children cannot attend?"

"Yes."

"And the most restrictive rating other than an X?"

"Correct. And they don't generally give X's for violence."

"Why the R, Mr. Boyle, if there was no violence in the films?"

"Mr. Whitwood has never been shy about sex, nudity, or strong language."

"So the lack of explicit violence could not have been motivated by the ratings?"

"No."

"Your Honor," said Hendricks in a weary tone, "this discussion of movies and ratings is all very interesting, but where is it getting us?"

"Is that an objection, Mr. Hendricks?"

"Just a question, Your Honor."

"Perhaps with fewer rhetorical questions we'll find out. Mr. Kowalski?"

"Thank you, Your Honor. Mr. Boyle, my client is accused of a very violent, very bloody crime. Grover Blunt was found dead in a pool of his own blood, the victim of multiple stab wounds in the face, chest, stomach, and legs. Is there any precedent for this brutal violence in the films of Gary Whitwood?"

"None."

"No scenes of such bloodiness and goriness?"

"None."

"And in the films of other present-day commercial directors?"

"Many. Far too many for queasy chaps like myself."

"Could a man of Whitwood's sensitivity, his abhorrence of violence, have committed such a crime?"

Prosecutor Hendricks seemed truly aroused for the first time. "Your Honor, I do object. Surely Mr. Boyle is not qualified to give a conclusion on such a question. He is not a psychiatrist."

"Objection sustained."

"Let me put it this way. Could a murderer capable of such a bloody and heinous crime, who was also a film director of crime films, find ample opportunity in the present cinematic climate to put such murderous interests on celluloid?"

"Objected to on the same grounds."

"Not quite the same situation. Overruled."

"Yes, of course he could."

"And does it not seem reasonable that a murderer so inclined would take such an opportunity to vent his violent nature on film?"

"Objection!"

"Sustained."

"No more questions." Kowalski sat down.

Hendricks rose and sighed deeply. "Your Honor, I don't know where to begin. I have never seen such a ridiculous defense."

"Objection!" cried Kowalski, shooting back to his feet.

"Mr. Hendricks, please. The time for closing statements will come. Do you wish to ask the witness any questions?"

"I do indeed. Mr. Boyle, do you think the murderer

could be a director of Walt Disney movies who killed because he had no chance to sublimate his hostility on film?"

"That's a ridiculous question, Your Honor," said Kowalski.

"It's not the first," Hendricks said under his breath but audible to the jury.

"Mr. Hendricks, your question is blatantly facetious, apart from calling for a speculation on the part of the witness. It will be stricken."

"Mr. Boyle, are you a close personal friend of the defendant?"

"Yes, I am," Martin replied without hesitation.

"Would you like to help him get off?"

"My purpose in testifying is to tell the truth to the best of my knowledge and ability."

"Do you usually find the directors' films reflect their private personalities?"

"Not always."

"Are directors of comedies usually funny men?"

"Sometimes. Often not."

"Are men who make violent films generally violent men?"

"No, not usually In my experience."

"Are makers of family films full of sweetness and light?"

"No, they're often quite cynical."

"And are makers of pacifist films usually themselves non-violent?"

"Yes."

"How do you explain this strange difference?"

"Purveyors of comedy, violence, and homely sentimentality are usually working in established commercial grooves, turning out films in certain ways that are known to be palatable to the public. Pacifist filmmakers on the other hand are not moving in the usual ways. They are inevitably going against the stream, offering non-commercial approaches when the opportunity for the usual mixture presents itself. To do that, their motives must be something other than the financial aspect that motivates most filmmakers. When a man takes a position in opposition to his best monetary interests, it says something for the sincerity of his beliefs."

"Oh. Have Gary Whitwood's films been box-office failures then?"

"Several have."

"But most of them have been successful, haven't they?"

"Oh, yes."

"Why?"

"He's a very gifted director. He makes good films."

"And he's commercial?"

"In many ways."

"And he's in his profession to make money?"

"Objection, Your Honor. Mr. Boyle can't be expected to know the defendant's motives."

"Can't he?" Hendricks responded sarcastically. "I thought that was what this was all about. Mr. Boyle opening up Mr. Whitwood's skull and telling us what a pussycat lives inside there."

"Your Honor, I must strenuously object to this continuous line of abuse from the prosecutor."

"Sustained. The question and Mr. Hendricks' remarks will be stricken and the jury is instructed to disregard them."

"Let's say this, Mr. Boyle," said Hendricks. "Mr. Whitwood's films are making money?"

"Undoubtedly."

"So his non-violent approach is making him money?"

"Not necessarily. If his films had explicit killings and maimings, he might be reaching a wider audience and making more money."

"Mr. Boyle, on the night of Mr. Blunt's murder was the defendant directing a movie?"

"Objection, Your Honor. Mr. Boyle can't be expected to know what Mr. Whitewood was doing on the night of Mr. Blunt's death."

"Sustained."

"Mr. Boyle, is it not possible for a man to believe one thing intellectually and be driven to another in a time of severe emotional and mental stress?"

"Objection, Your Honor. Now Mr. Hendricks seems to be expecting psychiatric judgments from the witness."

"Sustained."

"Let me ask you this then, Mr. Boyle. Do all the movie directors you know who express a certain point of view through their films live up to that point of view in their daily activities as you have observed them?"

"No."

"You have seen makers of very moral movies do immoral things?"

"Yes."

"And have you seen makers of non-violent movies do violent things?"

"No, but I have seen makers of violent films shrink from violence in real life."

"Have you ever had encounters with directors of movies to which you have given bad reviews, Mr. Boyle?"

"Of course. Frequently."

"Have they ever expressed any anger to you?"

"Yes, that's to be expected."

"Have they acted violently toward you?"

"Not usually."

"But sometimes?"

"Not murderously violent."

"Isn't it true, Mr. Boyle, that Spencer Kurtzman once attacked you in a New York nightclub after reading your review of one of his films?"

"Well, he'd had quite a bit to drink . . ."

"And subjected you to a violent attack?"

"I guess you could call it violent."

"Wouldn't you call breaking your nose violent, Mr. Boyle?"

"Yes, I would."

"So film directors have been known to react violently to criticism of their art?"

"Yes, but not Gary Whitwood in my experience."

"Well, perhaps your experience and Grover Blunt's experience have not been quite the . . ."

Kowalski shouted, "Your Honor, this is outrageous!"

"You know better, Mr. Hendricks. Jury will disregard the last remark."

"Mr. Boyle, you are a close personal friend of Gary Whitwood, is that correct?"

"Yes, I've said so."

"Have you ever panned one of his films?"

"Mr. Hendricks, my friendship for a director has no bearing on my . . ."

"Please, I am not impugning your integrity, Mr. Boyle, just asking a question. Have you ever panned a Gary Whitwood film?"

"Not precisely panned one, no."

"Have you ever given a bad review to one of his films?"

"Objection, Your Honor. That's the same question."

Hendricks explained. "I want an unqualified answer, Your Honor. Mr. Boyle has not given me one. The term 'panned' might be too subject to vague definitions to get a suitable response."

"Overruled. Witness may answer."

"No, I never have."

"Mr. Boyle, does the defendant have many friends among movie critics?"

"I don't think I can say. I don't know all the defendant's friends."

"Let me ask you this. Do you know of any other movie critics, besides yourself, who have formed a personal friendship with Gary Whitwood?"

"Well, yes. One."

"Who was that one?"

"Grover Blunt."

After pausing for effect, Hendricks answered.

"Grover Blunt, the deceased. Do you know of any other movie critics, other than Grover Blunt and yourself, who have been close friends of the defendant?"

"No, but that doesn't mean . . ."

"Then, to your knowledge, Mr. Boyle, the situation of a close personal friend of the defendant delivering a vicious attack on one of the defendant's films—films which the defendant might reasonably have looked on as his children, to be defended from attack—this situation, Grover Blunt's damning review, was a unique one?"

"Your Honor, that is objected to. It is outside the witness's scope of knowledge and sounds more like counsel's closing argument than a question."

"Sustained."

After more trips over the same ground, Martin Boyle's testimony was concluded and with it the case for the defense. In their summations, Hendricks emphasized the strength of his circumstantial case and expressed the view that the attack of a close friend on one of his "children" caused Gary Whitwood to act in a way ordinarily foreign to him while Kowalski emphasized that the circumstantial case was only that and that certainly the non-violent character of the defendant as brought out in the testimony constituted a more than reasonable doubt.

The jury agreed with Kowalski and after several hours of deliberation they found Gary Whitwood not guilty.

Several weeks after the trial, Martin Boyle, home from the screening of a disaster film worthy of the name, received a phone call from Gary Whitwood, whom he had not seen since the director's memorable acquittal party.

"Hello, Gary. How are you?"

"Fine, Marty, fine. And you?"

"Fine, just fine."

"I saw your review of *Close of Darkness*."

"Yeah, well, I . . ." Martin trailed off in embarrassment.

"Hey, it's all right, kid. I know you have to call 'em like you see em."

"Gary, I know you must have had a hard time concentrating on the picture with everything else you had on your mind, the trial and all, and I just thought for once your resistance to inherent societal violence reflected a retreat from reality into a world where everybody is as reasonable and understanding as you are. I just thought . . . Well, you know what I thought, I wrote it."

"And I wouldn't have you do anything else, Marty."

"No."

"Look, we haven't seen much of you lately, kid. How's about a weekend on the old sailboat like we used to do, just the three of us? It's all stocked up with our best booze and eats, and Judy would really like to see you again."

"Oh, well, sure, Gary. When?"

"See you about eight this Saturday morning at the marina, kid, usual place. Judy can't wait. Neither can I."

"Terrific, Gary. Thanks."

Hanging up, Martin chided himself. He'd almost turned the invitation down, and what a slap in the face that would have been to Gary. Such a warm, understanding, *civilized* guy.

But somehow he wasn't looking forward to the weekend.

Rumpole and the Female
of the Species

by John Mortimer

It may be said by those who read these memoirs, particularly by those of the female persuasion, that Rumpole is in some ways unsympathetic to the aspirations of women. This may be because, in the privacy of my own thoughts and when writing late at night in the solitary confines of my kitchen, I refer to my wife, Hilda Rumpole, as "She Who Must Be Obeyed." It is true that I have given her this title, but Hilda's character, her air of easy command, which might, if she had been born in other circumstances, have brought empires under her sway, and her undisputed government of our daily life at Froxbury Court, entitles her to no less an acclamation. Those who feel that I am not firmly on the female side in the Battle of the Sexes may care to consider my long struggle to get Miss Fiona Allways accepted as a member of our Chambers at Equity Court, and those who might think that I only engaged myself in this struggle to annoy the egregious Bollard and irritate Claude Erskine-Brown are guilty of a quite unworthy cynicism.

The dispute over the entry of Miss Allways into our close-knit group of learned friends arose during the time that our Chambers had a brief in the Pond Hill bank job. We were charged with the defense of Tony Timson.

I have written repeatedly elsewhere of the Timsons, the large family of South London villains who, many years ago, appointed me their Attorney-General and whose unending efforts have brought a considerable amount of work to Equity Court. Tony Timson belonged to the younger generation of the clan. He occupied a pleasant, semi-detached house on a South London estate with his wife, April, and their child, Vincent. His house was lavishly furnished with a large variety of video-recording machines, television sets, hi-fi equipment, spin-driers, eye-line grills, ultraviolet-ray cookers, deep freezes, and suchlike aids to gracious living. Many of these articles were said to be the fruit of Tony Timson's tireless night work.

When Inspector Broome called at the Timson house shortly after the Pond Hill bank job, he found the young master alone and playing "Home Sweet Home" on a newly acquired electric organ. He also found five thousand pounds in crisp, new, neatly packaged twenty-pound notes in the gleaming Super Snow White Extra Deluxe-model washing machine. Tony Timson was ripped from the bosom of his wife April and young Vincent, and placed within the confines of Brixton Prison, and I wondered if I should ultimately get the brief.

The appointment of Rumpole for the defense should, of course, have been a foregone conclusion. But the Timson Solicitor-General was Mr. Bernard, and between that gentleman and Rumpole there was a bit of a cold wind blowing, owing to a tiff which had taken place one day at the Uxbridge Magistrates Court. I had arrived at this particular Palais de Justice a little late one day, owing to a tailback on the Piccadilly Line, only to discover that the gutless Bernard had allowed our client of the day to plead guilty to a charge of handling. He had thrown in the towel!

I hadn't actually been rude to Mr. Bernard. I had merely improved his education by quoting Shakespeare's *Richard II.* " 'O, villain, viper, damned without redemption!' " I said to my instructing solicitor. " 'Would you make peace? Terrible hell make war upon your spotted soul for this.' " Mr. Bernard, it seemed, hadn't appreciated the quality of the lines and there was, as I say, an east wind blowing between us. So I wasn't greatly surprised when Henry gave me an account of what happened when Bernard came into our clerk's room and gave Henry the brief in R. *v.* Timson. Henry said that he supposed that would be for Mr. Rumpole.

"You suppose wrong, young man," Mr. Bernard said firmly.

"Do I?" Henry raised his eyebrows.

"The brief is clearly marked for the attention of Mrs. Phillida Erskine-Brown," Bernard pointed out, and Henry saw that it was so. "I can put up with a good deal, Henry, from members of the so called senior branch of our great profession," Mr. Bernard told him, "but I will not be called a villainous viper in the clear hearing of the clerk to the Uxbridge Magistrates Court."

At which point Mrs. Phillida Erskine-Brown, now an extremely successful lady barrister, entered the clerk's room and Henry handed her the papers.

"A wonderfully prepared brief, I don't doubt, like all Mr. Bernard's work." Phillida smiled with great charm at the glowing solicitor, and then asked tactfully, "How's your daughter, Mr. Bernard? Polytechnic going well still, is it?" Mrs. Erskine-Brown, since the days when she was plain Miss Phillida Trant, hadn't got where she was by legal ability alone; she was expert at public relations.

"Three A's," Mr. Bernard was delighted to say. "Thank you for asking."

"And *still* keeping up her figure skating, I bet. Chip off the old block, wouldn't you say so, Henry? See you in Brixton, Mr. Bernard."

She flashed another smile and went on her way, whereupon Bernard told Henry that he always thought that Mrs. Erskine-Brown had a real feeling for the law.

I had decided to improve the facilities in our mansion flat at Froxbury Court by erecting a shelf on our living-room wall to accommodate such necessities as *The Oxford Book of English Verse* (the Quiller-Couch edition), Professor Andrew Ackerman on *The Importance of Bloodstains in the Detection of Crime,* Archbold's *Criminal Pleading and Practice,* a little out of date, and a spare bottle or two of Chateau Thames Embankment of a fairly recent year. I celebrated my entry into the construction industry by buying what I think is known as a "kit" of Easy-Do Convenience Shelving and a few basic tools, and in no time at all, such was my natural feeling for woodwork, I had the shelf up and triumphantly bearing its load.

When I showed the results of my labors to Hilda, she didn't immediately congratulate me, but asked, unnecessarily I thought, if I had "plugged" the wall in accordance with the instructions that came in the Easy-Do box.

"I never read the instructions to counsel before doing a murder, Hilda," I told her firmly. "Rely on the facts, and the instinct of the advocate. It's never let me down yet in Court."

"Well, I do notice you haven't been in Court very much lately." Hilda took an unfair advantage.

"A temporary lull in business. Nothing serious," I assured her.

"It's because you're rude to solicitors." Hilda, of course, knew best. I didn't want to argue the matter further, so I told her that my new shelf was firm as a rock and added an air of distinction to our living room.

"Are you sure it's straight?" Hilda asked. "I think it's definitely at an angle."

"Oh, really, Hilda! It's because *you're* at an angle," I said, I'm afraid a little impatiently. "One small gin and tonic at lunchtime and you do your well known imitation of the Leaning Tower of Pisa."

"Well, if that's how you talk to solicitors—" Hilda was starting to tidy away my carpenter's tools and sweep up the sawdust "—no wonder I've got you at home all day." As I have remarked earlier, there is a good deal to be said in favor of She Who Must Be Obeyed, but she's hardly a fair opponent in an argument.

I left our improved home and went down to Chambers and, there being not much else to engage my attention before a five o'clock Chambers meeting, I took a little time off to instruct Miss Fiona Allways, who had proudly acquired a case entirely of her own, in the art of making a final speech for the defense. Picture us then, alone in my room, the teacher Rumpole standing as though to address the Court and the pupil Allways sitting obediently to learn.

"Soon this case will be over, members of the jury." I gave her my usual peroration. "In a little while you will go back to your jobs and your families, and you will forget all about it. At most it is only a small part of your lives. But for my client it is the *whole* of his life! And it is that life I leave with confidence in your hands, certain that there can be only one verdict in this case—'Not Guilty!'—Sink down exhausted, then, Fiona," I told her, "mopping the brow." I sat and plied a large red spotted handkerchief. "Good end to a final speech, don't you think?"

"Will it work just as well for me?" she asked doubtfully. "I mean, my man's only accused of nicking six frozen chicken pieces from Safeways."

"Goes just as well on any occasion!" I assured her.

And then Claude Erskine-Brown put his head round the door and told me that Ballard was upstairs and just about to start the Chambers meeting. Erskine-Brown then retired and Fiona looked at me in a despondent sort of manner.

"Is this when they decide—" she sounded desperately anxious "—if they're going to let me stay on here?"

"Don't worry. I shall tell them—" I promised her.

"What?"

"Well, let me think. Something like, 'The female of

the species is more deadly than the male.' Look on the bright side, Miss Allways. Perk up, Fiona. I've cracked far tougher Courts than that lot up there!"

I went to the door without any real idea of how to handle the case of Allways and then, as so often happens, thank God, inspiration struck. I turned back toward her.

"Oh, by the way," I said. "Just one question. You know old Claude, who just popped his head in here?"

"Mr. Erskine-Brown?"

"He doesn't tickle your fancy, does he, by any chance? You don't find him devastatingly attractive?"

"Of course not!" Fiona managed her first smile of the day. "He's hardly Paul Newman, is he?"

"No, I suppose he isn't." I must confess the news came to me as something of a relief. "Well, that's all right then. I'll see what I can do."

Ballard had made a few changes, none of them very much for the better, in Featherstone's old room. Guthrie's comfortable chairs had gone, and his silver cigarette-box, his picture of Marigold and the children, his comforting sherry decanter and bone-china tea service, and his perfectly harmless watercolors. Ballard had few luxuries except a number of etchings of English cathedrals in plain, light oak frames, the corners of which protruded in a Gothic and ecclesiastical manner, and an old tin of ginger biscuits which stood on his desk, and which he never offered about.

"Sorry. Am I late for Evensong?" I asked cheerfully as I sat beside Uncle Tom. Ballard, without a glance in my direction, continued with the business in hand.

"We have to consider an application by Fiona Allways for a permanent seat in Chambers," he said. "Mrs. Erskine-Brown, you were her pupil master."

"Mistress," I corrected him, but nobody noticed.

"It's an extremely tough life at the Bar for a woman," Phillida spoke from the depths of her experience. "I'm by no means sure that Allways has got what it takes. Just as a for instance, she burst into tears when left alone at Thames Magistrates Court."

"I know exactly how she felt," I said. "That was never my favorite tribunal."

"Of course. Rumpole's done a case with her." Ballard looked at me in a vaguely accusing manner.

"She took a note for me once. Something about her I liked," I had to admit. And when Hoskins asked me what it was, I said that she felt strongly about winning cases.

"Who is this fellow Allways?" Uncle Tom asked with an expression of mild bewilderment.

"This fellow's a girl, Uncle Tom," I told him.

"Oh, good heavens. Are we getting another one of them?" our oldest inhabitant grumbled, and Mrs. Erskine-Brown brought the discussion up to date by saying, "I really don't think that the mere fact that this girl is a girl should guarantee her a place at 3 Equity Court."

"Philly's perfectly right." Claude came in as a dutiful husband should. "We shouldn't take in a token woman, like a token black."

"Are we taking in a black woman, then?" Uncle Tom merely asked for clarity.

"This is obviously a problem that has to be taken seriously." Ballard spoke disapprovingly from the chair.

"Well, I think we should go for a well established man. Someone who's got to know a few solicitors, who can bring work to Chambers," Mrs. Erskine-Brown suggested politically.

"Steady on, Portia old fellow," I cautioned her. "Whatever happened to the quality of mercy?"

"I honestly don't see what mercy has to do with it."

"Dear God," I was moved to say. "It seems but yesterday that Miss Phillida Trant, white in the wig and a newcomer to the ladies' robing room, was accusing Henry of hiding the key to the laboratory as a sexist gesture! Can it be that now you've stormed the citadel you want to slam the door behind you?"

"Really, Rumpole!" Ballard called me to order. "You're not addressing a jury now. I don't think anyone could possibly accuse this Chambers of having the slightest prejudice against female barristers."

"Of course not. Provided they settle somewhere else, no doubt we find them quite delightful," I agreed.

"I believe I've told you all that I've applied for a silk gown." Erskine-Brown was never tired of telling us this.

"And I'm sure you'll look extremely pretty in it," I assured him.

"And from what I hear, quite informally of course—"

"In the bag, is it, Erskine-Brown?"

"That's not for me to say, but Philly is, of course, right behind me in this."

"Absolutely," his wife assured him. The Erskine-Browns were in a conjugal mood that day. And he rambled on, saying, "So with two Q.C.s at the top, it would be a great pity if these Chambers became weak in the tail."

"What would be a pity?" Uncle Tom asked me.

"If our tail got weak, Uncle Tom."

"Of course it would." It was a puzzling meeting for the old boy. Erskine-Brown didn't further enlighten him by saying, "I'm not interested in the sex side, of course." I noticed then that his wife was looking into the middle distance in a detached sort of way. "But I just don't feel that Allways is the right person to carry on the best traditions of these Chambers."

"I agree," Hoskins agreed.

"So Fiona Allways can swell the ranks of the unemployed?" I asked with some asperity.

"Oh, come on, Rumpole. She's got a rich daddy. She's not going to starve."

"Only miss the one thing she's ever wanted to do," I grumbled, but Ballard was collecting the final views of the meeting. He asked Uncle Tom for his considered opinion.

"I remember a Fiona. Used to work in the List Office." Uncle Tom wasn't particularly helpful. "She wasn't black, of course. No, I'm against it."

"Well, I think I've got the sense of the meeting. I shall tell Miss Allways that she'll have to look elsewhere."

It was time for quick thinking, and I thought extremely quickly. The best way to confuse lawyers is to tell them about a law which they think they've forgot ten.

"Just a moment." I hauled a diary out of my waistcoat pocket.

"What is it, Rumpole?" Ballard sounded impatient.

"This isn't the third Thursday of the Hilary Term!" I said severely.

"Of course it isn't." Erskine-Brown had not got my point, but I had, just in time. "Well!" I said positively. "We always decide questions of Chambers entry on the third Thursday of the Hilary Term. It was the rule of my sainted father-in-law's day. Guthrie Featherstone, Q.C., observed it religiously. Of course, if the new broom wants to make any *radical* changes—?" I looked at Ballard in a strict sort of way, and I must say he flinched.

"Well, no," he said, "I suppose not. Are you sure it's the rule?" He looked at Erskine-Brown, who couldn't say he remembered it.

"You were in rompers, Erskine-Brown, when this thing was first decided," I told him impatiently. "Our old clerk, Albert, said it was impossible otherwise, from a bookkeeping point of view. I do think we should keep to the rules, don't you, Bollard? I mean, we can't have anarchy at Equity Court!"

"That's in four weeks' time." Ballard was consulting his diary now.

"Exactly!"

Ballard put away his diary and came to a decision. "We'll deal with it then. It shouldn't take long, as we've reached a conclusion."

"Oh, no. A mere formality," I agreed.

"What are you playing at, Rumpole?" Mrs. Erskine-Brown was looking at me with some suspicion.

"Nothing much, Portia," I assured her. "Merely keeping up the best traditions of these Chambers."

The Pond Hill branch of the United Metropolitan Bank was held up by a number of men in stocking masks, who carried holdalls from which emerged a sawn-off shotgun or two and a sledgehammer for shattering the glass in front of the cashier. When the robbery was complete, the four masked men ran to the getaway car, a stolen Ford Cortina, which was waiting for them outside the bank, and it was this vehicle, the prosecution alleged, that Tony Timson had been driving. On the way to the car one of the men stumbled and fell. He was seized upon by an officer on traffic duty, and later found to be a Mr. Gerry Molloy—a remarkable fact when you consider the deep hostility which has always existed between the Timson family and the clan Molloy. Indeed, these two tribes have hated each other for as long as I can remember and I have already chronicled an instance of their feud.*

It seems that all the other men engaged on the Pond Hill enterprise were Molloys. They got away, so it was hardly to be wondered at that Mr. Gerald Molloy decided to become a grass and involve a Timson when he told his story to the police.

In the course of time, Mrs. Erskine-Brown and her instructing solicitor went to Brixton to see their client, but, as I later heard from him and from Mr. Bernard, Tony Timson seemed to have only one thing on his mind as he walked into the interview room and said, "Where's Mr. Rumpole?"

Phillida Erskine-Brown, in her jolliest "we're all lads together" voice, merely said, "Care for a fag,

*See "Rumpole and the Younger Generation" in *Rumpole of the Bailey,* Penguin Books, 1978.

Tony?" Tony didn't mind if he did, and when Phillida had lit it for him, Bernard broke the bad news.

"This is Mrs. Erskine-Brown, Tony," he said. "She's going to be your brief."

"I see they've charged you with taking part in the robbery, not merely the receiving. Of course, they've done that on Gerry Molloy's evidence." Phillida started off in a businesslike way, but Tony Timson was looking at his solicitor in a kind of panic and paying no attention to her at all.

"Mr. Rumpole's always the Timsons' brief," he said. "You know that, Mr. Bernard. Mr. Rumpole defended my dad and my Uncle Cyril and saw me through my Juvenile Court and my Borstal training—"

"Mr. Rumpole can't have done all that well for you if you got Borstal training," Bernard said reasonably.

"Well—" Tony looked at Phillida for support. "Win a few, lose a few, you know that, missus?"

"Any reason why Gerry Molloy should grass on you, Tony?" Phillida tried to return to the matter in hand.

"Look, it's good of you to come here, but—"

At which Phillida, no doubt in an attempt to reassure the client, lapsed into robbers' argot. "You ever had a meet with him where any sort of bank job was ever mentioned?" she asked. "Molly says in the deps that he was the sledge, two others had sawn-offs in their hold-alls, and you were the driver. He says you're pretty good on wheels, Tony."

"This is highly embarrassing, this is." Tony looked suitably pained at Phillida's personal knowledge of crime.

"What is it, Tony?" She did her best to sound deeply sympathetic.

"You being a woman and all. It don't feel right, not with a woman."

"Don't think of me as a woman, Tony," she tried to reassure him. "Think of me entirely as a brief."

"It's no good." Tony shook his head. "I keep thinking of my wife, April."

"Well, of course she's worried about you. That's only natural, seeing you got nicked, Tony."

"I don't mean that. I mean I wouldn't want a woman like my April to take on my job, would I? Briefs, and us what gets ourselves into a bit of trouble down the Bailey and that. It's all man's work, innit?"

Well, that may come as a shrewd shock to all readers of those women's pages which I have occasionally glanced at in Fiona Allway's *Guardian,* but I'm told that it is exactly what Tony Timson said. As a consequence, it was a rueful Phillida Erskine-Brown who walked away from the interview room, across the yard where the screws exercised the alsatians and the trusties weeded the flower beds, toward the gate.

"The Timsons are such *old-fashioned* villains." Mr. Bernard apologized for them. "They're always about half a century behind the times."

"It's not your fault, Mr. Bernard," said Phillida miserably.

"You wait till my wife gets to hear about this! They're pretty hot on women's rights in the Hammersmith S.D.P." Bernard was clearly deeply affronted.

"It's the client's right to choose." Phillida was taking it on the chin.

"It's decent of you to be like that about it, Mrs. Erskine-Brown. It's absolutely no reflection on you, of course. But—" Bernard looked deeply embarrassed "—I'm afraid I'll have to take in a chap to lead you."

They had arrived at the gatehouse and were about to be sprung when Phillida Erskine-Brown looked at Mr. Bernard and said she wondered who the chap would be exactly.

"It goes against the grain," said Bernard, "but we've really got no choice, have we?"

A good deal later that evening I was on my way home when I happened to pass Pommeroy's Wine Bar and, in the hope that they might be offloading cooking claret at a reasonable rate, I went in and saw, alone and palely loitering at the bar with an oldish sandwich and a glass of hock, none other than Claude Erskine-Brown. I saw the chance of playing another card in the long game of "Getting Fiona into Chambers," and I engaged the woebegone figure in conversation, the burden of which was that Phillida was so enormously busy at the Bar that the sandwich might well have to do for the Erskine-Brown supper.

"Of course," I said sympathetically, "your wife must be pretty hard pressed now she's taken the Timsons off me."

"She doesn't get home in the evenings until Tristan's gone to bed," Erskine-Brown told me, and I looked at him and said, "Just as well."

"Do you think so?" The man sounded slightly offended.

"Just as well young Fiona Allways isn't coming into chambers," I explained.

"You agree that we shouldn't take her?"

"In all the circumstances, well, perhaps I'd better not say anything."

"*What* do you mean, Rumpole?" Erskine-Brown was puzzled.

"It might have raised all sorts of problems. I mean, it might have got too much for you to handle."

"*What* might have got too much for me to handle?"

"It would create all sorts of difficulties, in the spring, and all that sort of thing. We don't want the delicate perfume of young Fiona floating around Chambers, do we?" I said, as casually as possible.

"Well, I don't suppose I'd've seen much of her."

"Oh, but you would, you know."

"Not as a silk."

"You'd've been thrown together. Chambers meetings. Brushing past each other in the clerk's room. Before you knew where you were, you'd be popping out for tea and a couple of chocky biscuits in the ABC." I looked as gravely concerned as I knew how. "Terribly dangerous!"

"Why on earth?" He still hadn't quite caught my drift.

"Well, you know exactly what these young lady barristers are—impressionable, passionate even, and enormously impressed with the older legal hack, especially one teetering on the verge of knee breeches and a silk gown."

"You don't mean—?" I could see that now he had perked up considerably.

"And she seems to find you extremely personable, Claude!" I laid it on thick. "You put her in distinct mind, so she has told me, of a film actor—'Newman,' could that be the name?" I asked innocently, and drained my glass. At which moment, Claude Erskine-Brown took off his spectacles and admired himself in one of the mirrors, decorated with fronds of frosty vegetation, that cover Pommeroy's walls. "Ridiculous!" he said, but I could see that the old fish was well and truly hooked.

"Of course it's ridiculous," I agreed. "But on second thoughts, far better she doesn't get into Chambers. Wouldn't you agree?" I left him then, but as I went out of Pommeroy's, Erskine-Brown was still looking at himself shortsightedly in the mirror.

The next day Henry gave me the glad news that I was to be leading the extraordinarily busy Mrs. Phillida Erskine-Brown in the Timson defense. It seemed that Mr. Bernard had seen sense on the subject of our little disagreement at Uxbridge, but Henry told me, extremely severely, that he couldn't go on clerking for me if I called my instructing solicitor a "viper" again. I asked him if he'd pass "snake," assured him I wasn't serious, and then went up to seek out our new Head of Chambers in his lair.

I was going to play the next card in the Fiona Allways game. I knocked at the door, heard a cry of "Who is it?" and found Ballard with a cup of tea and a ginger biscuit working on some massive prosecution involving a large number of villains who were all represented by different-colored pencils.

"Oh, it's you." Our leader didn't sound particularly welcoming. All the same, I came in, pushed Ballard's papers aside, and sat on the edge of his desk.

"Just thought I ought to give you a friendly warning," I started confidentially.

"Isn't it you that needs warning? Henry tells me that you've taken to being offensive to Mr. Bernard."

I lit up a small cigar and blew out smoke. Ballard coughed pointedly. "It doesn't do Chambers any good, you know, insulting a solicitor," he told me. By way of answer I closed my eyes and tried a vivid description.

"Fascinating character!" I began. "Marvelous hair, burnished like autumn leaves. Tender white neck, sticking out of the starched white collar—"

"Mr. Bernard?" Ballard was puzzled.

"Of course not!" I put him right. "I was speaking of Miss Phillida Trant, now Mrs. Erskine-Brown." I brought out the packet of small cigars and offered it. "You don't smoke, I suppose?"

"You know I don't."

"What *do* you do, I wonder?" There was a short diversion as Ballard blew my ash off his depositions and then I said thoughtfully, "Gorgeous creature in many ways, our Portia."

"With a most enviable practice, I understand," Ballard agreed. "Perhaps she's polite to solicitors."

"Determined to rise to the absolute top."

"I have the highest respect for Phillida, of course, but—"

"Devious." I supplied the word. "A brilliant mind, of course, but devious!"

"Rumpole, what are you trying to tell me?" Ballard seemed anxious to bring our dialogue to a swift conclusion.

"The way she got you to show your sexual prejudices at that Chambers meeting!" I said with admiration.

"My *what*?"

"Your blind and Victorian opposition to women in the legal profession. I believe she's writing a report on that to the Bar Council. Plus ten articles for the *Observer,* in depth."

"But, Rumpole, she spoke *against* Allways." Ballard was already arguing weakly.

"What a tactician!" For the sake of emphasis, I gave Ballard a brisk slap on the shoulder.

"She seemed totally opposed to the girl."

I slipped off his desk and took a turn round the room. "Just to lead you on, don't you see. To get *you* to show your hand. You walked right into it, Bollard. I can see the headlines now! 'Christian barrister presides over sexist redoubt!' 'Bollard, Q.C., puts the clock back fifty years!' "

"Ballard." He corrected me without too much conviction and said, "I didn't take that attitude, surely."

"You will have done," I assured him, "by the time our Phillida's finished with you. Don't cross her, Bollard, I warn you. She has the ear of the Lord Chancellor. I don't know if you were ever hoping for some sort of minor judgeship—" I went to the door and then turned back to Ballard. "Of course, you have one thing in your favor."

"What's that?" He seemed prepared to clutch at a straw. It was then that I played the ace. "Our Portia seems to have taken something of a shine to you," I told him. " 'Craggily handsome' I think was the way she put it. I suppose there's just a chance you might get round her. Try using your irresistible charm."

I left him then. The poor old darling was looking like a person who has to choose between a public execution and a heady draught of hemlock.

Whatever may be said about the equality of the sexes, there is still something about the nature of women which parts the average man almost entirely from his marbles. Faced with most problems, both

Erskine-Brown and Ballard might have proved reasonably resolute. When the question concerned a moderately personable young woman, they became as clay in the potter's hands. These thoughts passed through my mind as I lay in bed that night staring at the ceiling, while Hilda sat at the dressing table in night attire, brushing her hair before coming to bed.

"What are you thinking, Rumpole?" she asked. "I know you, Rumpole. You're lying there *thinking* about something!"

"I was thinking," I confessed, "about man's attitude to the female of the species."

"Oh, were you indeed?" Hilda sounded deeply suspicious.

"On the one hand, the presence of a woman strikes him with terror—"

"Really, Rumpole, don't be absurd," Hilda said severely.

"And fierce resentment."

"Is *that* what you were thinking?"

"And yet he finds her not only indispensable, but quite irresistible. Faced with a whiff of perfume, for instance, he is reduced to a state bordering on imbecility."

"Rumpole. Are you really?" Hilda's voice had softened considerably. The room became redolent with the smell of lavender water. Hilda was spraying on perfume.

" 'She is a woman, therefore may be woo'd/She is a woman, therefore may be won,' " I repeated sleepily.

I saw Hilda emerge from her dressing gown and make toward the bed. She said, "Oh, Rumpole," quite tenderly. But then sleep claimed me, and I heard no more.

One afternoon I turned up at the gates of Brixton Prison with my learned junior, Mrs. Phillida Erskine-Brown, and there was Mr. Bernard waiting for us and replying to my hearty greeting in a somewhat guarded manner.

"Hail to thee, blythe Bernard!" I said, and he replied, "We're taking you in on the express wishes of the client, Mr. Rumpole. Just for this case."

I then became aware of a pleasant-looking young woman with blonde hair and a small, rather plump child who was sitting slumped in a pushchair, regarding me with a wary eye.

"Mr. Rumpole." The lady introduced herself. "I'm April Timson. Tony's glad that you're going to be his brief."

My companion looked less than flattered, but I greeted our client's family warmly.

"Mrs. Timson, good of you to say so. And who's this young hopeful?"

"That's our young Vince. Been in to see his dad," said the child's proud mother.

"Delighted to meet you, Vincent," I said, and managed to leave a thought with April which might pay off in the course of time. "Let me know," I said, "the moment he gets into trouble."

"Straight up, it's a sodding plant," said Tony Timson, and then turned apologetically to my junior. "Pardon my French."

"Don't be so silly, Tony." Phillida didn't like not being taken for one of the boys. We were sitting in a small glass-walled room in the interview block at Brixton, and I felt I had to question Tony further as to his suggested defense.

"What sort of a plant are you suggesting?" I asked. "A floribunda of the Serious Crimes Squad or an exotic bloom cultivated by the Molloys?"

"That D.I. Broome. He's got no love for the Timsons," Tony grumbled.

"Neither have the Molloys."

"That's true, Mr. Rumpole. That's very true."

"A plant by the supergrass's family? I suppose it's possible." I considered the suggestion.

"I'd say it's typical."

"So some person unknown brought in the cash and popped it into your Super Snow White Extra Deluxe Easy-Wash?" I framed the charge.

"The jury may now wonder how Tony can afford all these luxuries out of window-cleaning," Phillida suggested.

"It's not a luxury. My April says it's just something you got to have," said Tony, the proud householder.

"You know how he affords these things, Portia?" I explained our case to one not expert in the Timson branch of the law. "Tony's a minor villain. Small stuff. Let's have a look at his form." I plucked a sheet of paper from my brief. "Warehouse-breaking, shop-breaking, criminal damage to a set of traffic lights—"

"I misjudged a turning, Mr. Rumpole," Tony admitted. It was the item of which he seemed slightly ashamed. But there was more to come.

"Careless driving, dangerous driving, failure to report an accident," I read out. "Look here, old sweetheart, if I get you out of this, do promise not to give me a lift home."

That same evening, Claude Erskine-Brown put his head round the door of my room, where Miss Fiona Allways was looking up a bit of law, and invited her to join him in a bottle of Pommeroy's bubbly. Naturally anxious to be on friendly terms with those who held her legal future in their hands, she accepted the invitation, and I am indebted to her for an account of what then took place.

Once ensconced at a corner table in the shadowy regions of the wine bar, Erskine-Brown took off his spectacles and sighed as though worn out by the cares of office.

"It can be lonely at the top, Fiona," he said. "I mean, you may wonder what it feels like to be on the verge of becoming a Q.C." Perhaps he was waiting for her to say something, but as she didn't he repeated with a sigh, "I'll tell you. Lonely."

"But you've got Mrs. Erskine-Brown." Fiona was puzzled.

Claude gave her a sad little smile. "Mrs. Erskine-Brown! I seem to see so little of Phillida nowadays. Pressures of work, of course. No," he went on seriously, "there comes a time in this job when a person feels terribly alone."

"I suppose so." Fiona felt the topic was becoming exhausted.

"I envy you those happy, carefree days when you hop from Magistrates Court to Magistrates Court, picking up little crumbs of indecent exposure."

"Frozen chicken," Fiona corrected him.

"What?" Erskine-Brown looked puzzled.

"I was doing a case about frozen chicken pieces. It seemed quite a responsibility to me."

As the subject had moved from himself, Claude's attention wandered. He looked across to the bar and said, "Is that old Rumpole over there?"

"Why?" Fiona asked, in all innocence. "Can't you see without your glasses?"

In fact, and this Erskine-Brown didn't notice, perhaps because she was hidden in the melee at the bar, I had come into the joint with Phillida in order that we might refresh ourselves after a hard conference at Brixton. I said I hoped she had no hard feelings about me being taken in to lead her in the Timson affair. She confessed to just a few hard feelings, but was then sporting enough to buy us a perfectly reasonable bottle.

"Criminals and barristers, Portia," I told her as Jack Pommeroy was uncorking the claret. "Both extremely conservative professions—"

But before she had time to absorb this thought, Phillida was off like a hound on the scent toward a corner of the room. Again I have to rely on Miss Allways' account for what was going on at the distant table.

"And if ever you have the slightest problem," Erskine-Brown was saying gently, "of a legal nature, or anything else come to that, don't hesitate, Fiona. A silk's door is always open to a member of Chambers, however junior."

"A member of Chambers?" Fiona repeated hopefully.

"I'm sure. I mean, some old squares are tremendously prejudiced against women, of course. But speaking for myself—" he put a hand on one of Fiona's which she had left lying about on the table "—I have absolutely no objection to a pretty face around Number 3 Equity Court."

"Haven't you, Claude?" Mrs. Erskine-Brown had fetched up beside the table and spoke with considerable asperity.

"Oh, Philly." Erskine-Brown hastily withdrew his hand. "Are you going to join us for a drink? You know Fiona, of course—"

"Yes. I know Allways." Phillida looked suspiciously at the gold-topped bottle. "What is it? Somebody's birthday? No, I'm not joining you two. I'm going to go straight back to Chambers and write a letter."

At which Phillida Erskine-Brown banged out of Pommeroy's, leaving her husband with a somewhat foolish expression on his face, and me with an entire bottle of claret.

Phillida, always as good as her word, did go back to her room in Chambers and started to write a lengthy and important letter to an official quarter. It was whilst she was doing this that there came a tap at her door, which she ignored, and then the devout Ballard entered uninvited.

This time I have to rely on our Portia for a full account of what transpired, and when she told me, over a rather hilarious celebratory bottle about a month later, her recollection may have grown somewhat dim, but she swears that it was a Ballard transformed who came gliding up to her desk. He was wearing a somewhat garish spotted tie (in pink and blue, as she remembered it), a matching silk handkerchief lolled from his top pocket, and surrounding the man was a fairly overpowering odor of some aftershave which the manufacturers advertise as Trouble-starter. He was also smiling.

"I saw your light on," Ballard murmured. Apparently Phillida didn't find this a statement of earth-shaking interest and went on writing.

"Mrs. Erskine-Brown," Ballard tried again. "You won't mind me calling you Phyllis?"

"If you want to, but it doesn't happen to be my name." Phillida didn't look up from her writing.

"Burning the midnight oil?"

"It's only half past six."

Although she had given him little encouragement, Ballard came and perched, no doubt as he thought jauntily, on the corner of her desk and made what seemed to Phillida to be an entirely unnecessary disclosure. "I've never married, of course," he said.

"Lucky you!" Phillida said with meaning as she went on with her work.

"I lead what I imagine you'd call a bit of a bachelor life in Dulwich. Decent-sized flat, though, all that sort of thing."

"Oh, good," Phillida said in as neutral a manner as possible.

"But I don't want you to run away with the idea that I don't like *women,* because I do like women—very much indeed. I am a perfectly normal sort of chap in that regard," Ballard assured her.

"Oh, jolly good." Phillida was still busy.

"In fact, I have to confess this to you. I find the sight of a woman wigged and wearing a winged collar surprisingly—well, let's be honest about this— alluring." There was a considerable pause and then he blurted out, "I saw you the other day, going up the stairs in the Law Courts, robed up!"

"Did you? I was on my way to do a divorce." Phillida was folding her letter with a grim determination.

"Well, I just didn't want you to be under any illusions." Ballard stood and gave Phillida what was no doubt meant to be a challenging look. "I'm thoroughly in favor of women, from every point of view."

"I'm sure the news will come as an enormous relief to the women of the world!" She licked the envelope and stuck it down. What she said seemed to have a strange effect on Ballard and he became extremely nervous.

"Oh, I don't want it published in the papers!" he said anxiously. "I thought I'd make it perfectly clear to you, in the course of private conversation."

"Well, you've made it clear, Ballard." Phillida looked him in the eye for the first time, and didn't particularly like what she saw.

"Please—'Sam,' " he corrected her skittishly.

"All right, 'Sam.' You've made it terribly clear."

"Look. Someday when you're not in Court—" he was smiling at her again "—why don't you let me take you out to a spot of lunch? They do a very decent set meal at the Ludgate Hotel."

Phillida looked at him with amazement and contempt. She then got up and walked past him to the door, taking her letter. "I've got to put this out to post," was all she had to say to that.

I had gone back to our clerk's room to pick up some forgotten papers and was alone there, Henry and Dianne having left for some unknown destination, when Phillida came to put her letter in the Post tray on Dianne's desk.

"What on earth happened, Portia?" I asked her. "You left me to finish the bottle."

"Has everyone in this Chambers gone completely out of their heads?" she replied with another question.

"Everyone?"

"Ballard just made the most disgusting suggestion to me." She did seem extremely angry.

"Bollard did? Whatever was it?" I asked, delighted.

"He invited me to have the set lunch at the Ludgate Hotel. And as for my so-called husband—" Words failing her, she went to the door. "Goodnight, Rumpole!"

"Goodnight, Portia."

It was then that I looked down at the letter she'd just written. The envelope was addressed to "The Lord Chancellor, The Lord Chancellor's Office, The House of Lords, London, S.W.I."

A good deal, I thought, was going on under the calm surface of life in our Chambers at Equity Court. I was speculating on the precise nature of such movements with considerable pleasure as I started to walk to the Temple station. On my way I found Miss Fiona Allways waiting for a bus.

"I say," she hailed me. "Any more news about my getting into Chambers?"

"There is a tide in the affairs of women barristers, Fiona," I told her, "which, taken at the flood, leads God knows where."

"What's that mean, exactly?"

"It means that they'll either let you in or they'll throw *me* out." I moved on toward Hilda and home. "Best of luck," I said, "to both of us."

His Honour Judge Leonard Dover was a fairly recent appointment to the collection of Old Bailey judges. He was a youngish man, in his mid-forties perhaps, certainly young enough to be my son, had fate chosen to inflict such a blow. He wore rimless glasses and was a fairly rimless character. He was the sort of judge who has about as many laughs in him as a digital computer, and seemed to have been programmed by the Civil Service. Press all the right buttons—you know the type—and he gives you seven years in the nick. I have often thought that if he were plugged into the mains,

Judge Dover could go on passing stiff sentences forever.

On my way into Dover's Court, I had passed Mrs. April Timson, made up to the nines and wearing a sky-blue trouser suit, come to celebrate her husband's day of fame. She accosted me anxiously.

"Tony says you've never let the Timsons down, Mr. Rumpole."

"Mrs. Timson!" I greeted her. "Where's young Vincent today? Otherwise engaged?"

"He's with my friend, Chrissie. She's my neighbor and she's minding him. What are our chances, Mr. Rumpole?"

"Talk to you later," I said, not caring to commit myself.

After the jury had been sworn in, Judge Dover leant toward them and said, in his usual unremarkable monotone, "Nothing that I am going to say now must be taken against the defendant in any way—"

I stirred in my seat. Whatever was going on, I didn't like the sound of it.

"This is a case in which it seems there is a particular danger of your being approached—by someone," Dover went on, sounding grave. "That often happens in trials of alleged armed robbery by what is known as a 'gang' of serious professional criminals."

It was time to throw a spanner in his programing. "My Lord," I said firmly, and rose to the hind legs, but Dover was locked in conversation with the jury.

"You will be particularly on your guard, and purely for your assistance, of course, you will be kept under police observation." He seemed to notice me at long last. "What is it, Mr. Rumpole? Don't you want this jury to be protected from interference?"

"I don't want the jury to be told this is a case concerning a serious crime before they'd heard one word of evidence," I said with all possible vehemence. "I don't want hints that my client belongs to a gang of serious professionals when the truth may be that he's nothing but a snapper-up of unconsidered trifles. I don't want the jury nobbled, but nobbled they have already been, in my respectful submission, by your Lordship's warning."

"Mr. Rumpole! That's an extraordinary suggestion, coming from you!"

"It was made to answer an extraordinary statement coming from your Lordship."

"What is your application, Mr. Rumpole?" Judge Dover asked in a voice several degrees below zero.

"My Lord, I ask that a fresh jury be empaneled, who will have heard no prejudicial suggestions against my client."

"Your application is refused." I had pressed the wrong button and got the automatic printout. There was nothing for it but to sit down, looking extremely hard done by.

"Members of the jury." The Judge turned back to them. "I have already made it perfectly clear to you that nothing I have said contains any suggestion whatever against Mr. Timson. Does that satisfy you, Mr. Rumpole?"

"About as much as a glass of cold carrot juice, old darling," I muttered to Phillida.

"I'm sorry, I didn't hear you, Mr. Rumpole."

"I said, I suppose it will have to, my Lord." I rose in a perfunctory manner.

"Yes, Mr. Rumpole," the Judge said, "I suppose it will . . ."

Back in the alleged mansion flat, things weren't going too well, either. Hilda, in the course of tidying up, found my old *Oxford Book of English Verse* on a chair (I had been seeking solace in the "Intimations of Immortality" the night before) and she put it on my excellent shelf.

No doubt she thumped it down a fair bit, for my elegant carpentry creaked and then collapsed, casting a good many books and a certain amount of wine to the ground. I have spoken already of the strength of my wife's character. Apparently she went out, purchased a number of rawlplugs and an electric drill, and started a career as a handyman, the full effects of which weren't noticed by me for some time.

In Court, the prosecution was in the hands of Mr. Hilary Onslow, a languid-looking young man whose fair curly hair came sprouting out from under his wig. In spite of his air of well born indifference, he could be, at times, a formidable opponent. One of the earliest witnesses was the supergrass, Gerry Molloy, an overweight character with a red face and glossy black hair who sweated a good deal and seemed about to burst out of his buttons.

"Mr. Molloy, I want to come now to the facts of the Pond Hill bank raid."

"The Pond Hill job. Yes, sir." Gerry sounded only too eager to help.

"How many of you were engaged on that particular enterprise?"

"There was two with sawn-offs. One collector—"

"And you with the sledgehammer?" Onslow asked.

"I was the sledge man, yes. There was five of us altogether."

"Five of you counting the driver?"

"Yes, sir."

"Did you *see* the driver?"

"Course I did." The witness sounded very sure of himself. "The driver picked me up at the meet."

"Had you seen him before?"

"Seen him before?" Molloy thought carefully, and then answered, "No, sir."

"Some weeks later did you attend an identification parade?" Onslow turned to me and asked languidly, "Is there any dispute as to whom he picked out at the I.D.?"

"No dispute as to that, no," I granted him.

"Thank you, Mr. Rumpole." The Judge gave me a faint look of approval.

"Delighted to be of assistance, my Lord," I rose to say, and sank back into my seat as quickly as possible.

"Did you pick out the defendant, Mr. Timson?" Onslow asked.

Tony Timson was staring at the witness from the dock. Gerry Molloy looked away to avoid his accusing eyes and met a glare from April Timson in the public gallery.

"Yes." The answer was a little muted. "I pointed to him. I got no hesitation."

"Thank you, Mr. Molloy."

Hilary Onslow sat and crossed his long legs elegantly. I rose, full of righteous indignation, and looked at the jury in a pained manner as I cast my questions in the general direction of the witness-box.

"Mr. Molloy. You have turned Queen's Evidence in this case?"

"Come again?" The answer was impertinent, so I put my voice up several decibels. "Translated into everyday language, Mr. Molloy, you are a grass. Not even a 'supergrass.' A common or garden ordinary bit of a grass."

There was a welcome stir of laughter from the jury, immediately silenced by the computer on the Bench.

"Members of the jury," Judge Dover reminded them, if they needed reminding, "this is not a place of public entertainment. This witness is giving evidence for the prosecution," he added, as though that covered the matter.

"You're giving evidence for the prosecution because you were caught." I turned to the witness-box then. "Not being a particularly efficient sledge, you tripped over your holdall in the street and missed the getaway car. You were apprehended, Mr. Molloy, in the gutter!"

"They nicked me, yes," Molloy admitted.

"And you have already been sentenced to two years for your part in the robbery?"

"I got a two, yes."

"A considerable reduction because you agreed with the police to grass on your colleagues," I suggested.

"I got under the odds, yes," he agreed, less readily.

"Considerably under the odds, Mr. Molloy, and for that you were prepared to betray your own family?"

"Come again?"

"Three of your colleagues were members of the clan Molloy."

"They were Molloys, yes."

"And only one Timson?"

"Yes."

"And as the Montagues to the Capulets, I put it to you, so are the Timsons to the Molloys."

"Did you say the 'Montagues,' Mr. Rumpole?" The Judge seemed puzzled by a name he hadn't heard in the case before, so my literary reference was lost on the computer.

"I simply meant that the Molloys hate and despise the Timsons. Isn't that so, Mr. Gerry Molloy?" I asked the witness.

"We never got on, no. It's traditional. Although—"

"Although what?"

"I believe my cousin Shawn's wife what he's separated from lives quite close to Tony Timson and his wife and—"

I interrupted a speech which I thought might somehow blur the picture I had just painted. "Apart from that, it's true, isn't it, that the Molloys are in a different league from the Timsons?"

"What league is that, Mr. Rumpole?" Judge Dover looked puzzled.

"The big league, my Lord." I helped him understand. "You and your relations, according to your evidence, did the Barclays Bank in Penge, the Midland, Croydon, and the NatWest in Barking—" I was back with the witness.

"That's what I've said." He was sweating more now, and two of his lower shirt buttons had gone off about their own affairs.

"Spreading your favors evenly round the money market. Have you ever known a Timson to be present at a bank robbery before, Mr. Molloy?"

"Not as I can remember. But my brother Charlie was off sick and we was short of a driver."

"Perhaps you were. Unhappily, all your Molloy colleagues seem to have vanished."

At which point my learned friend, Mr. Hilary Onslow, felt it right to unwind his legs and draw himself to his great height. "My Lord," he said, "I explained to the jury that determined efforts to trace the other participants in this robbery are still being made by the police."

"If my learned friend wishes to give evidence, perhaps your Lordship would like him to go into the witness-box," I said, and got the automatic judicial rebuke: "Mr. Rumpole, that comment was quite uncalled-for."

"Steady on, Rumpole. Don't tease him," Phillida whispered a bit of sound advice. So I said, with deep humility, "So it was, my Lord. I entirely agree." I turned back, with no humility at all, to Gerry Molloy. "With your relations all gone to ground you had to have a victim, didn't you, to justify your privileged treatment as a grass?" The jury, who looked extremely interested, clearly saw the point. The witness pretended that he didn't.

"A victim?" He was playing for time, I gave him none.

"So you decided to pick one out of the despised Timsons, and put him in the frame."

"Put him in the *what,* Mr. Rumpole?" The Judge affected not to understand. I hadn't time to teach him plain English.

"Put him in the driver's seat, where he certainly never was," I suggested to the supergrass.

"He was there. I told you." Gerry Molloy was growing indignant.

"Where did you meet?"

"One of the Molloy houses," he said, after a pause. "Which one?"

"I think it was Michael's. Or Vic's. I can't be sure."

"Can't you?"

"It was Shawn's," he decided.

"And having decided to frame Tony," I went on quickly, "was it some member of the Molloy family who planted a packet of stolen banknotes in the Timson home?"

"It couldn't have been him, could it, Mr. Rumpole?" The Judge was looking back in his notes. "This witness has been in custody ever since—"

"Since the robbery, yes, my Lord," I agreed, and then asked Molloy, "Did you receive visits in prison before you made your statement?"

"A few visits, yes."

"From your wife?"

"One or two."

"And was it through her that the word was sent out to plant the money on Tony Timson?"

I made the suggestion for the benefit of the jury, but it deeply shocked Gerald Supergrass Molloy. "I wouldn't ask my wife to do them sort of messages," he said, deeply pained.

Back at home, Hilda, swathed in an overall, was drilling the wall to receive a new consignment of Easy-Do shelving in a completely professional manner. I was also plugging away in Court, asking a few pertinent questions of Detective Inspector Broome, the officer in charge of the case.

"Gerry Molloy made his statement two days after the robbery, at about two-thirty in the afternoon?" I suggested.

"Two-thirty-five, to be precise," the D.I. put me right.

"Oh, please. I'm sure my Lord would like you to be very precise. You went straight round to Tony Timson's house?"

"We did."

"In a police car, with the siren blaring?"

"I think we had the siren on for some of the time. We were in a hurry."

"And you were lucky enough to find him at home?"

"Well, he wasn't out doing window-cleaning, sir."

There was a small titter from the jury. I interrupted it as soon as possible.

"My client opened the door to you at once?"

"Soon as we knocked. Yes."

"No sort of interval while he tried to move the money to a more sensible hiding place, for instance?"

"Perhaps he was happy with it where it was."

Before he got another laugh, I came in quickly with, "Or perhaps, Inspector, he had no idea that the money had been put there."

"I don't know about that."

"Don't you? One last matter. Was it Gerry Molloy who told you that Tony Timson was a dangerous member of a big-time robbery firm who might try and nobble the jury?"

"Molloy told us that, yes." Inspector Broome was a little reluctant to answer.

"So a solemn warning was given by the learned Judge on the word of a self-confessed sledgehammer man who has already been convicted of malicious wounding, robbery, and grievous bodily harm."

"Yes." The short answer came even more reluctantly from the Inspector.

"And doesn't that solemn warning give a quite unfair impression of Tony Timson?"

"Unfair, sir?" Broome did his best to look puzzled.

"You'd never put Tony Timson in for the serious-crime award, would you? He's a small-time thief who specializes in relieving householders of their home entertainment, video machines, teasmades, and the like."

"That would seem to be so, yes," the Inspector admitted.

"So if I said to you that this robbery was quite out

of Tony Timson's league, how would you translate that suggestion?"

"I would say it's out of his character, sir. Judging by past form." So I sat down with some heartfelt thanks to Detective Inspector Broome.

At the end of the day I went with Phillida and Bernard to visit our client in the cells. He appeared pleased with our progress, but I hadn't yet an answer to what seemed to me the single important question in the case.

"The money in the washing machine, Tony," I asked him. "It must have been put there by someone. Does April go out much?"

"She takes young Vince round her friend's."

"Her friend Chrissie?" The question seemed important to me, but Tony answered vaguely, "I think that's her name. I don't know the woman."

"Money found in the kitchen," I said thoughtfully. "I don't suppose you do much cooking, do you, Tony?"

"Oh, leave it out, Mr. Rumpole!" Tony found the suggestion highly diverting.

"Never wash up?"

"Course I don't!" He could hardly suppress his laughter. "That's April's job, innit?"

"I suppose it's only barristers who spend the evenings up to their wrists in the Fairy Liquid. Yes, and of course you don't run young Vince's smalls through the washing machine?"

"Now would I be expected to do a job like that?" He looked to Mrs. Erskine-Brown for support. "Would I?"

"You mean it would be a bit like having a woman defend you?" Phillida asked in a pointed sort of way. Tony Timson had the grace to look apologetic.

"I never meant nothing personal," he said. "It just doesn't seem natural."

"Really." Phillida was unappeased. "As a matter of fact, my husband is quite a good performer on the spin-drier."

"Poor bloke!" Tony was laughing again.

I interrupted the badinage. "Let's take it that you leave such matters to April. When does she do the washing, Tony? On a Monday?"

"Suppose so." He didn't sound particularly interested.

"The bank raid was on Monday. Gerry Molloy made his statement on Wednesday afternoon and the police were round at once. Whoever put it there didn't have much time."

"I don't know," and he added hopelessly, "I just never go near the bleeding washing machine."

I gathered up my brief and prepared to return to the free world.

"See you tomorrow, Tony," I said. "Come on, Portia. I think we've got what we wanted."

When I left the Old Bailey that evening and stepped off the pavement, a small white sportscar, driven with great speed and expertise, flashed past me, almost cutting me off somewhere past my prime, and, passing two or three slowly moving taxis on the inside, zipped off and was lost in traffic. I caught sight of a blonde head behind the wheel and deduced that the driver was none other than that devoted housewife, Mrs. April Timson.

I didn't sleep much that night. I was busy putting two and two together to make about five thousand nicker. Around dawn I drifted off and dreamt of washing machines and spin-driers, and Ballard was bringing me a bouquet of roses and inviting me to lunch, and Fiona Allways had decided to leave the Bar and take up life as a coal miner, saying the pay was so much better.

So I arrived at the Old Bailey in a somewhat jaded condition. Having robed for the day's work, I went up to the canteen on the third floor and bought myself a black coffee and a slightly flaccid sausage roll. I wasn't enjoying them much when Erskine-Brown came up to me in a state of considerable distress, holding out a copy of *The Times* in a trembling hand. The poor fellow looked decidedly seedy.

"The silk list, Rumpole!" he stammered. "Have you seen the new Q.C.s?"

"Haven't got beyond the crossword." I opened the paper and found the relevant page. "Well, here's your name. What are you worrying about?"

"*My* name?" Erskine-Brown asked bitterly.

"Erskine-Brown. *Mrs.*!" I read the entry more carefully. "Oh, I do see." I felt for the man, my heart bled for him.

"She never warned me, Rumpole! I had no idea she'd applied. Had you?"

"No." I honestly hadn't. "Haven't you asked her about it?"

"She left home before the paper came. And now she's gone to ground in the ladies' robing room!" Then he asked with a faint hope, "Do you think it might be some sort of misprint?"

I might have sat there for some time commiserating with Claude, but I saw a blonde head and a blue trouser suit by the tea-urns. I rose, excused myself to the still suffering, still junior barrister, and arrived alongside Mrs. April Timson just in time to pay for her coffee.

"You're very kind, Mr. Rumpole," she said.

"Sometimes," I agreed. She moved to a table. I went with her. "Young Vincent well this morning, is he? Chrissie Molloy looking after him properly?"

"Chrissie's all right." She sat and then looked up at me and spoke very quietly. "Tony doesn't know she's a Molloy."

I sat down beside her and took my time in lighting a small cigar. "No, Mrs. Timson," I said. "Tony doesn't know very much, does he?"

"We were at school together. Me and Chrissie. Anyway, she and Shawn Molloy's separated."

"But still friends," I suggested. "Close enough for the Molloy firm to meet at Chrissie's house." I blew out smoke and then asked, "When did you know they were short of a driver?"

"I may have heard—someone mention it." She looked away from me and stirred her coffee. So I told her the whole story, as though she didn't know. "Your husband wouldn't have been the slightest use in a get-away car, would he?" I said. "He'd have had three parking tickets and hit a milk float before they'd got clear of the bank. You, on the other hand, I happen to have noticed, are distinctly nippy driving through traffic." A silence fell between us. It lasted until I said, "What was the matter? Tony not ambitious enough for you?"

"Why ever should you think—?" She looked up at me then. Whatever it was meant to be, the look was not innocent.

"Because of where you put the money," I told her quietly. "It was the one place in the house you knew your husband would never look."

She had the nerve of an accomplished villain, had Mrs. April Timson. She took a long swig of coffee and then she asked me what I was going to do.

"The real question is," I said, "what are *you* going to do?" And then I gave her my legal advice. "Leave it out, April," I said. "Give it up, Mrs. Timson. Keep away from it. It's men's work, you know. Let the men make a mess of it." I paused to let the advice sink in, then I stood up to go. "It was the first time, I imagine. Better make it the last."

I got into Court some time before the learned computer took his seat on the Bench. As soon as Phillida arrived, I gave her, believing it right to take my junior into my full confidence, my solution to the case, and an account of my conversation with April Timson.

She thought for a moment, and then asked, "But why didn't Gerry Molloy identify *her*?"

"He was ashamed, don't you understand? He didn't

want to admit that the great Molloys went out with a *woman* driver!"

"What on earth are we going to do?"

"We can't prove it was April. Let's hope they can't prove it was Tony. The jury don't much care for the mini-grass, and the Molloys *might* have planted the money."

Hilary Onslow came in then, gave us a cheerful "Good morning," and took his place. I spoke to Phillida in a whisper.

"Only one thing we can do, Portia. I'll just give them the speech about reasonable doubt."

"No. *I* will," she said firmly.

"What?" I wasn't following her drift.

"I'm *your* leader now. Don't you read *The Times,* Rumpole? I have taken silk!"

At which point the usher shouted, "Be upstanding," and Judge Dover was upon us. He looked at the defense team, said, "Yes, Mr. Rumpole?" and then saw that Phillida was on her feet.

"Mrs. Erskine-Brown. I believe that certain congratulations are in order?"

"Yes, my Lord, I believe they are," said our Portia, and announced that she would now call the defendant.

Tony gave evidence. As he denied knowing anything about the money, or the whereabouts of the Pond Hill bank, or even the exact situation of his own washing machine, he was a difficult witness to cross-examine. Onslow did his best, and made a moderately effective final speech, and then I sat quietly and listened to Mrs. Phillida Erskine-Brown, now my learned leader. I smiled as I heard her reach a familiar peroration.

"Members of the jury." She was addressing them with carefully controlled emotion. "Soon this case will be over. In a little while you will go back to your jobs and your families, and you will forget about it. At most it is only a small part of your lives, but for my client, Tony Timson, it is the *whole* of his life! And it is that life I leave with confidence in your hands, certain that there can be only one verdict in this case, 'Not Guilty'!"

And then Phillida sank down in her seat exhausted, just as I had taught her to, as I had taught Fiona Allways, and anyone else who would care to listen.

"Good speech," I congratulated Phillida as we came out of Court when the Timson case was over.

"Yes. It always was."

"Portia of Belmont—Phillida Erskine-Brown, nee Trant—and Fiona Allways. The great tradition of female advocates should be carried on!" I lit a small cigar.

Phillida looked at me. "It's not enough for you that we won Timson, is it? Not enough that you got the jury to disbelieve Gerry Molloy and think the money may have been planted. You want to win the Allways case as well."

"Well," I said reasonably, "why shouldn't we take on Fiona?"

"Over my dead body!"

She moved toward the lifts. I followed her.

"But *why?*"

"She was making a play for Claude. I found them all over each other in Pommeroy's. That's when I got so angry I applied for silk."

"Without telling your husband?" I asked sorrowfully.

"I'm afraid so."

"I'd better come clean about this." I took off my wig and stood looking at her. She looked back at me, deeply suspicious. "What've you been up to, Rumpole?"

"Well, I just wanted your Claude to look on Miss Allways with a warm and friendly eye. I mean, I thought that'd increase her chances of getting in, so—"

"You wanted Claude to *warm* to her—?" Phillida's voice was rising to a note of outrage.

"I thought it might help, yes," I admitted.

"Rumpole! I suppose you told him that she fancied him."

"Now, Portia. Would I do such a thing?" I protested.

"Very probably. If you wanted to win badly enough. I imagine you told him she thought he looked like Robert Redford."

"No. I protest!" I was hurt. "That is utterly and entirely untrue! I told him she thought he looked like a fellow called Newman."

"And had Allways actually said that?" Phillida was still uncertain of the facts.

"Well, if you want me to be entirely honest—"

"It would make a change," she said.

"Well, no, she hadn't."

And then, quite unexpectedly, our Portia smiled. "Poor old Claude," she said. "You know what you were doing, Rumpole? You can't rely on a girl to get in on her own talents, can you? You have to manipulate and rely on everyone else's vanity. You were simply exploiting the male sex."

"So now you know," I asked her, "will you vote for Fiona?"

"Tell me one good reason."

"Ballard's against her."

"I suppose that's one good reason. And because of you I've ended up a silk. What on earth can I tell Claude?" She seemed, for a delightful moment, overcome with guilt and blushed very prettily, as though she had to admit the existence of a lover.

"Tell him," I suggested, "that the Lord Chancellor just thought there weren't enough women silks. So that's why you got it. He'll feel better if he thinks there's no damn merit about this thing."

"I suppose so." She looked a little disappointed as she asked me, "Is that true?"

"Quite possibly," I told her. After all, I hadn't undertaken to tell her the *whole* truth about anything.

When I got home that night, Hilda asked me if I had noticed anything. Suspecting that she had had a new hairdo or bought a new dress, I said of course she was looking extremely pretty.

"Not me," she said. "Look at the walls."

The shelf I had put up was not only firmly screwed and looking even better than usual, it seemed to have pupped and there were shelves all over the place, gamely supporting potted plants and glasses, telephone directories and bottles of plonk.

"What did you do, Hilda?" I asked her. "Did you get a man in?"

"Yes," she said. "Me."

It all ended once again with a Chambers party. The excuse for that particular shindig was the swearing-in at the House of Lords of Mrs. Phillida Erskine-Brown as One of Her Majesty's Counsel. She made a resplendent figure as she came to split a few bottles of champagne with us in Ballard's room. Her handsome female face peeped out between the long spaniel's ears of her full-bottomed wig. She wore a long silk gown with a black purse on her back. There were lace cuffs on her tailed coat, and lace at her throat. Her black skirt ended with black stockings and diamond-buckled shoes. She carried white gloves in one hand and a glass of Mercier (on offer at Pommeroy's) in the other. Just when matters were going with a certain amount of swing, Ballard took it upon himself to make a speech. "In our great profession," he was saying, "we are sometimes accused of prejudice against the female sex."

"Shame!" said Erskine-Brown.

"That may be true of some sets of Chambers, but it cannot be said of us at 3 Equity Court," Ballard continued. "As in many other things, we take the lead and set the example! Today we celebrate the well deserved promotion of Mrs. Phillida Erskine-Brown to the front row!"

"Philly looks very fine in a silk gown, doesn't she, Rumpole?" the proud husband said to me.

"Gorgeous!" I agreed.

"And we welcome a new member of our set, young Fiona Allways," Ballard concluded. All around me barristers were toasting the triumph of women.

"You know, between ourselves, Philly got it because it's the Lord Chancellor's policy to appoint more *women* Q.C.'s," Erskine-Brown told me confidentially.

"How appalling." I looked on the man with considerable sympathy. "You're a victim of sexual discrimination!"

"But Philly's made me a promise. Next year she's going to take some time off."

"Good. I might get my work back."

"We're going to have—" his voice sank confidentially "—a little companion for Tristan."

"Isolde?" I suggested.

"Oh, really, Rumpole!"

I moved away from him as I saw Phillida in all her glory go up to Fiona, who was wearing wide trousers which, coming to just below the knees, had the appearance of a widish split skirt.

"Well done, Allways!" Phillida gave the girl an encouraging smile. "Welcome to Chambers."

"Thank you, Mrs. Erskine-Brown." Fiona seemed genuinely pleased. But Phillida had stopped smiling.

"Oh, just one thing, Allways. No culottes!"

"Oh," said Fiona. "Really?"

"If you want to get on at the Bar, and it is a pretty tough profession," Phillida told her, "just don't go in for those sort of baggy trouser arrangements. It's just not on."

"No. Remember that, Fiona," I put my oar in. "A fellow looks so much better in a skirt."

Hanged for a Sheep

by Henry Slesar

They would call him Boze here.

It was Phil Boswell's first thought when the elevator shivered to a halt on the third floor of the County Criminal Courts Building. Nothing had changed in the past nine years. There was still the same smell of sweat and stale air. There was still no way of telling grain from grime on the marble floor. There was still the same crackle and hum, almost below the threshold of audibility, like the murmur of high-tension wires. Everything was just as it was when he had been a ferrety kid new to the District Attorney's office, so why wouldn't his nickname be the same?

He was disappointed when the first person he met called him "sir," looking at his grey Armani suit and taking him for an attorney—right about that, of course, but Phil hadn't handled a criminal case in the last eight of his years in private practice. He gave the preppy young man an avuncular grin and asked if Donny Donahue still did his dirty work out of the same corner office. Yes, he was told, Donny was there, but in a different corner. He pointed east, toward the area of the building they had once called Siberia.

It still deserved the name. Donny's star had obviously dimmed. He had sounded like his old self on the phone, but Phil had done some arithmetic in the taxi and figured that his old boss must be past sixty now—not a good age for bad politicians like Donny. But, hell, he didn't look all that different, and he bounced out of his swivel chair and gave Phil a crushing bear hug. And sure enough, he said: "Hey, *Boze!*"

Donny had a face full of parentheses, lines carved mostly by pure merriment. But the lines became question marks when he heard the favor Phil had come to ask.

"Why? What for?" he said. "This guy is looney-tunes, Boze. Why do you want to see him?"

"I'm interested in the case," Phil answered. "That's all it is. I prosecuted a serial killer my second year on the job, remember?"

"Rat droppings," Donny growled. "Myron Wechsler did the 'prosecuting.' All you did was the coolie labor."

"But I still spent five months on the case, putting the package together, and it made me curious about this guy, Wortman." It sounded lame even as he spoke the words, so Phil shifted gears and said: "Come on, Donny, you always told me I had markers with you. Did I ever call one in before?"

"No," he admitted. "But I never thought you'd need anything, not from this office. What are you getting from those uptown clients these days? I read a million for your new divorce case, or is it palimony?"

"It's divorce," Phil said. "And, believe me, I'm earning every nickel. You think matrimonial law is a piece of cake, try spending six months with a hysterical, bloodthirsty woman."

"Maybe that's why you never married," Donny grunted. "Seeing so much of these Bitches from Hell." His eyes narrowed. "Hey, is that what this is all about? You trying to get back into criminal law?"

For a moment, Phil was tempted to smile mysteriously and let Donny keep his assumption. Donny had seen it often enough, lawyers looking for showcase clients, willing to defend the undefendable, so headline-hungry that they'd get into bed with an axe murderer or rapist or even a housewife strangler like Carl Wortman. Only so far, nobody had tried. So far,

Wortman's icy-calm confessions had paled the resolve of even the hardiest of the publicity-minded attorneys in town.

"No," Phil said, "I haven't touched a criminal case in years, and I sure wouldn't start with the Wortman case if I wanted back in. This is a kind of—journalistic interest. I've been putting some things on paper, you know the itch you get. Nizer, F. Lee Bailey—I don't know if I'll ever finish the damned book, probably burn it before I reach chapter two, but it's something I want to try."

Maybe Donny believed him, maybe he just decided not to press for more explanations. Whatever it was, he said he would do what he could, and Phil knew it would be enough. Donny would make the right calls and Phil would get admitted to the county detention center where Carl Wortman was still busily engaged in police interrogations, trying to delay his trial and inevitable sentencing as long as he could, maybe even enjoying the spotlight, no matter how white and hot it shone in his bright, intelligent, maniac eyes.

Three day later, Phil faced those eyes across a scarred wooden table in a room that reeked of old cigarettes and a few other odors he didn't care to identify. Oddly, the aroma exuded by the prisoner was one of clean soap and shaving lotion. Wortman's blue-cotton prison clothes were freshly laundered, his long straight hair damp from a recent shower, his expression amiable, even eager. It didn't matter that he was uninformed of Phil Boswell's purpose. He had been grilled by dozens of strangers since his arrest; by now he was a professional grillee.

Phil introduced himself with a business card, one that didn't mention his specialty. Wortman made a lucky guess. With a wide, crinkly smile he said: "I know who sent you here. It was Charlene, am I right?"

Phil had done his homework, so he knew who Charlene was. Wortman had an estranged wife living in a trailer park in Abilene. There was also a four-year-old daughter he hadn't seen since the night her croupy cough and endless bawling had caused him to slam out the door and hitchhike his way to Fort Worth, where, according to the police, he had taken the notion of sexually assaulting and murdering his first housewife. Phil had read some glib theories about how Wortman had redirected his rage against his wife, and maybe his mother if not his teddy bear, but he intended to ignore Carl Wortman's psyche and concentrate on his mission.

"I don't know your wife," Phil said. "I'm not here on her behalf. If anything, I'm here because of your little girl. I'm afraid I don't remember her name." He did, but Phil had a little test in mind.

"Her name is Rachel," Wortman said. "Same name as my grandmother." If there was any alteration in the luminescence of his eyes, Phil couldn't detect it.

"You left when she was only ten months old. Have you thought about her in all this time? Visited her maybe?"

Wortman surprised him by nodding affirmatively. Then he asked Phil for a cigarette, but Phil didn't smoke. A guard came out of the shadows and handed Wortman one, lighting it for him. The service was good here.

"I was passing through Abilene," Wortman said. "I went to the trailer park, but I didn't see Charlene there. Hell, I didn't even *want* to see her. Somebody told me she was working in a coffee shop and Rachel was in a day-care center. I went to the place. The kids were outside, in a yard all fenced in with chicken wire. I picked her out right away. Rachel. More like me than Charlene. Me in a little red dress."

He grinned and stubbed out the cigarette, only half smoked. Phil saw the hole in the back of his hand and Wortman explained it almost with pride. "She did that. Woman named Cleo. Stabbed me with a pair of scissors, had me pinned down on her coffee table." He chuckled softly, as if in fond remembrance. Phil hadn't heard this gruesome detail, but the case name was familiar. Cleo Barnes, housewife, mother of two. She had been Wortman's fourth or fifth victim. He couldn't remember which, and wasn't sure that Wortman could, either.

"When the police caught you," Phil said, "in Abilene, last April—were you trying to see your little girl again?"

Wortman shrugged.

"Do you care about Rachel? Do you care what happens to her, how she grows up, whether she goes to school, has enough to eat?"

Some of Wortman's affability was waning now that the subject was no longer himself, and Phil hurried up his argument. "What I mean is, there's a lot more to you than the things you did wrong, the things you couldn't help doing, am I right? No matter what they say, you've got feelings. You would never have gone to that day-care center if your little girl didn't mean something to you."

"Well, hell, yes. That's the truth of it," Wortman said. Then he grinned. "Hey, you sure you're a lawyer, not a preacher? They snuck in one of those on me and I told him to go save the sinners. Me, I'm just 'disturbed.' "

He dropped a wink and leaned back.

"I'm not a preacher," Phil said softly. "And I'm not a social worker, either. Although you might say I represent a charitable organization interested in the welfare of kids like your daughter Rachel. Because, let's face it, Carl, she's the child of a victim, just like the kids of Cleo Barnes."

Wortman was getting restless. Words like "welfare" struck discordant notes with him. But the name Rachel seemed to create a blip in the black intensity of his eyes, so Phil said it a few more times. *Rachel* is going to need help, he said. *Rachel* is going to need money— her own money, not his wife's.

"Damn right," Wortman said, his lips thinning.

"Charlene won't do a damn thing for that kid, I know her only too well."

"Then here's what we're offering," Phil said. "This is how we would like to help Rachel."

Before he went on, he glanced at the guard in the shadowy corner of the interrogation room. His arms were folded, straining all the threads in his uniform. His back was curved into the recess of the wall. His eyes were closed and his lips parted; if the acoustics had been better, Phil was sure he would hear the faint whistle of his shallow breath. He was a man dozing on his feet, and Phil's last concern was gone.

"This is the offer," he said again. "A trust fund for Rachel. A nice tight trust fund in the Bank of Abilene, so tight that her mother can't touch a single nickel of it. It'll be payable to Rachel Wortman in escalating installments from the age of, say, fifteen, eighteen, twenty-one. Enough to take care of her through school, even college if she wants it."

"How much?" Wortman said, the blip more pronounced. "How much will this fund be worth?"

"One hundred thousand dollars," Phil said carefully. "One hundred big ones, Carl. How many kids have that kind of start in life? How many fathers can offer them a start like that?"

"Why?" Wortman asked, a reasonable suspicion in his voice. "Why would you do all that for her? Don't give me that 'charity' stuff, that's all cow flop. I know charities."

"I'm sure you do. I can tell when a man's been around, Carl. So I'll give you the bottom line. Just tell me one thing. Have you ever heard the expression 'hanged for a sheep' . . ."

Barry didn't answer the door after three long indentations of the buzzer, and Phil thought he might have decided to disobey his instructions and leave the apartment. Barry brought the explanation for his delay with him when he opened the door. Two explanations. One was the terrycloth robe he was wrapping around his body. The other was the faint fragrance of good Scotch whisky. Phil recognized his own robe and his own whisky, but he didn't complain. A man with Barry's problems, sweating out the last three hours in what must have been agonizing suspense, was entitled to a hot bath and a cold drink.

"I've been going crazy," he said. "I kept looking at my watch every five minuets. I took it into the tub with me and dropped it twice. Now I'll find out how true that waterproof claim is. Do you want a drink? Don't ask for the Glenlivet, this is the last of it."

"Sit down," Phil said. "I've got things to tell you."

"Good things, for God's sake. Make it something I want to hear, Boze."

He was Boze here, too. He had known Barry Lewin for a dozen years, worked across the same cluttered desk with him at the D.A.'s office until Barry had switched to defense work, had copped a nice light plea for a Wall Street criminal and ended up in his law department two years later, making nice money, marrying the prettiest girl they both knew, moving into a nice country house. The house was out of bounds now, haunted by the press, so Phil had offered his own city apartment as a hideout.

Phil checked his phone messages first. There were four shrill calls, all from his divorce client. There were two messages from his secretary. A robot voice told him that he just might be the winner of a sweepstakes. He switched off the machine and looked at Barry, huddled in a wing chair, his naked feet and hands like a sixteen-year-old's, his face like an old man's. Twelve years ago he had been the office pretty boy, with a mop of gold ringlets. Girls were always dropping by. Now there were only scribbles of hair atop a high wrinkled forehead. Phil said: "I didn't want to tell you what I was doing until I knew it was feasible. I'm still not sure it's going to work. I've got hopes, but hopes don't always keep people out of the slammer." He paused. "Which is where I was this morning."

"Where?" Barry said.

"I went to the detention center to see a man named Carl Wortman. Maybe you don't know the name, but you know the case. The Housewife Strangler? Did he kill six, did he kill ten? Are there twenty victims still unidentified? Stay tuned. Bulletins on the hour. Film at eleven."

He went to see if Barry had told the truth about the Glenlivet. He had. Phil poured himself some vodka on ice and then sat down wearily, never touching the glass again.

"I made Wortman an offer," he said. "I told him that I'd guarantee his daughter a trust fund worth a hundred thousand dollars. All he had to do was agree with the old proverb that you might as well hang for a sheep as a lamb. Now see if that giant Wall Street brain of yours can figure out the rest."

Barry only needed five seconds. His tightened features began to inflate, his jaw slackened, his blue eyes rounded.

"Tracey," he said. "You asked him to take the blame—for what happened to Tracey."

"I got the idea three weeks ago when Joey Lopez leaked the story to me about Wortman being caught in Texas. I had to check it out first—the logistics, I mean. What Wortman's itinerary was, whether he could have been in the vicinity around the time Tracey was killed. Joey told me that the guy was hazy about his travels, that he hopped buses when he saw them, that he just let the wind blow him in every direction. All he cared about was his next date with some lonely housewife. He liked to kill them in the kitchen, did you know that? He dragged them all into the kitchen and murdered them over the sink. That was the only thing that didn't fit about Tracey, but I don't think it's crucial."

"My God," Barry whispered. "Can this really work, Boze?"

"It might," Phil said. "It just might. I told him some things he had to know. About your house, your neighborhood, about Tracey. Wortman's smart, believe it or not. A smart maniac. Had two years at Abilene Christian, studied engineering, dropped out when he got married. He knew what I was talking about. He remembered the little things I told him. About your unfinished garage, your bay windows, the Navajo rugs Tracey collected. I told him what Tracey looked like, the turquoise-and-silver necklace she always wore. The necklace that strangled her."

He looked up to see if Barry winced, but Barry's rapt expression hadn't changed.

"He said he'd do it? He said he'd confess to Tracey's murder?"

"I told him it wouldn't matter to him, but it would matter to his little girl. When she found out how well he'd provided for her. I told him she'd grow up thinking her old man was one hell of a guy no matter what other people said."

"When will we know?" Barry asked. "When will we find out? They're breathing down my neck, Boze. There's a homicide cop named Riggs who knew me in the old days. He'd like nothing better than to nail my ass to the electric chair."

"We won't know until Wortman decides to let us know. Until we read it in the papers or hear it on the Six O'Clock News."

He saw Barry look at his watch again. It was five-thirty.

There was nothing on the television news that night, at six or eleven, and nothing in the midnight edition of the newspaper. There was nothing more about Wortman until the following evening, when the *Post* headlined a story on page three that said: THREE MORE VICTIMS CITED BY HOUSEWIFE SLAYER. The first was the wife of an insurance broker who had broken her neck in what had been mistaken for a household accident, slipping on the terrazzo tiles of her kitchen. The second was a woman in Boise, Idaho, who seemed an unlikely victim of sexual assault, being stout and sixty-eight. The third was described as thin, pretty, dark-eyed like an Indian, with Indian rugs all over the house. He'd broken her neck, too. She had been wearing a necklace he described perfectly; it was the kind of jewelry he used to see for sale around Santa Fe and Albuquerque and places like that. He even recalled that he had killed her in the living room, that she had struggled so much he could neither rape her or strangle her over the kitchen sink. The *Post* didn't hesitate to jump to the right conclusion. This third victim was local. She was Tracey Jean Lewin of 200 Roylston Road, Allenville.

Barry returned to Royalston Road the next morning, but Phil telephoned before coming out that evening, assuming that he might be having visitors. He was right. Riggs himself had been there to question Barry about Carl Wortman. Barry gleefully reported that Riggs had been deferential, even remorseful. The press had called, too, of course, but Perry had taken Boze's advice and invoked his "no comment" privilege. The relief in Barry's voice made him sound ten years younger.

Phil showed up at ten that night. Barry looked bleary-eyed, but at peace. He wasn't drunk, as Phil thought he might be, just pleasantly muddled by alcohol. The television set was on, a situation comedy giving itself lots of laughs. Phil found the sound obscene in this room, but he said nothing about it.

"I still can't believe it," Barry said. "That it's over, that it's really over. For two months—it's almost three, isn't it?—all I could think about was being in a courtroom, being the defendant this time. Me, the defendant! It was a nightmare, Boze. I used to have dreams like that when I was in criminal law, me sitting there and someone else defending. And it would have happened just that way if it wasn't for you."

For a moment Phil thought he was going to be on the receiving end of a sloppy embrace, but he slid away from the threatened lunge and went to the dry bar. There was no Glenlivet, but there was a bottle of medium-priced Scotch, one-third empty. He filled a glass and dropped in a couple of ice cubes. He was still watching them swim in the amber liquid when he said:

"Now keep your promise and tell me the truth. All of it, right from the beginning."

He didn't turn, even when Barry remained silent. Then he heard the click of a remote button on the TV set. The laughter died, and Barry said, "What I told you right off was the truth, Boze. I didn't mean to kill Tracey. As God is my witness, it was the last thing in my mind that night."

"Afternoon," Phil said. "It happened in the afternoon, didn't it?"

"Yes. That's right. It was a Wednesday afternoon. I was in my office. It was about two-thirty. I'd just had lunch with Nat Seely, the Senior V.P. Heavy hitter, Nat. Three Gibsons for lunch, and I kept up with him, he gets insulted if you don't. I was shot for the afternoon—not that I cared. Half the time I had nothing to do anyway. That was bad for me, because it gave me too much time to think. And all I thought about was Tracey. All I ever thought about in those days was Tracey. And the goddamn white roses."

"White roses?" Phil repeated.

"You remember Donny Donahue's office, right? When Tracey was his secretary? There were flowers on his desk every morning. Tracey brought those flowers—paid for them herself. I know, everybody thought she was a tough little cookie, always trying to be one of the guys, but she was like a hard piece of candy with a soft center. Maybe that was the problem. Maybe I never stopped thinking of Tracey, as you know, strong, self-reliant. I thought she could take anything. If I didn't come home some nights, if I went out of town a lot, Tracey would understand, you know what I mean? I couldn't picture her as a 'neglected house-wife,' one of those weepy, complaining women. Even after she lost the baby, she didn't mope around as if her life was over. Yes, we had a few fights then, because she wanted to adopt and I hated the idea, you never know what you'll get out of the goddamn gene pool. Oh—about the roses."

He picked up his abandoned drink.

"The way I found out about Donny's office and the flowers, I was going to work one morning when I saw Tracey coming out of a florist's. I asked her how she got a hardnose like Donny to spend money on flowers, and she broke down and told me the truth. She asked me not to tell anyone at the office, and I said I wouldn't. It gave us a secret together. We had a date a couple of nights later, and it was terrific. I was crazy about her. The next day I sent her a dozen red roses, and when I asked her if she liked them she said next time make them white."

"Did you?" Phil asked.

"No," Barry said. "The truth is, I never sent Tracey flowers again. I don't know why. I just didn't think about it. I mean, three weeks after we started dating, we decided to get married. Then I had that job offer in Chicago and there was all the fuss about relocating. Then came the Loomis case, and my new job, and the baby business, and all the other things—"

Phil was still studying the ice cubes.

"Maybe nobody ever realizes when a marriage starts going sour," Barry said. "Not until it's too late to do anything about it. Only don't ask me what I could have done, Boze. I was still crazy about Tracey, I never stopped being crazy about her. If I thought a bunch of flowers would have changed things for us, I would have sent them by the truckload."

Barry sat down for the first time, clutching his glass with both hands. "I don't know when I first got the idea that there was somebody else. It was before I noticed the rose, I'm sure of that much. The white rose in a skinny vase next to Tracey's bed. There was nothing unusual about Tracey having flowers around."

He seemed to be waiting for Phil to ask a question, but Phil didn't.

"One day," Barry said, "I was at the airport about to catch a plane for a meeting in L.A. when I realized I had left all the papers I needed in my study. I could have called Tracey, asked her to messenger them out to me, but something made me decide to go back home. Without calling first. I can't explain how I felt. There was something perverse about it. I was actually hoping I'd find somebody with Tracey. I was so sick of my doubts that I wanted them to be certainties. And I wasn't disappointed."

"You saw the man?"

"No," Barry said. "I saw the roses.

"Tracey wasn't home when I arrived. She was subbing at the local high school—she did that sometimes. She had brought in the mail before she left. There were letters, junk mail, bills. And the white roses. Half a dozen of them, wrapped in white paper. You could just make out the florist's logo printed in light grey. It was Reiner Brothers. Our local florist is called Evergreen. There was no address label, no card, so I knew they had to have been hand-delivered.

"When I got back from L.A. the next day, the white roses were in a little vase on the coffee table. I even asked a casual question about them. I said I didn't know roses were still in season. I asked her did Evergreen get them from a hothouse or something? She said yes—yes, they did. The way she answered, the way she looked away from me, Boze, that told me everything. Everything I needed to know, everything I didn't want to know.

"In the next couple of days, the roses withered and died and Tracey threw them out. The next day, I went to Reiner Brothers in the city and bought half a dozen white roses. I took an early train home, and when I handed them to Tracey her face went as white as the flowers. I said, 'What's the matter? You once told me to bring you white roses. Or am I the wrong delivery boy?' I thought she was going to faint, but she did something worse. She stood tall and straight, she put that look on her face she used to wear around the office when things weren't going right—you remember that look, Boze, her eyes like black marbles, death-ray eyes we used to call them. And she said, 'You're right, Barry. It's too late for a delivery, and you're the wrong boy. The right one isn't a boy at all. He's a *man*.'

"I hit her, Boze. I hit her just once, I swear it was only once. But I hit her hard. I hadn't used my fist like that since I got into a schoolyard fight when I was fifteen. At first it felt good, it was satisfying—all the anger that was building up in me went into that fist, Boze. But I knew it was too hard when my hand started to hurt, when I saw Tracey on the floor, her head twisted at that funny angle. I don't know if she hit something on her way down, the corner of the coffee table maybe. I tried to pick her up by her shoulders, and maybe that was another mistake. I could hear the bones in her neck grinding against each other. It was horrible.

"I ran out of the house. I was too scared to stay there. I drove back to the train station without even thinking about the plan that was already formulating in my mind. To wait for the train to arrive, my usual train. To act as if I'd just gotten off the train, to say hello to people I knew, neighbors. To walk to the parking lot with them as if I hadn't been home at all.

"That's what I did, Boze, but you know what happened. The cops always suspect the husband first—why wouldn't they? Riggs even asked around about the train, about the possibility that I had done exactly what I did do. It was just going to be a matter of time, Boze, you and I know that. Until you did what you did. Until you did this thing for me, this great thing. I never knew what a friend you were, Boze. Now tell me what I can do for you."

Phil took the first swallow of his drink, a sizable one. Then he put it down and said: "You can write me a check. Two checks, as a matter of fact. One for a hundred thousand, the other for five hundred. The first one will be for the little girl's trust fund. The second is my fee."

"That's not enough. Not nearly enough!"

"It'll cover my expenses."

"Why are you doing this, Boze? Why? It's not your responsibility—"

"Isn't it?"

Barry wrote the checks and Phil left the house a few minutes later. Then he went home, mulling over ways to create the anonymous trust for Rachel Wortman. In the morning, he stopped off at Reiner Brothers and picked up a half dozen white roses for his visit to Tracey's grave.

The Decision

by Joe L. Hensley

By his tenth year on the bench, Judge Cleve Marshall had become a judge's judge. His decisions were sought after all over his area of the state. Bright lawyers filed change-of-venue motions and requested him. Life was interesting and busy. He had never married and now, at forty-three, thought he never would. There had been women, and still were, in and around the small town of Avalon where he'd lived all his life. He maintained an active life style. He played fair golf and better tennis. But much of his time was spent, black-robed, listening intently to evidence, studying casebooks for precedent, or mulling over knotty decisions.

He wasn't surprised, therefore, when he was chosen to hear the Fielder murder case. He'd read about it in the area papers and wondered if it would fall to him to sit as presiding judge in it. He *was* surprised, however, when Prosecutor Hanks and Defense Attorney Baron announced to him, at an omnibus hearing, that he'd hear it without jury.

"Now hold on, boys," he said. "I know and admire both of you and I've read a bit about the case in the local paper. I can maybe see one of you wanting a non-jury trial, but not both of you."

Lester Baron rose and smiled at him. "Judge, this woman is accused of deliberately poisoning her husband and daughter. My feeling is that a jury would be swayed by the mere fact she's accused, would disregard the flimsiness of the evidence, and would want to punish Alice Fielder because her husband and child are dead. So I'm asking that you alone hear it. My client has agreed."

George Hanks nodded. "The prosecution is willing to go along because the evidence is circumstantial, with inferences arising out of inferences. We think it requires a judicial mind to realize the full perfidy of what Alice Fielder did to her family." He smiled like a half open knife. He'd always been an effective but vicious prosecutor.

"So be it then," Judge Marshall said. "How long do you foresee it will take to try the matter, gentlemen?"

"A few days. Certainly no more than a week," Baron said. "Much of the evidence could even be stipulated, but won't be because of a circumstance. That circumstance is, of course, a separate page asking for the death penalty. Prosecutor Hanks is also willing to go along because of that possibility. Mrs. Fielder is a very handsome woman. He believes a jury might convict her but not sentence her to death. And he wants the death penalty."

Hanks nodded. "Will you do it, Judge?"

Cleve Marshall folded his hands. "I've never turned down a case, but I want both of you to know I'd like to turn this one down. My difficulty is that I can find no reason in the judicial code of ethics why I should."

They set a June trial date.

"One more thing, Judge," Baron said. "Do you know Alice Fielder?"

"Not to my knowledge. If she grew up around here, I *might* know her. I vaguely knew her deceased husband."

"She was a Linip before she was married," Hanks told him.

"I don't remember the name," Marshall said. "I still might know her, but it doesn't mean anything to me. If I find out anything which might bias me before trial, I'll get out."

Both lawyers nodded, satisfied.

After they'd gone, Judge Marshall read the file. There wasn't much there to satisfy his aroused curiosity. There was the information charging Alice Fielder with killing her husband and daughter. There were some discovery motions from both sides and lists of witnesses, most of them the expected people—the police officers who'd made the original run to the Fielder home after the frantic call from Alice Fielder, doctors who'd examined the bodies, a toxicologist who'd run tests on body fluids, some neighbors.

If the prosecution was correct, Alice Fielder had poisoned her husband and fifteen-year-old daughter. Judge Marshall wondered what kind of monster could do that. Then, in the middle of the file, he came across two police photos of Alice Fielder, one taken front face, the other from the side. She was a most pleasant-looking woman, not yet forty. Her face seemed vaguely familiar to him. he tried to remember why, but nothing came. He got his magnifying glass out of his desk and studied the face, giving particular attention to the eyes. They stared at the camera. He couldn't tell whether they were sorrowful, bewildered, or merely cunning. It still seemed as if somewhere, some time long ago, he'd seen it—and forgotten it.

Doctor Leybeck was an aging medical-expert boor. Marshall had heard him many times and had once stated, only half in joke, that the man could put a jury to sleep while describing the results of an axe murder. Leybeck was a forensic pathologist much used by the prosecutor.

When the veteran police officer who'd made the run had seen the two victims, he'd called Doctor Leybeck and he had arrived on the scene in the company of the coroner.

"The poison was nicotine, pure nicotine, distilled somehow either from some old pesticides we found in a shed outside the house or from tobacco itself. Edgar

Fielder managed a tobacco warehouse and it was the height of the season when it happened. Both victims were found in their bedrooms. The dishes from a table in the dining room had been removed, but traces of the poison were found in the food remaining on two of the dinner plates. The family had eaten some sort of Mexican meal, very hot and spicy. After Sergeant Jones read her Mirandas to her, Mrs. Fielder said it was enchiladas and she had prepared it."

"What effect would nicotine have upon someone who ingested it?" the prosecutor asked.

"A fatal dose could be as little as one drop. It would first stimulate, then depress the cells of peripheral autonomic ganglia, particularly the midbrain, and the spinal cord. Initially, there'd be a burning of the mouth, throat, and stomach, then nausea, tachycardia, elevation of blood-pressure, respiratory slowing, coma, and finally death. These symptoms would follow each other with great rapidity. And from my tests, that's how Edgar and Joan Fielder died." The doctor stared out into the warm, crowded courtroom. It was almost full. Murder cases still drew crowds.

"Did you do tests on the plates found in Mrs. Fielder's kitchen?"

"Yes."

"And the results?"

"The food on them was liberally doused with pure nicotine. Enough to kill ten people. I estimated a time of death for each victim about ten to thirty minutes after the drug was ingested."

Lester Baron asked on cross-examination: "You saw nothing in the house to indicate that Mrs. Fielder had prepared some sort of apparatus to distill pure nicotine?"

"No. I didn't look."

After Doctor Leybeck, there came a parade of neighbors and acquaintances of the Fielders. They testified concerning public quarrels and threats. Close neighbors testified to the sounds of strife emanating almost constantly from the Fielder home and to occasional marks they'd seen on Mrs. Fielder after the battles. Once her arm had been broken. Once she'd apparently scalded her husband so severely with hot coffee that he'd been laid up for a week. The daughter had sometimes come to school with bruises and lacerations.

The most telling witness for the prosecution was a next-door neighbor, Janet Robbins. She and Mrs. Fielder were close.

"She said one day she was going to kill Edgar," Mrs. Robbins said.

"Did she say it more than once?"

"Oh, yes. Many times—every time they had a fight. He was always picking on her or the daughter. Joan ran away several times, but was found and sent back home."

Co-workers at the warehouse testified that Mrs. Fielder had been in and out of the place many times and that she and her husband had had arguments there. They attested to Mrs. Fielder's interest in tobacco and the availability of raw tobacco leaves in the warehouse. As one co-worker described an attempt she'd made to hit Fielder with a hammer while at the warehouse, Judge Marshall studied the woman from the bench.

She seemed calm enough now. She was wearing inexpensive clothes and smiled only when her lawyer asked a telling cross-question. Her features were good, her teeth perfect. She had apparently been difficult to live with, and yet it seemed to have been a two-way street she and her now deceased husband had so tempestuously ridden upon. He'd hurt her and she'd hurt him in return. The daughter had probably been dominated and kept in fear by both of them, but there were questions about that which weren't being asked and that puzzled him.

A teacher had said of her: "She was kind of withdrawn and strange, you know? She was bright enough in some areas, uninterested in others. Her grades ran from Fs to As. She liked science and reading. Until around the time she died, she was like a little girl, though she'd matured physically over the last summer vacation. She didn't take part in any of the extra-curricular activities at the school. She read a lot—those dreadful things they write for young adults now. She came to school, she went home. She was a pretty child, but she seemed afraid of boys. Several times she broke down and cried in class. I took her aside and asked her if she was ever beaten at home, but she'd never admit it to me or any of the other teachers, even when she came to school with bruises."

Police Sergeant Jones testified about going to the house and finding the two bodies in the bedrooms. When he had arrived, Mrs. Fielder had shown almost no emotion. She'd politely invited him inside the quiet house, saying her husband and daughter had gotten sick after supper and were in bed. She willingly allowed Jones to enter the bedrooms where he'd found the still-warm bodies.

"I read her the Miranda warning and she said she'd fixed the meal. When I asked her other questions, she said she'd like to have a lawyer first so I stopped."

"Did you search the house?"

"Yes, later. That's when we found the poison on the closet shelf in her bedroom, sitting right out in plain sight."

"Did you find anything to indicate that it had been distilled inside the house?"

"There were some old chemistry things down in the basement—you know, bottles and retorts and tubing. One of those kid sets you can buy in a toy store. We analyzed them, but they were clean. I checked the local night school and found out Mrs. Fielder had taken some chemistry courses there, but I don't know if the stuff we found in the basement was hers or her daughter's." He shrugged. "Or her husband's."

A teacher from the night school testified that Mrs. Fielder had taken enough courses to understand how to distill the poison and would be likely to know of its highly toxic nature. Avalon was a tobacco town and workers in the warehouses had suffered chronic, but curable, poisoning, and those poisonings had been reported in the local newspaper.

The prosecution rested.

Defense Counsel Baron made the obligatory motion for judgment and Marshall politely overruled it, pointing out that there'd been three people in the Fielder house, that two of them were dead, and that a prima facie case had been established.

"You may begin your evidence," he said.

Baron nodded and went back to the defense table. For a time he and his client held a low-voiced discussion—seemingly amiable until Marshall saw that Baron was becoming red-faced and somewhat angry.

Finally, Baron approached the bench. "Could we break until tomorrow morning? I need to talk with my client concerning her defense."

George Hanks got to his feet. "I'll have to object, Your Honor," he said smoothly. "Mr. Baron and his client have had some months to prepare strategy."

Marshall nodded and looked at his watch. It was almost four. "True, but I'll give Mr. Baron until the morning."

At the courtroom door, Marshall saw Alice Fielder look back at him—calculating him, perhaps. A tiny memory came and again he thought he might barely remember her. There had been a time after his freshman year in college when he'd summered as a lifeguard at the local municipal pool. There had been dozens of girls around that summer, some older than he was, some his age, many younger. He thought he remembered a face like Alice Fielder's somewhere in that lost crowd. He wondered if she'd been one of his "summer girls." It had been a lot of years.

In the morning, a sullen Baron rested without introducing any evidence. The two lawyers made closing argument and Marshall returned the defendant to the dirty, aging county jail while he considered the case.

For days, he sat in his law library, smelling the dampness and decay and rereading his case books. He vacillated. Sometimes he was sure Alice Fielder was guilty but at other times he was not. He did know that two people had died and that a third who'd been present had not and that that was strong circumstantial evidence.

On a day in early July he ordered the court back into session. The prosecutor came smiling into the courtroom and the defense counsel arrived scowling. Neither expression lasted long.

"I find," Marshall announced, "after careful consideration, that there is insufficient evidence against the defendant to convict Mrs. Fielder of murder. At times, in considering this case, I have had the feeling that the defendant probably committed the crime, but I have never been able to say to myself, beyond a reasonable doubt, that she committed the double murder of her husband and daughter. Therefore, I now order that she be released from custody."

He nodded down at the deputy who was guarding Alice Fielder. "I'm sure she has personal belongings at the jail. Return her there and allow her to pick them up." He nodded at her. "You're free, Mrs. Fielder. I hope I've done the right thing. I know I've done the legally right thing."

She nodded back at him, not smiling. There were tears in her eyes. It was the first sign of strong emotion he'd observed in her.

He didn't see Alice Fielder for some months after the trial. Lester Baron told him she'd gone off somewhere to escape the publicity. There had been a substantial amount. Marshall had caught the brunt of it, smiling and repeating "Insufficient evidence" until the public interest finally moved on to fresher news.

He encountered her at a restaurant he favored. He'd never seen her there before. She sat at the bar, drinking a tall icy drink, wearing a tailored dress that set off her figure and face far better than the drab apparel she'd worn in the courtroom. Her eyes were as he remembered them, lost and forlorn, and it struck him that, strangely enough, she might be there hoping to speak with him.

"I see you survived my release," she said when he went over to her. "I want to thank you for it." She smiled without humor. "Some in town still think I'm guilty. I'm about to move away—I've given up hope for a normal life here."

He nodded and waited, sensing she wanted to say more.

"Why did you find me innocent?" she asked. "My lawyer was sure you wouldn't when I refused to take the witness stand."

"You had a constitutional right not to testify," Marshall said. "I found you not guilty because I could see another way the deaths could have happened. Your husband could have poisoned the plates and then gotten a poisoned one by mistake, having meant the poison for you and your daughter. You have studied chemistry, so I didn't think you would leave plates with poison on them in the sink until the police came, invite the police officer in, admit your prepared the dinner, and let him enter the bedrooms without objection." He shook his head. "The only thing that puzzled me about the trial is why you, yourself, didn't say on the witness stand what I'm saying now."

She smiled. "There was a reason. And you have a right to know. I wasn't going to get on the witness stand and tell what happened, not even if I had to die for it, but I'll tell you if you promise you'll tell no one else. I want you to know and understand."

He nodded, his curiosity aroused. Besides, he found himself attracted to her. He knew she couldn't be for him, but he was still attracted. "You were one of my summer girls, weren't you?"

She nodded. "I didn't think you remembered that."

"It took me a while," he admitted.

She looked into her glass, her face somber again.

"He always beat on us. Maybe it was something that went wrong in his childhood. I could take his viciousness to me, but he was also vicious to Joan. I threw that scalding coffee on him when he was beating her, not me. I could take care of myself, she couldn't. I was physically about as strong as he was. Then, when Joan started to grow up, he changed subtly toward her. He patted her and kissed her and she didn't know how to handle that. It got worse. What he did damaged her.

"Joan carried the plates to the table that night. She must have distilled the poison. The chemistry set was hers—I bought it for her one Christmas when she was about twelve. She was very good at things like chemistry and physics. I heard her tinkering with the set in the basement again in the weeks before it happened and I saw evidence down there that she was distilling something. It never occurred to me . . ."

"One never suspects the obvious," Marshall said. "Or the very young."

"Yes." She nodded. "And I wanted it kept like that. I remembered your kindness when you were a lifeguard. You never really saw me that summer, but I saw you. I loved you that summer I was only fourteen and you were eighteen or nineteen. Love's very difficult at that age. Joan's age. I couldn't sit in your court and say that my sexually brutalized daughter had poisoned her father and herself. I doubted I'd be believed anyway, but whether I was believed or not I couldn't make myself do it. I couldn't for her and I couldn't for me. They were both dead and it was over.

"But I want you personally to know before I move on that you made the right decision. If you can keep it secret I'll be very grateful."

"Where will you go?"

"Someplace new."

He smiled at her. "Stay in touch with me."

"All right." She set the unfinished drink down and got up as if to leave. She looked at him and said again, "All right."

The Prisoner's Defense

by Arthur Conan Doyle

The circumstances, so far as they were known to the public, concerning the death of the beautiful Miss Ena Garnier, and the fact that Captain John Fowler, the accused officer, had refused to defend himself on the occasion of the proceedings at the police court, had roused very general interest. This was increased by the statement that, though he withheld his defense, it would be found to be of a very novel and convincing character. The assertion of the prisoner's lawyer at the police court, to the effect that the answer to the charge was such that it could not yet be given, but would be available before the Assizes, also caused much speculation.

A final touch was given to the curiosity of the public when it was learned that the prisoner had refused all offers of legal assistance from counsel and was determined to conduct his own defense.

The case for the Crown was ably presented, and was generally considered to be a very damning one, since it showed very clearly that the accused was subject to fits of jealousy, and that he had already been guilty of some violence owing to this cause. The prisoner listened to the evidence without emotion, and neither interrupted nor cross-questioned the witnesses. Finally, on being informed that the time had come when he might address the jury, he stepped to the front of the dock. He was a man of striking appearance, swarthy, black-mustached, nervous, and virile, with a quietly confident manner. Taking a paper from his pocket he read the following statement, which made the deepest impression upon the crowded court:

I would wish to say, in the first place, gentlemen of the jury, that, owing to the generosity of my brother officers—for my own means are limited—I might have been defended today by the first talent of the Bar. The reason I have declined their assistance and have determined to fight my own case is not that I have any con fidence in my own abilities or eloquence, but it is because I am convinced that a plain, straightforward tale, coming direct from the man who has been the tragic actor in this dreadful affair, will impress you more than any indirect statement could do.

If I had felt that I were guilty I should have asked for help. Since, in my own heart, I believe that I am innocent, I am pleading my own cause, feeling that my plain words of truth and reason will have more weight with you than the most learned and eloquent advocate. By the indulgence of the Court I have been permitted to put my remarks upon paper, so that I may reproduce certain conversations and be assured of saying neither more nor less than I mean.

It will be remembered that at the trial at the police court two months ago I refused to defend myself. This has been referred to today as a proof of my guilt. I said that it would be some days before I could open my mouth. This was taken at the time as a subterfuge.

Well, the days are over, and I am now able to make clear to you not only what took place, but also why it was impossible for me to give any explanation. I will tell you now exactly what I did and why it was that I did it. If you, my fellow-countrymen, think that I did wrong, I will make no complaint, but will suffer in silence any penalty which you may impose upon me.

I am a soldier of fifteen years' standing, a captain in the Second Breconshire Battalion. I have served in the South African Campaign and was mentioned in despatches after the battle of Diamond Hill. When the war broke out with Germany I was seconded from my regiment, and I was appointed as adjutant to the First Scottish Scouts, newly raised. The regiment was quartered at Radchurch, in Essex, where the men were placed partly in huts and were partly billeted upon the inhabitants. All the officers were billeted out, and my quarters were with Mr. Murreyfield, the local squire. It was there that I first met Miss Ena Garnier.

It may not seem proper at such a time and place as this that I should describe that lady. And yet her personality is the very essence of my case. Let me only say that I cannot believe that Nature ever put into female form a more exquisite combination of beauty and intelligence. She was twenty-five years of age, blonde and tall, with a peculiar delicacy of features and of expression.

I have read of people falling in love at first sight, and had always looked upon it as an expression of the novelist. And yet from the moment that I saw Ena Garnier, life held for me but the one ambition—that she should be mine. I had never dreamed before of the possibilities of passion that were within me. I will not enlarge upon the subject, but to make you understand my action—for I wish you to comprehend it, however much you may condemn it—you must realize that I was in the grip of a frantic elementary passion which made, for a time, the world and all that was in it seem a small thing—if I could but gain the love of this one girl.

And yet, in justice to myself, I will say that there was always one thing which I placed above her. That was my honor as a soldier and a gentleman. You will find it hard to believe this when I tell you what occurred, and yet—though for one moment I forgot myself—my whole legal offense consists of my desperate endeavor to retrieve what I had done.

I soon found that the lady was not insensible to the advances which I made to her. Her position in the household was a curious one. She had come a year before from Montpelier, in the South of France, in answer to an advertisement from the Murreyfields, in order to teach French to their three young children. She was, however, unpaid, so that she was rather a friendly guest than an employee.

She had always, as I gathered, been fond of the English and desirous to live in England, but the outbreak of the war had quickened her feelings into passionate attachment, for the ruling emotion of her soul was her hatred of the Germans. Her grandfather, as she told me, had been killed under very tragic circumstances in the campaign of 1870, and her two brothers were both in the French army. Her voice vibrated with passion when she spoke of the infamies of Belgium, and more than once I had seen her kissing my sword and my revolver because she hoped they would be used upon the enemy.

With such feelings in her heart it can be imagined that my wooing was not a difficult one. I should have been glad to marry her at once, but to this she would not consent. Everything was to come after the war, for it was necessary, she said, that I should go to Montpelier and meet her people, so that the French proprieties should be properly observed.

She had one accomplishment which was rare for a lady: she was a skilled motorcyclist. She had been fond of long, solitary rides, but after our engagement I was occasionally allowed to accompany her. She was a woman, however, of strange moods and fancies, which added in my feelings to the charm of her character. She could be tenderness itself, and she could be aloof and even harsh in her manner. More than once she had refused my company with no reason given, and with a quick, angry flash of her eyes when I asked for one. Then, perhaps, her mood would change and she would make up for this unkindness by some exquisite attention which would in an instant soothe all my ruffled feelings.

It was the same in the house. My military duties

were so exacting that it was only in the evenings that I could hope to see her, and yet very often she remained in the little study which was used during the day for the children's lessons, and would tell me plainly that she wished to be alone. Then, when she saw that I was hurt by her caprice, she would laugh and apologize so sweetly for her rudeness that I was more her slave than ever.

Mention has been made of my jealous disposition, and it has been asserted at the trial that there were scenes owing to my jealousy, and that once Mrs. Murreyfield had to interfere. I admit that I was jealous. When a man loves with the whole strength of his soul it is impossible, I think, that he should be clear of jealousy. The girl was of a very independent spirit. I found that she knew many officers of Chelmsford and Colchester. She would disappear for hours together upon her motorcycle. There were questions about her past life which she would only answer with a smile unless they were closely pressed. Then the smile would become a frown.

Is it any wonder that I, with my whole nature vibrating with passionate, wholehearted love, was often torn by jealousy when I came upon those closed doors of her life which she was so determined not to open? Reason came at times and whispered how foolish it was that I should stake my whole life and soul upon one of whom I really knew nothing. Then came a wave of passion once more and reason was submerged.

I have spoken of the closed doors of her life. I was aware that a young, unmarried Frenchwoman has usually less liberty than her English sister. And yet in the case of this lady it continually came out in her conversation that she had seen and known much of the world. It was the more distressing to me as whenever she had made an observation which pointed to this she would afterwards, as I could plainly see, be annoyed by her own indiscretion, and endeavor to remove the impression by every means in her power.

We had several small quarrels on this account, when I asked questions to which I could get no answers, but they have been exaggerated in the address for the prosecution. Too much has been made also of the intervention of Mrs. Murreyfield, though I admit that the quarrel was more serious upon that occasion.

It arose from my finding the photograph of a man upon her table, and her evident confusion when I asked her for some particulars about him. The name "H. Vardin" was written underneath—evidently an autograph. I was worried by the fact that this photograph had the frayed appearance of one which has been carried secretly about, as a girl might conceal the picture of her lover in her dress.

She absolutely refused to give me any information about him, save to make a statement which I found incredible, that it was a man whom she had never seen in her life. It was then that I forgot myself. I raised my voice and declared that I should know more about her life or that I should break with her, even if my own heart should be broken in the parting.

I was not violent, but Mrs. Murreyfield heard me from the passage, and came into the room to remonstrate. She was a kind, motherly person who took a sympathetic interest in our romance, and I remember that on this occasion she reproved me for my jealousy and finally persuaded me that I had been unreasonable, so that we became reconciled once more. Ena was so madly fascinating and I so hopelessly her slave that she could always draw me back, however much prudence and reason warned me to escape from her control.

I tried again and again to find out about this man Vardin, but was always met by the same assurance, which she repeated with every kind of solemn oath, that she had never seen the man in her life. Why she should carry about the photograph of a man—a young, somewhat sinister man, for I had observed him closely before she snatched the picture from my hand—was what she either could not, or would not, explain.

Then came the time for my leaving Radchurch. I had been appointed to a junior but very responsible post at the War office, which, of course, entailed my living in London. Even my week-ends found me engrossed with my work, but at last I had a few days' leave of absence. It is those few days which have ruined my life, which have brought me the most horrible experience that ever a man had to undergo, and have finally placed me here in the dock, pleading as I plead today for my life and my honor.

It is nearly five miles from the station to Radchurch. She was there to meet me. It was the first time that we had been reunited since I had put all my heart and my soul upon her. I cannot enlarge upon these matters, gentlemen. You will either be able to sympathize with and understand the emotions which overbalance a man at such a time, or you will not. If you have imagination, you will. If you have not, I can never hope to make you see more than the bare fact.

That bare fact, placed in the baldest language, is that during this drive from Radchurch Junction to the village I was led into the greatest indiscretion—the greatest dishonor, if you will—of my life. I told the woman a secret, an enormously important secret, which might affect the fate of the war and the lives of many thousands of men.

It was done before I knew it—before I grasped the way in which her quick brain could place various scattered hints together and weave them into one idea. She was wailing, almost weeping, over the fact that the allied armies were held up by the iron line of the Germans. I explained that it was more correct to say that our iron line was holding them up, since they were the invaders.

"But is France, is Belgium, *never* to be rid of them?" she cried. "Are we simply to sit in front of their trenches and be content to let them do what they will with ten provinces of France? Oh, Jack, Jack, for God's sake, say something to bring a little hope to my heart, for sometimes I think that it is breaking! You English are stolid. You can bear these things. But we others, we have more nerve, more soul! It is death to us. Tell me! Do tell me that there is hope! And yet it is foolish of me to ask, for, of course, you are only a subordinate at the War office, and how should you know what is in the mind of your chiefs?"

"Well, as it happens, I know a good deal," I answered. "Don't fret, for we shall certainly get a move on soon."

"Soon! Next year may seem soon to some people."

"It's not next year."

"Must we wait another month?"

"Not even that."

She squeezed my hand in hers. "Oh, my darling boy, you have brought such joy to my heart! What suspense I shall live in now! I think a week of it would kill me."

"Well, perhaps it won't even be a week."

"And tell me," she went on, in her coaxing voice, "tell me just one thing, Jack. Just one, and I will trouble you no more. Is it our brave French soldiers who advance? Or is it your splendid Tommies? With whom will the honor lie?"

"With both."

"Glorious!" she cried. "I see it all. The attack will be at the point where the French and British lines join. Together they will rush forward on one glorious advance."

"No," I said. "They will not be together."

"But I understood you to say—of course, women know nothing of such matters, but I understood you to say that it would be a joint advance."

"Well, if the French advanced, we will say, at Verdun, and the British advanced at Ypres, even if they were hundreds of miles apart it would still be a joint advance."

"Ah, I see," she cried, clapping her hands with delight. "They would advance at both ends of the line, so that the Boches would not know which way to send their reserves."

"That is exactly the idea—a real advance at Verdun, and an enormous feint at Ypres."

Then suddenly a chill of doubt seized me. I can remember how I sprang back from her and looked hard into her face.

"I've told you too much!" I cried. "Can I trust you? I have been mad to say so much."

She was bitterly hurt by my words. That I should for a moment doubt her was more than she could bear.

"I would cut my tongue out, Jack, before I would tell any human being one word of what you have said."

So earnest was she that my fears died away. I felt that I could trust her utterly. Before we had reached Radchurch I had put the matter from my mind, and we were lost in our joy of the present and in our plans for the future.

I had a business message to deliver to Colonel Worral, who commanded a small camp at Pedley-Woodrow. I went there and was away for about two hours. When I returned I inquired for Miss Garnier, and was told by the maid that she had gone to her bedroom, and that she had asked the groom to bring her motorcycle to the door.

It seemed to me strange that she should arrange to go out alone when my visit was such a short one. I had gone into her little study to seek her, and here it was that I waited, for it opened on to the hall passage, and she could not pass without my seeing her.

There was a small table in the window of this room at which she used to write. I had seated myself beside this when my eyes fell upon a name written in her large, bold handwriting. It was a reversed impression upon the blotting paper which she had used, but there could be no difficulty in reading it. The name was Hubert Vardin.

Apparently it was part of the address of an envelope,

for underneath I was able to distinguish the initials S.W., referring to a postal division of London, though the actual name of the street had not been clearly reproduced.

Then I knew for the first time that she was actually corresponding with this man whose vile, voluptuous face I had seen in the photograph with the frayed edges. She had clearly lied to me, too, for was it conceivable that she should correspond with a man whom she had never seen?

I don't desire to condone my conduct. Put yourself in my place. Imagine that you had my desperately fervid and jealous nature. You would have done what I did, for you could have done nothing else.

A wave of fury passed over me. I laid my hands upon the wooden desk. If it had been an iron safe I should have opened it. As it was, it literally flew to pieces before me. There lay the letter itself, placed under lock and key for safety, while the writer prepared to take it from the house.

I had no hesitation or scruple. I tore it open. Dishonorable, you will say, but when a man is frenzied with jealousy he hardly knows what he does. This woman, for whom I was ready to give everything, was either faithful to me or she was not. At any cost I would know which.

I could hardly bear to look at it.

A thrill of joy passed through me as my eyes fell upon the first words. I had wronged her. "Cher Monsieur Vardin." So the letter began. It was clearly a business letter, nothing else. I was about to replace it in the envelope with a thousand regrets in my mind for my want of faith when a single word at the bottom of the page caught my eyes, and I started as if I had been stung by an adder.

"Verdun"—that was the word. I looked again. "Ypres" was immediately below it. I sat down, horror-stricken, by the broken desk, and I read this letter, a translation of which I have in my hand:

Murreyfield House,
Radchurch

DEAR M. VARDIN,—Stringer has told me that he has kept you sufficiently informed as to Chelmsford and Colchester, so I have not troubled to write. They have moved the Midland Territorial Brigade and the heavy guns towards the coast near Cromer, but only for a time. It is for training, not embarkation.

And now for my great news, which I have straight from the War Office itself. Within a week there is to be a very severe attack from Verdun, which is to be supported by a holding attack at Ypres. It is all on a very large scale, and you must send off a special Dutch messenger to Von Starmer by the first boat. I hope to get the exact date and some further particulars from my informant tonight, but meanwhile you must act with energy.

I dare not post this here—you know what village postmasters are, so I am taking it into Colchester, where Stringer will include it with his own report which goes by hand.—Yours faithfully, SOPHIA HEFFNER.

I was stunned at first as I read this letter, and then a kind of cold, concentrated rage came over me. So this woman was a German and a spy! I thought of her hypocrisy and her treachery towards me, but, above all, I thought of the danger to the Army and the State. A great defeat, the death of thousands of men, might spring from my misplaced confidence.

There was still time, by judgment and energy, to stop this frightful evil. I heard her step upon the stairs outside, and an instant later she had come through the doorway. She started, and her face was bloodless as she saw me seated there with the open letter in my hand.

"How did you get that?" she gasped. "How dared you break my desk and steal my letter?"

I said nothing. I simply sat and looked at her and pondered what I should do. She suddenly sprang forward and tried to snatch the letter. I caught her wrist and pushed her down onto the sofa, where she lay, collapsed. Then I rang the bell, and told the maid that I must see Mr. Murreyfield at once.

He was a genial, elderly man, who had treated this woman with as much kindness as if she were his daughter. He was horrified at what I said. I could not show him the letter on account of the secret that it contained, but I made him understand that it was of desperate importance.

"What are we to do?" he asked. "I never could have imagined anything so dreadful. What would you advise us to do?"

"There is only one thing that we can do," I answered. "This woman must be arrested, and in the meanwhile we must so arrange matters that she cannot possibly communicate with anyone. For all we know, she has confederates in this very village. Can you undertake to hold her securely while I go to Colonel Worral at Pedley and get a warrant and a guard?"

"We can lock her in her bedroom."

"You need not trouble," said she. "I give you my word that I will stay where I am. I advise you to be careful, Captain Fowler. You've shown once before that you are liable to do things before you have thought of the consequence. If I am arrested all the world will know that you have given away the secrets that were confided to you. There is an end to your career, my friend. You can punish me, no doubt. What about yourself?"

"I think," said I, "you had best take her to her bedroom."

"Very good, if you wish it," said she, and followed us to the door.

When we reached the hall she suddenly broke away, dashed through the entrance, and made for her motorcycle, which was standing there. Before she could start we had both seized her. She stooped and made her teeth meet in Murreyfield's hand. With flashing eyes and tearing fingers she was as fierce as a wild cat at bay.

It was with some difficulty that we mastered her, and dragged her—almost carried her—up the stairs. We thrust her into her room and turned the key, while she screamed our abuse and beat upon the door inside.

"It's a forty-foot drop into the garden," said Murreyfield, tying up his bleeding hand. "I'll wait here till you come back. I think we have the lady fairly safe."

"I have a revolver here," said I. "You should be armed." I slipped a couple of cartridges into it and held it out to him. "We can't afford to take chances. How do you know what friends she may have?"

"Thank you," said he. "I have a stick here and the gardener is within call. You hurry off for the guard."

Having taken, as it seemed to me, every possible precaution, I ran to give the alarm. It was two miles to Pedley, and the colonel was out, which occasioned some delay. Then there were formalities and a magistrate's signature to be obtained. A policeman was to serve the warrant, but a military escort was to be sent in to bring back the prisoner. I was so filled with anxiety and impatience that I could not wait, but I hurried back alone with the promise that they would follow.

The Pedley-Woodrow Road opens into the high-road to Colchester at a point about half a mile from the village of Radchurch. It was evening now and the light was such that one could not see more than twenty or thirty yards ahead. I had proceeded only a very short way from the point of junction when I heard, coming towards me, the roar of a motorcycle being ridden at a furious pace. It was without lights, and close upon me.

I sprang aside in order to avoid being ridden down, and in that instant, as the machine flashed by, I saw clearly the face of the rider. It was she—the woman whom I had loved. She was hatless, her hair streaming in the wind, her face glimmering white in the twilight, flying through the night like one of the Valkyries of her native land.

She was past me like a flash and tore on down the Colchester Road. In that instant I saw all that it would mean if she could reach the town. If she once was allowed to see her agent we might arrest him or her, but it would be too late. The news would have been passed on. The victory of the Allies and the lives of thousands of our soldiers were at stake.

Next instant I had pulled out the loaded revolver and fired two shots after the vanishing figure. I heard a scream, the crashing of the breaking cycle, and all was still.

I need not tell you more, gentlemen. You know the rest. When I ran forward I found her lying in the ditch. Both my bullets had struck her. One of them had penetrated her brain.

I was still standing beside her body when Murryfield arrived, running breathlessly down the road. She had, it seemed, with great courage and activity scrambled down the ivy of the wall; only when he heard the whir of the motorcycle did he realize what had occurred.

He was explaining it to my dazed brain when the police and soldiers arrived to arrest her. By the irony of fate it was me whom they arrested instead.

It was urged at the trial in the police court that jealousy was the cause of the crime. I did not deny it, nor did I put forward any witnesses to deny it. It was my desire that they should believe it. The hour of the French advance had not yet come and I could not defend myself without producing the letter which would reveal it.

But now it is over—gloriously over—and so my lips are unsealed at last. I confess my fault—my very grievous fault. But it is not that for which you are trying me. It is for murder. I should have thought myself the murderer of my own countrymen if I had let the woman pass.

These are the facts, gentlemen. I leave my future in your hands. If you should absolve me, I may say that I have hopes of serving my country in a fashion which will atone for this one great indiscretion, and will also, as I hope, end forever those terrible recollections which weigh me down. If you condemn me, I am ready to face whatever you may think fit to inflict.

"P."

by Robert Twohy

Some years ago a professor of law at an Ivy League university married a girl from a nearby town, where everyone who knew her thought he must be a damn fool. He wasn't, but he was a lot more naive about women than a forty-two-year-old man should be.

The champagne bubbles were still spinning around in his head when she had her first extramarital affair.

With one of his students.

Time passed, bringing other adventures into her life. The professor wasn't even slightly upset. He never had an inkling.

His little blonde bride thought that theirs was the perfect marriage. She had prestige, a darling little house on campus, and proximity to acres of sturdy young swains ripe and ready for the picking—and her husband told her that he'd never been happier. What more could be asked of a marriage?

None of his colleagues tried to tip him off, because they had always considered him a stuck-up prig and rather enjoyed seeing him sprouting horns.

He had no idea how the wind blew until almost a full school year had slipped by—when, in April, the lady failed to destroy a note.

It lay on the floor of their bedroom. How she had got so careless after disposing of all previous evidence isn't known. But there it was, right in the open, and the professor picked it up and read it.

"Winnie—I'll cut The Worm's lecture Tues. and be over 8 sharp. We'll have 2 hr. of *zowee*!—P."

He didn't know who P. was, but could guess what *zowee* was, and had no doubt who The Worm was—himself. He was due to give a lecture at 8:00 that evening, which was Tuesday.

He didn't say anything about the note to Winnie as she bounced around, partially smashed as usual on secret sherry. She was busy fixing him a dinner of sorts and kissing the air in his direction and giving off bubbly noises, and did not observe that for once he wasn't in a condition of simpering idiocy at her cavortings. He sat still and silent, in his eyes the look of someone who's been savoring a mouthful of gooey candy and suddenly realized that all his fillings have been jerked out. But with the glow she had on, and excited by the prospect of a really fun evening, she failed to catch the change in the wind.

Eight o'clock. The professor sat at his desk in the lecture room, gazing at the scholarly assemblage. He didn't see it. He saw nothing. Nothing but his wife's sparkling, lying eyes.

His own eyes had gone flat and shiny and strange.

He didn't take the roll. Which was too bad—he could have found out later which young men weren't in attendance. At the time it seemed of no importance—he planned to meet P. in person in just a few minutes.

He stood up suddenly and grabbed his lean belly. The class looked moderately interested for perhaps the first time all semester. "Sudden attack—old chronic illness—class dismissed for tonight—"

He lurched to the door and out, got in his car, and whipped on home.

He parked half a block away and took the lug wrench from the trunk. He slid up the block, ducking as he passed neighbors' hedges, through his own gate and up the walk, got out his key, turned it and the knob, pushed the door open, stepped inside, and shut it softly behind him. At the foot of the stairs he paused.

From above came soprano and baritone giggles and murmurs.

He climbed toward them.

What he saw in the bedroom was what he'd expected to see.

Dim moonlight shone through the window on pale flesh quickly untangling. Winnie's thin voice implored, "Joseph? Don't, Joseph, don't! *Please* don't—"

He had a glimpse of a waxy shape sliding from the bed in one rapid motion, but his attention was on the huddled, cringing form of his wife. Forward with the lug wrench, smash, scream, crash, crush, scream. Slash, crash, scream, groan, sigh. Worm in eruption.

He was alone in the room with his wife. She lay flat on the bed as if stuck there by her blood. Her wide blue eyes were far away—they wouldn't be back.

After the rapid movement of pallid flesh fleeing, the professor hadn't noticed anything—only his wife. Had stood over her and watched the juices bursting out of her as the wrench did its work.

Dumbly he turned from her savaged body, looked around. There was no evidence P. had ever been there. No heap of men's clothes—not even a stray sock. He went to the door and looked down the stairs. No red tracks led down. Apparently no blood had stained P.'s nimble feet—he'd gotten away clean.

The professor laid the wrench on the floor, went to the phone, and called the police.

The trial was three months later. P. was the missing ingredient that gave the case a certain glamour and mystery: did he or did he not exist?

Yes, said the defendant's lawyer.

No, said the prosecutor. "A note is said to have triggered this night of horror, a note signed P. But no note has been produced in evidence—no note exists. And P. does not exist."

The professor could never remember what he had

done with the note. With everything depending on it, he couldn't remember.

The State did not challenge the evidence that the bride had had numerous affairs. "Indeed," the prosecutor said, "they were undoubtedly the motive for this horrible crime. The defendant, becoming aware finally of what had been known to a great many—that his wife had consistently flouted her marriage vows— decided to avenge himself upon her—she would pay for her infidelity with her life!"

He paced about, a small man with a heavy black moustache, shooting dark glances at the professor, who sat very still in his chair, looking more than ever (thought his students present) like a worm.

"Professor Millby is an intelligent man. He knew well that her murder would come home to him—there was no escape from that inevitability. But still she must pay. He had to make her pay! A score must be settled!"

He crouched, his luminous eyes darting in various directions, plucking his moustache as if seeking to rid it of fleas, and scuttled furtively back and forth— presenting a crude quick sketch of a dastard plotting dastardy. Ludicrous? Certainly to the detached observer. But the prosecutor gave not a rat's foot for the opinion of the detached observer. He was after the jury's attention.

He got it. They watched him, enthralled.

This prosecutor set no worth on appeals to a jury's intelligence. "Save your time," was his advice to new assistants. "Hit 'em in the gut—that's where they live. You think a summation is hokey? Great! Make it hokier. The more you pour it on the more they'll believe. They don't want reality, facts, reason, all that dull stuff—give 'em entertainment! They'll love you for it, and when it's verdict time, they'll reward you for not boring them or making them think!"

He was partly joking—but only partly. This prosecutor, like most comedians, carried a fair load of cynicism.

"So," he resumed to the Millby jury, leaving off the pacing and moustache-tweaking and impaling them now on the rays that seemed to dart from his luminous eyes, "he gets an idea. He'll invent a story, a cover story—a man was with her! A lover was with her! And he came home early from class and found them together—and a red rage came over him! He was in the grip of an uncontrollable fury!"

Maddened grimaces, clutching fingers, fantastically rolling eyes. The jury loved it. The spectators did too.

He calmed down somewhat. "Never mind that Millby had brought the lug wrench upstairs with him— never mind that. The defense says he has no memory of bringing it up. He has no memory of anything after leaving the classroom until he stood in the door of the bedroom and saw his wife and her lover there. And then, we are told, his red rage took over."

He gifted the jury with a thin, sardonic smile. "Let us talk of red rage, of uncontrollable fury. Not insanity—oh, no, we've heard no plea that Joseph Millby was insane—no, he's too obviously completely sane. They could not hope to foist *that* fraud off on you!" A quick, contemptuous smirk at the defense table. "No, what is promulgated here is not insanity but a brand-new doctrine—what perhaps I can coin a phrase for, and refer to as *diminished capacity.* In other words, this defendant is completely sane, yes, but you see—" his voice developed a wheedling whine "—he suddenly got an attack of *diminished capacity,* which naturally left him unable to refrain from smashing his wife thirty-seven times with a lug wrench—"

"Objection! The defense never used any such term *diminished capacity!*"

"You can't object during my summation. I never said you said it. I just made it up—giving a name to your amazing new doctrine. Maybe—" a conspiratorial leer to the jury "—it'll catch on. A great new ploy to get guilty murderers off when they're obviously sane. Don't bet it won't be picked up on—not again in our state, I trust, but maybe in one of the weirder states like California. May I proceed?" he inquired with stately coldness.

The defense muttered, "I wish you'd base some of your summation on the evidence."

"Evidence? *Evidence*? You speak of evidence?" His voice had risen to the pitch of a demented rat. He whirled to the jury. "He *gives* us no evidence! He tells of a note but gives us no note—no note signed P., or D., or XYZ! He speaks of a lover and gives us no evidence of a lover—no fingerprints, no bloodstains, no personal possessions, no scrap or stitch of clothing to show that a lover was in that room! No eyewitnesses to the lover's arrival or departure. The entire eight o'clock class has been interviewed individually, and no knowledge of P. is discovered. All students in the class with first, last, or middle names beginning with P. have been investigated as to their possible connection with the victim and their whereabouts at eight o'clock that night—and all have been cleared."

He plucked his moustache, this time slowly, ruminatively. Then, as if light had suddenly dawned, he whirled, pinioned the defendant with his eyes, and spoke in a deadly whisper that could be heard throughout the courtroom.

"Is this a sinister, obscene joke by you, Joseph Millby? Do you think to laugh at the law and society, and arrogantly assume that no one will see through your superior wit and intelligence? Did you not decide on the letter P. because—*P stands for phantom*?"

Several jurors gasped audibly as this dazzling insight was stunningly brought forth.

The professor sat still, gazing back at the prosecutor, his face without expression. He knew what the prosecutor was doing to him, that this was theater of the absurd as staged by a master—and things had reached such a point that any expression he assumed would be taken as proof of perfidy and intellectualism. No expression at all was no better, really—but there you were. Or there *he* was.

He had been sketched, by deft strokes of the prosecutor throughout the trial, as a man any decent juror would love to hate. So they did—they adored him for his villainy. He knew that they were righteously going to throw the book at him. They cared not for red rages—and they didn't believe in P.

The prosecutor, leaving his pinioned prey, turned back to the jury. His voice was now low, with a superb quaver. "Can you imagine any student of our great university—even the lowest, the most abject—can you imagine him leaping from that bed, grabbing his clothes, rushing away into the night—doing nothing to aid his beloved in her agony? You cannot. I cannot. The world cannot. But *he* can!" Dreadful finger outthrust at the professor. "*He* can imagine it! And did! He imagined it all! Carefully, deliberately, like a writer plotting a story—and the story is fiction. Fiction—all fiction! P. is fiction. No lover was there in that room of blood and carnage—only Millby's wife, alone in the bed, sweetly asleep, when he came on the scene with his lug wrench and his diabolical thirst for vengeance. There was no rage, red or any other color—just the cold, systematic slaughter of a defenseless woman who, whatever her faults, did not deserve to die like that!"

He gripped the edge of the jury box, and his eyes were huge, yearning for the jurors to reach into the deep well of understanding and wisdom that resided within the bosom of each and every one of them. "Throw it back to him! Throw the lie back to him! Tell him No, Professor Joseph Millby! No, no—NO!" He smashed a fist on the edge of the jury box, heedless that the blow might fracture some small bones. Perhaps it did—he flopped his hand at the wrist and for a second looked a little appalled. Then, thrusting his hand into the front of his coat, he paced, hooked his lip with

his teeth, shook his head quickly, rising above personal
pain, and carried on, in tones now grim and sonorous.

"No. No, Joseph Millby, we've had enough! We reject your smiling lies! You will not prance from this
American courtroom with a grin and a chuckle to, on
some later date perhaps, lay your steaming hand on another lug wrench—"

"Objection!"

"This is still summation! On another lug wrench, or
maybe even the *very selfsame lug wrench,* still stained
with the blood of your first victim—"

"Objection!"

"—and smash and destroy another beautiful young
woman deep in the depths of tender, vulnerable sleep!"

He staggered, moisture in his haunted eyes—his
hand hurt like hell—toward his chair, then paused to
fling one last harpoon.

"Enough, Joseph Millby! The ordinary, the decent,
the non-intellectual citizens of this great state cry out
to you. *We have had enough!*"

The jury did not applaud as he fell into his chair, but
they looked as if they wanted to.

And after a decent interval they came back and
found the defendant guilty of everything the prosecutor
had laid on him. The judge saw no particular reason
not to give him life, and did.

Thirteen years later, in 1971, he was released.

He became a freelance odd-job man and a permanent
drunk. He stumbled haphazardly across the country
and wound up in a California town called Lindenvale.
Nine years later he was still there—on welfare now,
and a regular fixture at a low-grade bar called Pete's
Place, where many of the broken-down old wrecks of
the town spent most of the time they had left. There he
drank ale, read the local and San Francisco papers,
talked with other ancient mariners, and off and on
wondered who P. was, or if maybe the prosecutor had

been right and he *had* imagined it all—the note and the pallid body moving swiftly away from the bed.

One day in May he had an answer.

Turning the pages of the wretchedly edited *Lindenvale Standard,* he came on a feature story, bylined Barbara Miles—a gushy interview with a famous San Francisco attorney, Herman N. Wandworth. The professor had heard of him—who in the Bay Area had not? You read in the San Francisco papers of his court activities and his social and charitable activities, you read tidbits in the gossip columns, you saw him on local talk shows. (The professor never had—he had a TV in his room, but it didn't work.) A broad faced man with round cheeks, amused eyes, a head of fine hair, prematurely and elegantly white. Some called him the greatest criminal lawyer in the whole Golden State.

He was known as a friend of the poor, taking cases for no fee. He received a good deal of publicity for that, and between these freebies managed to slide in a good number of lucrative jobs. He had made a great deal of money and there was some speculation that he was considering a run for governor. This particular article in the Lindenvale rag tied in with that notion—a trial balloon. As with a play that might or might not make it to Broadway after seeing how it plays in the sticks, Wandworth might be launching an announcement that he could be available.

The professor, glancing along the article with moderate interest, reached a paragraph that told of the illustrious man's educational background—a notable Eastern prep school, a renowned university.

The professor's booze-bleary old eyes widened and he took a quick breath—he and this eminence had something in common. He hadn't known Wandworth was an Easterner. But there it was, the name of his own university, and damned if the years didn't coincide. Wandworth had been there in 1957, '58.

The professor frowned at the smiling photo above the article, but he couldn't place the face as that of one of his students, which was not surprising—it was a lot of years ago, a lot of booze.

He read on.

> One's impression of Herman Wandworth is that he is a man who, for all his acumen, loves to laugh. His clear blue eyes seem to have a permanent crinkle. Those eyes, something in his voice, and certain mannerisms, bring to mind a particular Hollywood actor.
>
> With some impertinence, perhaps, this reporter asked the famous attorney if he has ever been told he looks just a little like Paul Newman.
>
> He responded, "I can't remember ever having been told that."
>
> He seemed a little embarrassed, and a touch of red showed in his cheeks. The subject was quickly changed. One sees in him an attractive modesty one all too seldom sees in a handsome man . . .

The professor looked again at the photograph. Round face, pleasant smile. He put his hand over the face, under the eyes, and concentrated on the eyes. If they were clear blue . . . Take away twenty-two years, thin down the cheeks, assume a clean-cut chin and jawline, color the hair light-brown . . . Yes, as a young man he might have borne a resemblance to the actor.

The professor sat still as if, should he move, the thoughts in his head might go tumbling out his ears and scatter around on the bar.

Herman. Not a romantic name. Winnie had been a wayward child—a romantic. To her, Herman would seem heavy, solemn, suggestive of ponderous movements and middle-age. She wouldn't want to call a lover Herman. If she had a lover of that name she might give him a private name, a love-name that would please her, a name that seemed youthful, lively, appropriate for someone with clear blue eyes that crinkled.

Paul might seem a fit name.

And when the gushy reporter's dumb question had

poked into that area, Wandworth had seemed "embarrassed, and a touch of red showed in his cheeks. The
subject was quickly changed." Yes. Twenty-two years
ago—and not a memory to be proud of. Good reason
not to look back on that long-ago spring when a beautiful, silly blonde housewife might have gifted him
with the love-name Paul.

The professor put down his empty glass, got up, and
went on rickety old legs out the door.

He went home to his room a few blocks from Pete's
Place. It was over a garage. Inside were his furnish-
ings—a cot, the TV that didn't work, a suitcase. The
suitcase was a desk if he wanted to write something—
like fill out a welfare form. He knelt and opened it and
pawed in among a few old books and law magazines
and various junk he'd carried around for the nine years
since leaving jail. Pulling out a manila envelope, he
went to the cot and perched there and shook the contents of the envelope out on the bed.

Clippings from newspapers of 1958—articles, photos. A souvenir menu from the wedding dinner. Photos
of a few university affairs. An old program from the
Brown game in 1957 (why had he kept that?). Photos
of Winnie—bouncing short blonde hair, dimples, shining teeth, shining, lying eyes. He looked through everything, feeling nothing in particular; too much time
gone by, too much booze the past nine years. He put
the stuff back in the envelope, set it on the floor, lay
down, and let the ale in his brain carry him gently out
on a soft, deep sea.

Time. The sea had no time. P. owed him time. If P.
had come forward, the jury would have seen P. there in
bed with Winnie. That could have made all the
difference—they might have accepted his red rage. Ten
years' difference, maybe. Time. But his time was almost spun out. His insides were shot—a few hundred
more ales at Pete's, a few more aimless conversations

. . . His time was almost gone, and a good thing. But P. owed him—something.

Then again, maybe not. Maybe P. owed him nothing. But P. owed—somebody. Who or what? The law? The spirit of justice? Had his own punishment—thirteen years, or rather a life—had that been justice?

Maybe. The prosecutor *had* been a master of the absurd, but maybe justice works that way sometimes—absurdly. But in the end giving you what you've earned. One way or another, giving you your fair pay.

A stupid remark by a reporter, from which Millby had pulled a thread and stretched it out to become a theory. A frail thread, easily snapped—absurd to try to tie it to Wandworth. But maybe Wandworth was meant to be caught in something absurd, as the professor had been. Maybe that was the way justice would come to him too—absurdly. If he were P.

The famous attorney had the cab drive him past the Post Street entrance around the block. He paid, tipped, gave his wide, warm smile. The driver was of the people, and the attorney would make his run, if he did, as the candidate of the people. A campaign begins with a smile.

He crossed an alley and headed for a discreet, unmarked door near the rear of the building that contained his offices—a door that led directly into his private sanctum.

A bum stood near the door, looking toward him. Shabby jacket, squashed canvas hat, bloated drinker's face. Bums are everywhere—and some are voters. The attorney, briskly approaching, put a good-natured look on his face.

As he walked past he heard, in a low voice, the name of his university.

Key in the lock, he turned. "What did you say?"

"You knew my wife there. In the biblical sense."

I knew his wife . . . He had known numerous wives

through the years. In the biblical sense. But only one wife had he known in that way at the university.

He looked at the seamed, pouched face, and it was as if the eroded flesh fell away. The nose seemed to thin, the lips tightened, slack folds under the chin and jaw disappeared, and a cold, supercilious face was before him. Instead of the squashed hat he saw thin dark hair; instead of the worn jacket a dark suit, white shirt, precise tie. Millby at his lecture stand. The Worm.

He whispered, "My God!"

And ran.

Inside, he slammed the door, shot the bolt, and stood there shaking. He leaned on the door, thinking back to that night . . .

Flat, polished eyes staring. The lug wrench—up, down, up, down—striking flesh, the flesh of the woman.—What was her name? She screaming. He'd slid from the bed, crouched, weak, trembling, naked— incredibly, not noticed. The murderer smashing down on the flesh before him on the bed up, down, up, down—spurts of blood from the white body. Himself across the room, shaking, grabbing up his clothes, dropping a shoe. The murderer didn't hear, the murderer and the woman—Winnie, that was her name— locked in a circle that he dared not break into. That terrible curved steel . . . He seized the shoe, and with his bundle lurched out the door and down the stairs to his car, parked in back. Nobody was passing, nobody saw. He got in, drove home to his fraternity house—a nude man driving across campus—parked in the yard behind the house, put on his clothes. Then he sat for a long time until the house was dark and quiet before letting himself in the back door and going up the stairs to his room.

Nobody knew. Some of the guys had suspected he was having a thing with her, but he hadn't bragged— and he wasn't her only lover. And no one knew her love-name for him.

Everyone liked him, admired him—he was good-looking, muscular, a gymnast, bright and articulate, with a great future—why mention that he might have been involved with her? It would just cause unpleasantness for him. There'd be police with questions, snoopy reporters—general messiness. And all for no good, because Millby was lying, that was plain. No one had been in the bedroom with his wife that night. If someone had been, that person wouldn't have run— he'd have fought. As the prosecutor said.

Which was why Wandworth could never speak up. Because everyone admired him, he had a great future—and he had run. Not hurt, not even hit, he had run like a naked rabbit. While the woman, screaming, was being smashed to death.

He came back from that night, and only a few seconds had passed. Knocking came on the door he leaned against—not loud, but steady and insistent.

"You hear me. You know I'm here.'

The attorney whispered, "Why are you here?"

"You were her lover. You're P. You were there on campus that spring, and you have clear blue eyes."

"You're a crazy old man. I don't know what you're talking about. I'll call the police."

"All right. There'll be reporters. I'll tell them how it was. How you ran. How afterwards you wouldn't stand up and say you'd been there with her."

"Who would believe you?"

"It doesn't matter. It'll get known. In time it'll get known."

"Absurd—this is all absurd!"

"Yes—absurd. Maybe from it will come justice for you. If you're P."

Why was he sagging here against the door? He must straighten up, get hold of himself! The man outside was nothing, an old bum—Millby the bum—and it had happened twenty-two years ago. Was he afraid he had a lug wrench under his wretched jacket? Was he afraid

Millby would attack him through the door? He must straighten up!

—*Be a man! Stop lying—you do a bad thing and then lie that you haven't! I hate a sneak who lies! Take your punishment when you're bad! Be a man!*

He slid down the door. He lay there, looking up. His father stood over him—thin lips and incredible coldness in his eyes . . . There was his cane, going up. Whack—the boy screamed, writhed—whack, whack, whack—

—*You're a sneak! You're a coward! Take your punishment! Be a man!*

They heard it in the outer offices, shot startled looks at each other. A young assistant attorney hurried to the door, calling the famous man's name. He faltered a little at the door. Someone had sneaked in the private street door. Wandworth was being attacked. Secretaries, colleagues were in the hall, their eyes were on him . . . Was this a moment of truth for him? Was he brave inside, really brave? He had a future—was this moment the key to it? Turn the knob and step in, or turn away, wait for help, the police? Does a future hang on a particular second? Was this his? He turned the knob and threw open the door.

He saw Wandworth on the floor. He stood at the door, didn't go any farther. Those watching him perceived that there was no danger to cringe from, but something to see.

They crowded up the corridor to peer through the door. They saw Herman N. Wandworth writhing on the floor, hands imploring, wide eyes staring up and out at them, beyond them, and the famous rich voice now a dull, steady scream—

"Don't—don't—please don't! I'm sorry—don't—don't hurt me—don't *hurt* me—don't! I didn't mean it—don't—"

The shabby man at the street door stood listening as voices gradually sounded at the edges of Wandworth's screams.

"Get him up."—"No, leave him, call his doctor."—
"Who's his doctor?"—"It's in his book."—"Where's
his book?"—"How would I know?"—"His doctor's
Crankshaw, on Sutter."—"Why are you laughing?"—"I'm not—am I? It's just—I can't believe it!—
look at him! He's a little kid! A little kid, shaking and
drooling—"

Steadily the dull screaming went on.

The man at the back door was gone before the am-
bulance came. He walked slowly south, to Market, and
up to Seventh, where he caught the bus back to
Lindenvale.

Later word came from the hospital that the noted attorney, Herman N. Wandworth, had been stricken with
an acute gastric disturbance. He was resting comfort-
ably, and expected to be back at his office in a few
days.

Some days later his doctor reported that Wandworth
was suffering from exhaustion due to overwork and
was returning to his family home in the East for a complete rest.

Some months passed. The plan to run him for governor was shelved. His condominium on Russian Hill
and his law practice were sold. As time went on, the
question was heard less and less—"I wonder what *really* happened to Herman Wandworth?"

Joseph Millby lingers on. He can be found almost
any day at Pete's Place, near the tracks in Lindenvale.
A blotchy, shabby old man, mild of manner, drinking
ale.

Debbie, the day barperson, thinks he looks a lot better than he used to—"much more relaxed, like things
are pretty much taken care of and he can take it easy,
read the papers, chat a little, drink his ale."

She could be right. Absurd as it seems, he may know
that justice has been done—and that the Millby case is
closed.

A Matter of Conscience

by Gary Alexander

Children do have some rights in this country, but most of the legal ones protect only the child's physical well-being. One cannot, for example, mug one's child too often, too severely, too conspicuously. One cannot deprive one's child of adequate nourishment either. A parent accused of such crimes can be and is occasionally prosecuted in a court of law.

Unfortunately, tragically, parents who subject their child to more subtle forms of deprivation will seldom be held accountable. A child unloved has no legal redress. The sheriff will not intervene, nor will a social worker.

Only when this emotional barrenness erupts into violence does the System step in, as it did last Thursday night when Peter Callison, Junior, was arrested for the murder of his mother, father, and sister.

It was unusual for the Public Defender's Office to be assigned the defense of a millionaire. Peter Callison, Junior, age fifteen, was heir to an estate worth millions, but Peter was a minor, so the funds were frozen. In effect, he was a pauper.

On Monday morning, Alvin Harris called me in and handed me the Callison file.

"Dave, as of now you are my Chief Deputy, Juvenile Division."

We are a small office in a medium-sized town: Harris and three underlings, including myself. Harris has been here for twenty years, in charge for the last twelve. He is hopelessly addicted to the security of civil service. We peons are typical of the Deputy Defenders whom Alvin has had over the years. We signed on at low pay, partly for the experience, partly to purge the idealism from our systems before moving on to the big bucks.

"How long have we had a Juvenile Division, Alvin?"

Harris glanced at his watch. "About five minutes. I'll call somebody to have it lettered on your door if you'd like."

I gave him a wide-eyed expression of mock gratitude. He was doing this to me for two reasons. He personally loathed any case that smacked of controversy or sensationalism. He also loathed any deputy who was overly questioning or argumentative toward him. I fit snugly in the latter category.

"Looks to me like a walk-through, Dave," he went on. "Open and shut. His preliminary hearing is scheduled for Friday. You'll argue that he shouldn't be tried as an adult. You'll lose, of course. Then you'll defend him in Superior Court, going with the incompetency angle. From what I know of the kid so far, you might be solid in that area."

I paged through the file. On top were photos of the three victims—Peter's mother, father, and sister. All had gunshot wounds in their heads and elsewhere. Seems that the neighbors heard the shots. At first they dismissed them as backfires, but there were too many, so they called the police. The officers found the bodies on the living-room floor within feet of one another. Peter Callison, Junior, was located upstairs in his room, reading. He claimed he hadn't heard anything because his stereo was playing. There was no sign of forcible entry and every door and window in the house was locked. The boy was impassive, even when escorted downstairs past the victims. One officer had made reference to "ice water in his veins"; hyperbole wasn't normally found in official investigative reports.

"The weapon?" I asked.

"A Smith and Wesson .38. It's a huge house and it's landscaped like a jungle. They're still looking for it."

"Eight shots altogether, I see. Which means he reloaded before finishing the job."

Harris raised his eyebrows. "Very good, Clay. Sweet kid, isn't he?"

"Why us?" I asked. "No close relatives?"

Harris shook his head. "No living grandparents. Mrs. Callison was an only child. Peter Senior has one brother five years older. His name is Paul and he lives in Portland. He's been checked out. He seems as poor as these people were flush. Evidently alienated from them too. Essentially, he told the detectives to go to hell."

I saw relief in Harris' eyes when I stood up with the file. "So you're asking me to go through the motions?"

Harris sighed. "I want the *appearance* of a good fight, Dave, even though it's hopeless. The media is going to be living with this one and I don't want any trouble. They haven't had anything so juicy since the kickbacks in the Assessor's Office. Go by the book and *please* don't make waves. I've already ordered a psychiatric evaluation, so half of your work's already done. Good luck."

I left, knowing who I was really defending: Alvin Harris, his reputation and august office.

I drove out to the Callison home, which was part of an exclusive suburban development. The area was new money, ostentatious money. Most of the houses were Twenty-first Century Gothics, ultra contemporary, with hardly a right angle in sight. The Callison residence was atop a hill, at the end of a cul-de-sac. It afforded a grand view of the city. Obviously, Peter Senior, as owner of Callison Air Freight, held his own in the neighborhood.

The place was still crawling with detectives, presumably in search of the weapon. The captain in charge gave me permission to go inside and look around, with a warning not to touch anything. They always say that, so I don't.

The foyer led directly to a huge, sunken living room. The large patches of bloodstain would never come out of that lush beige carpet. The images in those grisly photos projected themselves onto the spots. I shuddered, absolutely certain that when I left the Public Defender's Office, criminal law would not be my specialty.

I climbed a sweeping staircase, looking for Peter Junior's room. The first room past the landing was some sort of den, although it had more the appearance of a sports hall of fame—plaques, trophies, photographs, and framed certificates cluttered the shelving and walnut paneling.

The memorabilia provided a brief family history. Peter Senior had been a football star at Stanford during the early fifties. The pictures of him in a menacing lineman's stance depicted a large determined man. More recent photos proved him only slightly heavier and every bit as physically imposing. He had played no-handicap golf and was a terror on local squash courts.

Mollie, his wife, struck me as being classically Nordic, very athletic, yet lovely and feminine. All the hardware on the shelves confirmed that she had been a formidable tennis opponent.

Julie, the daughter, a junior at Radcliffe, was new money in pursuit of old, chasing it on horseback. A clipping described her as an Olympic hopeful in dressage.

Peter Junior, the surviving Callison, was notably absent in this shrine. I scanned everything twice, just to be sure. Nothing, not even a Little League certificate, the kind everyone receives whether they ever get off the bench or not.

His room was at the end of the hall. The detectives had it pretty well torn apart, so I couldn't determine if he was tidy or if he was an average teenager in that respect.

The walls were plastered with posters of aircraft, rockets, and robots that had starred in science-fiction movies. Model airplanes hung willy-nilly from the ceiling. The bedroom was decorated to the gills, but every single piece was inanimate—machines, past, present, and future. If the boy had had contact with another human being in his life, there was no evidence of that in his room.

I almost walked out before I noticed it. On the top of a bookcase, stuffed behind a plastic ICBM, was an old black-and-white photograph in an upright frame. A smiling man in flight gear sat on the wing of a Korean War vintage jet. At first glance I thought it was Peter's father, but I studied it more closely and saw that it wasn't. There was a definite resemblance but the man was smaller and his eyes weren't carnivorous.

I wasn't entirely a bad boy. The captain had ordered me to touch nothing. I touched only one item, the photo, which I stuffed inside my shirt.

I made arrangements to visit Peter Callison, Junior, at the Juvenile Detention Center. After all, if I was to go through the motions, I should go through the motions.

Alvin Harris intercepted me on the way out of the office.

"The shrink saw him this morning," he said. "So did the prosecution's. We should have a written report before Friday's hearing. What are you going to talk to the kid about?"

"The customary attorney-client stuff," I said with a shrug. "I'll play it by ear."

"Nothing fancy, okay? Just feel him out and explain the situation. I've had media people in and out all day. Just don't do anything that would embarrass me, okay?"

The best method of breaking loose from Alvin when

he's in one of his uptight moods is to act smart. He'd rather walk away than deal with it.

"After I give him his hacksaw-layer cake we'll have a harmless little chat. That's all."

I strode out, enjoying the after-image of Harris' face. It was a haunted, totally exhausted expression, the kind you see on marathon runners at the end of the race.

As I headed for the Juvenile Detention Center I digested the few facts I had gleaned from the Prosecuting Attorney's Office earlier. We usually get along with them because our clients and their crimes are mostly minor league, so nobody's career is on the line. Of course the Callison case was different. Peter Senior was a leading citizen and our fair city had not been subjected to a triple murder for many a year.

The Chief Criminal Deputy assigned the case to himself. Scuttlebutt around town had him running for the top job this fall. He needed an adult trial, a conviction, and consecutive life sentences. He couldn't ask for the death penalty for a fifteen-year-old. An incompetency ruling would not enhance his reputation; an acquittal would destroy it.

He had placed himself in a box and the tension showed. He gave me ten minutes, lukewarm coffee, and Peter Junior's school records, including sketchy interviews with teachers and fellow students.

Peter attended a public high school, had an IQ of 153, and a C-minus grade average. He participated in no activities. He had no real friends. His teachers characterized him as quiet and obedient. His peers pegged him as weird. A loner.

Our Juvenile Detention Center was frayed around the edges and chronically understaffed, but they tried. I'd been there before on behalf of runaways who had got into mischief. Today, as then, the noise was random and continuous. It was not a happy place.

I was taken to the isolation wing, where the heavy felonies and drug overdoses were housed. The cells were small and padded. Most of the kids were kept at the other end in Army-style barracks.

I asked the counselor a stupid question. "Is Callison isolated for security reasons or has he been disruptive?"

The counselor smiled tolerantly. "Everyone here should behave so well, but he's not here for stealing hubcaps, you know."

A police officer sat outside Peter Junior's door. I wasn't sure if he was there to keep Callison in or reporters out. He let me in and locked the door.

Somehow I wasn't surprised by Peter's appearance. He had a pasty complexion, was short for his age, slender, and almost feminine. He was no chip off the old block.

"Dave Clay," I said. "From the Public Defender's Office. If it's all right with you, we'll be going into your hearing together."

He got up from his bunk, nodded politely, and offered a limp handshake. His eyes struck me immediately. They were merely optical instruments, with no emotional backlighting. He gestured for me to take a seat on the bunk, as if one businessman were inviting another into his office to discuss routine matters. Peter was fifteen going on fifty. I didn't need professional training to determine that the boy was a psychological cripple of some sort.

I explained the procedure to him, outlining the possibilities he might have to face.

Then I trotted out the clichés used in the movies to delineate attorney-client relationships, emphasizing confidentiality and the need for absolute frankness between us.

He replied with a patronizing smirk. I deserved it since I had patronized him, but I hate that response from anyone, let alone a fifteen-year-old.

"Did you do it or didn't you?" I asked bluntly.

Peter shrugged. "Maybe, but not that I recall. They say I did, so I could've blacked out or something."

"They haven't found the gun yet," I said. "Let's say you did do it and don't remember. Where might you hide something you don't want discovered? Do you have a special hiding place for things?"

"Dirty books and stuff like that?"

"Yeah."

"Nope. I don't think Mom ever cared enough to snoop."

"I doubt that very much," I said.

Another patronizing smirk. Again I was repaid in kind.

I tried the shock method. "Peter, I want you to realize that the death penalty is back on the books in this state. We have to help each other."

He nodded and said, "It's the electric chair, isn't it? I was curious about that. Do they do it with high voltage or is it the amps? I've experimented with electric motors on my model planes, but they're really too heavy for the power they put out and—"

I interrupted with a reference to the psychiatrists who had seen him, risking total loss of rapport. People are quite sensitive when their innermost feelings are probed. They don't want to admit that they're walking around with a head full of stripped gears. I told him that the ability to stand trial is a subjective thing and that he'd best plant both feet on the floor and level with me.

He was amused rather than offended. "Those doctors were nice guys. It was stimulating."

Stimulating!

"What did you talk about?"

"Mom, Dad, and Sis, mainly. They wanted to know how we got along."

"How did you?"

He patted an empty pocket on his coveralls. "Do you have a cigarette?"

"I don't smoke."

"Very sensible. Oh, we got along fine. My parents had obligations toward me. Food, clothing, shelter, education. You know. They took care of all that. My obligation was to behave, attend school regularly, and make a bed. We all did our jobs."

It was early June and Peter's cell was sweltering. My arms were moonscapes of goose pimples. I wished I'd brought a sweater.

"I was impressed with your den. A vigorous family."

Peter chuckled. "Oh, the Holy Room? I guess I didn't fill up much space in there."

I thought of Peter Senior, of his athletic prowess, of the business he had built. I doubted if he had had much truck with losers, with noncompetitive types. To have a weak son, a product of his seed, must have been intolerable.

"I imagine you and your father shared a common interest in aviation. His business. What I saw in your room."

The smirk tilted higher. "Are you kidding? Dad didn't fly. He didn't even like to get on an airliner. He knew how to make money and there's lots of money in air cargo, you know."

I took the photo I had lifted from his room and gave it to him. "I had to remove it from the frame. Even so, it's still considered contraband here, but I thought you would like to have it."

Peter flushed. I had rung an emotional bell, but most of the emotion stayed beneath the surface.

"I appreciate this, Mr. Clay."

"It's Dave. Anyone you know?"

"Sure, Uncle Paul."

"Your father's brother who lives in Portland?"

"Yeah. It's an old picture of him but my favorite. That's his F-86. Did you know he shot down four MiGs? Got two in one day. One more and he'd have been an Ace, but they strafed his runway. His unit was being scrambled and while he was running out to his ship, he caught some bullets in a leg, so he got shipped home."

"Sounds like a helluva guy. Did you see much of him?"

Peter didn't answer for nearly a minute. The temperature in the room dropped another ten degrees.

He said finally, "I'm getting kind of tired. Can we do this some other time?"

"Friday's closing in on us, Peter."

He shrugged once more. "You know where I'll be."

Psychiatric evaluations frequently coincide with the wishes of the side ordering them. You can expect to enter court knowing that the bad guys have an opinion one-hundred-and-eighty degrees out of phase with your own.

If you're defending, your client will be as lucid as a cantaloupe. If you're prosecuting, he'll be normal but antisocial to an extreme. Like Heinrich Himmler.

Occasionally the opposing doctors take umbrage at the remarks of the other. Old grievances may appear. The attorneys, bless their evil minds, exploit these differences. We sometimes reach the threshold of threats and counterthreats, of possible slander charges, of complaints filed with whatever professional societies the doctors are members of. In a dull, protracted murder trial where the evidence is inconclusive and the witnesses numerous, such fireworks are about all that keep any of us awake.

I had written off the hearing. It was a leadpipe cinch that Peter Junior was going to be remanded to Superior Court to stand trial as an adult. My only hope was testimony from our psychiatrist. I wasn't happy with the prospect of the kid whiling away the years with the Mad Hatter and March Hare, munching tranquilizers six times a day; but if he went to the state pen the old hands would scoop him up in five minutes.

I don't have to tell you why. He'd be Queen of the Hop.

In his office Dr. Pelfrey, our guy, ruined my whole day. He said, "He's a textbook sociopath. Dissertations have been written with less material than he alone provides."

"I don't seem to have Webster with me."

"A psychopath and a sociopath are similar. They manifest their needs, their whims, with an utter lack of concern for any other creature on this planet. Say a sociopath is in a bar and runs out of money; though he would prefer to stay and drink more, he'll excuse himself, hurry out and stick up a gas station. If it happens that the attendant recognizes him and the sociopath knows he is recognized, he may put a bullet in the attendant's head. He's aware that what he's doing is wrong. There's no confusion, no departure from reality. He wants something, he gets it. So sorry about the flotsam left in his wake.

"The psychotic personality differs. He has a nodding acquaintance with reality, but when his mind is made up on something, Nellie bar the door. To use a technical term, he's a brick short of a load. He wanders between Earth and a parallel universe."

"Aside from what's in your report, what can you tell me about Peter? Did he do it?"

Dr. Pelfrey's hands flew up in mock surrender. "If he confessed, I can't say. We're in the doctor-patient realm there."

Alvin Harris, to his credit, instructed me not to waltz with Pelfrey. Our office did ten grand a year with him.

"Hippocrates won't roll over in his grave if you give me a teensy-weensy clue, Dr. Pelfrey," I said. "I have to go in there Friday like a Super Bowl coach with twenty-five of my best players out with knee injuries. Alvin got next year's budget last week. He says it's brutal. We'll have to shut down the office coffee pot. Among other cutbacks. We can be coy if you like. You know, is it larger than a breadbox and so forth. You pick the format. So long as the information emerges."

Dr. Pelfrey slammed his palms down on his polished rosewood. He took a deep breath, and glared at me. "I can read between the lines. Get out your bamboo splints because it ain't no free lunch! Clay, hell, you should pay him my fee. I stumbled out of there and he knew more about me than I did about him. I haven't a glimmer!"

Alvin Harris cried out in imagined pain, then laid his head on his desk and buried it with his arms. By and by he sat up, saying, "You want to plead that little squirrel *not guilty*? Clay, the house was sealed, the alarm system was functioning!"

I'd picked up one of Peter's mannerisms. I shrugged and offered a tight smile. I sure as hell didn't have anything else going on this case. "Have they found the gun yet?" I asked.

"It'll turn up. The damn thing isn't biodegradable, you know. But that's the least of your problems. What you have to do is get over to what's-his-name, the Chief Criminal Deputy, and extend a formality. He's not gonna fry the kid. Even if he wanted to, his campaign manager wouldn't let him. If you want to be a hero, maybe you can get concurrent terms instead of consecutive. The kid will be up for parole before all his hair has fallen out. By then no one will care.

"Do *something*, for Pete's sake, and make it positive. That guy from Channel Three was over about an hour ago, the one who does those editorials on how the pollution from the chemical plant affects us. He was trailing this dame from the network who was mumbling about doing a documentary. Clay, get the kid in there Friday, tell him to behave himself, and maybe we can lighten the problem for him a tad."

Alvin wasn't in an ideal frame of mind for a debate, but I felt I had to present the facts, or the lack of them.

"No gun. No powder burns. No nothing. He was just there."

"Circumstantial evidence isn't bad in this one," Harris fired back. "They don't have to have a smoking pistol here."

"Whatever. I have my doubts. You know he'll be

handed over Friday. You also know that if Pelfrey says he's competent, their guy will too. What you're saying is for me to make a deal with the P.A.'s office and trade a plea so Peter has to spend only fifty years in the can instead of a hundred."

"I'm telling you to be reasonable. If we had *anything* to go on, I'd say fight. But we don't."

"Yes, we do," I said. "The boy is, uh, strange, but I'm not entirely convinced he's a killer."

Alvin closed his eyes and moaned. I got out of his office before he opened them again.

Thursday was on me in what seemed like a hurry. I'd planned to see Peter in the afternoon and outline my strategy. I stopped over at the Chief Criminal Deputy's, hinting that I was in a flexible mood, then asking if the investigation had turned up the gun or any other information.

He shook his head and served me another cup of lukewarm coffee. He began discussing concurrent sentences when I told him that he needed a new coffee pot and that I was going to let a jury decide this one. I'm not certain which assertion he thought was so hilarious because I left his office without further conversation.

I had some time to kill so I called the business editor of one of the newspapers to learn more about Callison Air Freight. Undoubtedly the police had covered this territory by now and if a skeleton had fallen out of a corporate closet, our office would have been notified, so my efforts were in the realm of idle curiosity.

The editor had done an article on Callison Air Freight a month ago when they won a contract that connected them to Malaysia and Singapore. Callison was financially healthy, he said, and growing like a weed.

I wondered if he knew who the other corporate officers were and who besides Peter Senior owned large blocks of Callison stock. He didn't, but he gave me a number to call at the capital.

The woman I talked to worked in the Secretary of State's office, in the department that processed corporation charters. She couldn't tell me much except the date of incorporation, the names of the officers, and the changes to the charter that had taken place over the years.

She may have told me a great deal more than she realized.

Peter and I small-talked for a while, then I told him what I wanted to do. He was agreeable, maddeningly so, as if we'd just decided where to have lunch.

I said, "I learned something interesting this morning. Did you know that Callison Air Freight was formerly Callison Brothers Air Cargo, that your father bought out your Uncle Paul in 1964?"

He nodded blankly. "Yeah. They were small back then. One beat-up old DC-3. Uncle Paul was the chief and only pilot. I told you before that Dad didn't fly."

"I'll bet your Dad bought him out cheap."

"Could be. I don't know."

"Paul was probably sorry he did after the company took off."

"I don't know."

"I hear Paul hasn't been doing very well lately."

Peter's eyes widened. "That's not his fault! His leg that got shot up in Korea, he needed an operation on it two years ago. He couldn't fly any more."

"I didn't say it was his fault, Peter. Lucky, though, that he lives in a nearby town, isn't it? Having his family close enough to help him through the rough spots."

"Why don't you drop it, okay?" he snapped. "That guy who's going to try me and that other guy from your office were by yesterday to talk to me. All they asked about Uncle Paul was when I last saw him."

I squeezed my hands together and remained outwardly calm. "When did you last see Uncle Paul?"

"I don't know. Last fall, I think."

"That's odd for brothers who live only a few hours

apart. But your father was a busy man. I suppose he mailed Paul a check now and then."

That cockeyed smirk returned. "Are you kidding? They hated each other's guts. I'll bet Dad cheated him when Uncle Paul sold out. That's what I think."

I took a deep breath. If there was such a thing as a right time to draw to an inside straight, this was it.

"Is that why Paul killed your father? Did he come over for money? Was there an argument? Did tempers flare? Maybe he really didn't mean to fire the gun. Maybe there was a struggle. Maybe your mother and sister got involved. Maybe one of them ran to the phone. In any event, they were witnesses. You were upstairs alone, as you usually were. In the heat of it Paul probably wasn't aware that you were in the house. Lucky for you, otherwise he may have—"

"He would not," Peter screamed. "He'd never have hurt *me*."

The boy was trembling. His eyes were moist.

"Then after Paul left," I went on, "you locked up and waited for the police. The gun hasn't been located because Paul took it with him. Everything so obviously points toward you that Paul wasn't even suspected."

I had brought a pack of cigarettes this time. I waited until he smoked one.

"Well, Peter?"

He lit another one and stared at the opposite wall.

"Do you know what my folks got me last Christmas? Football pads and a tennis racket. They wouldn't say anything. They'd just watch to see if I'd use the stuff. Then it would go into a closet with every other present they got me but really got for their own egos. Nobody ever yelled at me, Mr. Clay. Not that I can remember. Nobody ever hit me. They just disapproved of me.

"When they finally gave up and accepted the fact that I was different and that I'd never change, they just left me alone. It was real hard for Dad to even talk to me. When he did, it was like he was talking to a stranger on the street."

I fought back tears, then a surge of nausea. "Uncle Paul. Did he pay attention to you?"

"The best he could. He wasn't welcome in the house, so we talked on the phone a lot. Those model airplanes you saw in my room, they were presents from him. He never sent me the easy kind either, that plastic junk. These were wood and tissue. Uncle Paul said I'd appreciate them more if I had to work to put them together."

"Did you really intend to take the blame for him?"

"I don't know. Uncle Paul probably won't let me anyway when he finds out I'm in trouble. I just figured I'd play along for a while."

"And subject yourself to all that goes with being an accused killer?"

He lit another cigarette. "Why not?" he said with a casual shrug. "All kinds of people are interested in me now. People listen when I say something. What's wrong with that?"

I walked out, happy that Peter would soon be free. But that didn't prevent me from almost losing my lunch in the parking lot.

There was no hearing. I related my story to Alvin, who passed it on to the Chief Criminal Deputy, who immediately called the Portland police.

When the coroner arrived at Paul Callison's fleabag room, his initial guess was that Paul had been dead for about twenty-four hours. The missing .38 was on the floor beside the pillow he'd fired it through. On the bed a Portland newspaper was opened to an article about Peter's upcoming hearing.

I surmised that Paul had picked suicide as the only way to handle his problem and Peter's too. He knew that he and his gun would be discovered sooner or later; when that happened, both he and his nephew would be free.

Peter stayed at the Juvenile Detention Center for several more weeks, while foster home arrangements were made. I visited him every few days and noticed that he had become a minor celebrity with his peers. He lived in the open wing now and seemed to enjoy the attention.

A family east of the mountains who volunteered to take him was approved. They had eight hundred acres of winter wheat and the consensus was that the fresh air, country living, and Middle American values would do the boy a world of good.

I doubted it. Peter had passed into adolescence emotionally stunted. As with anybody who had an untreated childhood-growth disorder, I felt it was much too late.

I drove Peter to the airport. When his flight was called, we shook hands. I gave him to the stock pitch about regarding his new life as an adventure. He asked me if I planned to go into private practice soon.

"Why?"

That same smirk. "I'll probably need a good lawyer when my inheritance clears. Just because these people are farmers doesn't mean they won't try to get their grubby paws on it."

I didn't know how to reply, so I didn't. I waited until his plane broke ground, then entered the nearest lounge, and had a couple of stiff drinks.

Odds were I'd never see Peter Callison, Junior, again. The probability that *someone* in the criminal justice system would at another time and place was, unfortunately, much better.

The Affair of the Reluctant Witness

by Erle Stanley Gardner

Jerry Bane knuckled his eyes into wakefulness, kicked back the covers and said, "What time is it, Mugs?"

"Ten thirty," Mugs Magoo told him.

Bane jumped from the bed, stood in front of the open window, and went through a series of quick calisthenics.

Magoo surveyed the swift, lithe motions with eyes that had been trained to soak in details as a fresh blotting paper absorbs ink.

Jerry Bane straightened, extended his arms from the shoulder, and bending his knees, rapidly raised and lowered his body.

"How am I doing, Mugs?"

"Okay," Magoo said without enthusiasm. "I guess you just ain't the type that puts on weight. What's your waist?"

"Twenty-eight."

Mugs's comment was based on fifty years of cynical observation. "It's all right while you're young," he said, "and the girls are crazy about a good dancer, to be slim-waisted, but when you get up to what I call the competitive years, it takes beef to flatten out the opposition. When I was on the police force, the boys used to figure you needed weight to have impact. Not fat, you understand, but beef and bone."

"I understand," Bane said, smiling.

Mugs surveyed the empty sleeve of his right arm. "Of course," he added, "I've only got one punch now, but that one punch will do the work if I can get it in the right place and at the right time. What do you want for breakfast?"

"Poached eggs and coffee. What's the right time for the punch, Mugs?"

"First," Mugs said laconically.

Jerry chuckled.

"Better take your orange juice before you have your shower," Mugs advised, "and remember your friend, Arthur Arman Anson, is coming this morning."

Bane laughed. "Don't call that old fossil a friend. He's an attorney and the executor of my uncle's estate, that's all. He disapproves thoroughly of everything I do. . . . What's in the mail?"

"Did you order a package of photos from the Shooting Star News Photo Service?"

Bane nodded.

Mugs cocked a quizzical eyebrow.

"It's an idea I had," Jerry said. "It's the answer to Anson, Mugs. The Shooting Star outfit has photographers who cover all the news events. Now, with your photographic memory, your knowledge of the underworld, the confidence men, the slickers and the hypocrites, it occurred to me it might be a good plan for us to study the news photographs. In other words, Mugs, we might build up a business, an unorthodox business to be sure, but a profitable business."

"And a dangerous business?" Mugs asked.

Jerry merely grinned.

"It's an expensive service?" Mugs asked dryly.

"A hundred bucks a month," Jerry said cheerfully. "Do you know, Mugs, Arthur Arman Anson had the colossal effrontery to tell me that since he's the trustee of a so-called spendthrift trust under my uncle's will he can withhold every penny of the trust fund if he sees fit.

"The ten thousand we got in a lump sum from my uncle's estate must be about gone. Anson is going to be difficult, so I thought we'd better do a little sharp-shooting. He lives by his brains. We'll live by our wits."

"I see," Mugs said without expression.

"That ten grand *is* about gone, isn't it?" Jerry asked.

Mugs headed for the kitchenette. "I think I'd better look at the coffee."

"Okay," Bane said cheerfully.

He seated himself in front of the mirror, opened the package of photographs Mugs brought him, drank his orange juice, then connected the electric shaver.

Magoo said, "Anson is going to be here any minute now. Hope you don't mind my saying so, but he won't like it if he finds you still in pajamas. It irritates him."

"I know," Jerry said. "The old fossil thinks he has a right to order my life just because he's the executor of a spendthrift trust. How much money is left in the account, Mugs?"

Magoo cleared his throat. "I can't remember exactly," he said.

Bane disconnected the razor so that he could hear better. "Mugs, what the devil's the matter?"

"Nothing."

"*Phooey*! Let's have it."

"I'm sorry," Magoo blurted, "but you're overdrawn three hundred and eighty-seven dollars. The bank sent a notice."

"I suppose the bank also advised Arthur Anson," Jerry said, "and he's coming up to pour reproaches over me and rub them in the open wounds."

"He'll relent and tide you over," Mugs said without conviction. "That's why your uncle made him trustee."

"Not Anson. That old petrified pretzel wants to run my life. If I'd do what he wants I'd become another Arthur Arman Anson, puttering around with a brief-case, a cavernous, bony face, lips as thin as a safety-razor blade, and about as sharp . . . well, Mugs, I don't know what I'm going to do about salary, and today, I believe, is payday."

"You don't need to bother about salary," Magoo said

feelingly. "When you picked me up I was selling pencils on the street."

"It isn't a question of what you *were* doing, but what you *are* doing," Jerry said. "Well, we'll finish with the whiskers, then the shower, then breakfast, then finances."

He resumed his shaving and as he did so started studying the pictures which had been sent out by the Shooting Star News Photo Service, photographs on eight-by ten, with a hard, glossy finish, each photograph bearing a mimeographed warning to watch the credit line and a brief description of the picture so that news editors could make and run their own captions.

Jerry Bane tossed aside a picture of an automobile accident. "I guess the idea of this picture stuff wasn't so good, Mugs. It seems they're running around like mad, shooting auto accidents with all of the gruesome details."

"Part of a publicity campaign to educate the people," Mugs explained.

"Well, *those* photographs certainly don't interest me," Bane said. "Here, Mugs, you're the camera-eye man of the outfit. Run your eye through these pictures while I shower. I can't look at gruesome, mangled bodies and smashed-up automobiles on an empty stomach. See if you can't find the picture of some crook who's crashed into the news, someone you can tell me about. Then we may be able to figure out an angle."

Mugs said deprecatingly, "Of course, I'm an old-timer, Mr. Bane. There's a whole crop of newcomers in the crime field since I—"

"I know," Bane interrupted, laughing. "You're always apologizing, but the fact remains you have the old camera eye. That's where you got your nickname, Mugs, from being able to remember faces. They tell me you've never forgotten a face, a name, or a connection."

"That was in the old days. I had both arms when I was on the force and—"

"Yes, yes, I know," Jerry interrupted hastily, "and then you got mixed up in politics. Then you lost an arm, took to drink, and wound up selling pencils."

"There was an interval with a gentleman by the name of Mr. Pry," Mugs Magoo said somewhat wistfully. "He was a fast worker, that lad—reminds me of you. But I got to drinking too much and—"

"Well, you're on the wagon now," Bane said reassuringly. "You look over these pictures and see if you find anyone you know."

Still clad in pajamas, Bane seated himself at the breakfast table and said, "What about the photographs, Mugs?"

Magoo said, "A neat bit of cheesecake, sir. You might prefer this to the auto-accident pictures."

"Let's take a look."

Mugs Magoo passed over the picture of a girl in a bathing suit.

Bane looked at the picture, then read the caption underneath aloud:

"Federal Court proceedings were enlivened yesterday when, during a bathing-suit patent case, Stella Darling, nightclub entertainer, modeled the suit. 'Remove the garment and it will be introduced as plaintiff's Exhibit A,' said Judge Asa Lansing, then added hastily, 'Not here! Not here!' while the courtroom rocked with laughter."

Bane surveyed the photograph. "Some doll!"

Mugs nodded.

"Nice chassis."

Again Mugs nodded.

"But somehow the face doesn't go with the legs," Bane said. "It's a sad face, almost tragic. That expression could have been carved on a wooden mask."

Mugs Magoo said, "Nice kid when I first knew her. Won a beauty contest and was Miss Something-or-other in nineteen forty-three. Then things happened to her fast. She cashed in on what prosperity she could get, married a pretty good chap, then fell in love with another guy. Her husband caught her cheating, shot the other man, couldn't get by with the unwritten law, and went to jail. She came out west and turned up in the nightclubs. Nice figure, but gossip followed her from back east. Too bad the kid can't get a break and begin all over again. Gossip has long legs."

Bane nodded thoughtfully. "When you come right down to it, Mugs, there's not so much to differentiate her from a lot of the people who look down on her."

"Just a mere thirty minutes," Magoo said. "How's your coffee?"

"The coffee's fine. Why the thirty minutes, Mugs?"

"Her husband's train could have been late."

Bane grinned. "What else, Mugs? Anything else?"

"One here I don't get," Mugs said.

"What is it?"

Mugs handed him a photograph. It showed a young woman standing in a serve-yourself grocery store, pointing an accusing finger at a broad-shouldered man who, in turn, was pointing an accusing finger at the woman. At the woman's feet a dog lay sprawled. A pile of groceries on the counter by the cash register were evidently purchases made by the man.

"Why the double pointing?" Bane asked.

"Read it," Mugs said.

Bane read the story:

ACCUSER ACCUSED—In a strange double mix-up yesterday afternoon, Bernice Calhoun, 23, 9305 Sunset Way, accused William L. Gordon, 32, residing at a roominghouse at 505 Monadnock Drive, of having held up a jewelry shop known as the Jewel Casket, 9316 Sunset Way. When the suspect entered her Serve-Yourself Grocery Story, Miss Calhoun notified police, explaining she had seen Gordon, carrying a gun, backing out of the jewelry shop, forcing the proprietor, Harvey Haggard, to hold his hands high in the air. Then Gordon, alarmed by an approaching prowl car, entered the grocery store, apparently as a customer, picked up a shopping basket, and started selecting canned goods.

Police, answering Bernice Calhoun's call, rushed to the scene, only to encounter complications. Not only was no loot found on Gordon, but Harvey Haggard, casually reading a magazine in the Jewel Casket, said it was all news to him. So far as he knew, no one had staged a stickup. Gordon accused the woman of blackmail and is starting suit for defamation of character.

Bernice Calhoun, who is well liked in the neighborhood and who inherited the grocery store from her father, is frankly disturbed over her predicament. This photograph was taken just a few minutes after police arrived on the scene and shows Bernice Calhoun, right, accusing Gordon, left, who is, in turn, accusing Miss Calhoun. Gordon was taken into custody by police, pending an investigation.

"Now that," Bane said, "is *something*! Know anything about it, Mugs?"

"This Gordon," Mugs said, placing a stubby finger on the picture of the man, "is a slick one. They call him 'Gopher' Gordon because he's always burrowing and working in the dark."

"You think it's a frame-up to shake Bernice Calhoun loose from some change?"

"More probably Gopher Gordon and Harvey Haggard are in it together and want to get the grocery-store lease."

"Seems a rather crude way of doing it," Bane said.

"Anything that works ain't crude," Mugs insisted doggedly.

"I wish you'd look into this, Mugs," Jerry Bane said thoughtfully. "It has possibilities. Here we are fresh out of cash, and this crook . . . and a beautiful woman . . . Check up on it, will you, Mugs?"

"You want me to do it now?"

"Right now," Jerry Bane said. "The way I look at it, haste is important. Get started."

* * *

Ten minutes after Mugs Magoo had left, Arthur Arman Anson knocked on the door.

His cold knuckles tapped with evenly spaced decision.

Jerry Bane let him in.

"Hello, Counselor," he said. "I've just finished breakfast. How about having a cup of coffee?"

"No, thank you. I breakfasted at six thirty."

"You look it," Bane said.

"How's that?"

"I said you looked it. You know, early to bed, early to rise, and all that sort of stuff."

Anson settled himself with severe austerity in a straight-backed chair, depositing his briefcase beside him.

"I come in the performance of a necessary but disagreeable duty," Anson said, his voice showing that he relished his errand, despite his remarks.

"Go right ahead with the lecture," Jerry Bane said.

"It's not a lecture, young man. I am merely making a few remarks."

"Go ahead and make them, then, but remember the adjective."

"You are living the life of a wastrel. By this time you should have recovered from the harrowing experiences of the Japanese prison camp. You should have recovered from the effects of your two years of malnutrition. In other words, young man, you should go to work."

"What do you suggest?" Jerry asked.

"Hard manual labor," Anson said grimly.

"I don't get it."

"That is the way *I* got *my* start. I worked with pick and shovel on railroad construction and—"

"And then inherited money, I believe," Jerry said.

"That has nothing to do with it, young man. I began at the bottom and have worked my way to the top. You are wasting your time in frivolity. I don't suppose you go to bed before eleven or twelve o'clock at night! I find you at this hour of the morning still lounging around in pajamas.

"Furthermore, I find you associating with a disreputable character, a one-armed consort of the underworld, who has sold pencils on the streets of this city."

"He's loyal and I like him," Jerry said.

"He's a dissipated has-been," Anson snapped. "Your uncle left you ten thousand dollars outright. The bulk of his estate, however, he left to me as trustee. I am empowered to give you as much or as little of that money as I see fit, the idea being that—"

"Yes, yes, I know," Jerry interrupted. "My uncle thought I might spend it all in one wild fling. He wanted you to see that it was passed out to me in installments. All right, I'm broke right now. Pass out an installment."

"I do not know what your uncle wanted," Anson said, "but I do know what I intend to do."

"What's that?"

"You have squandered the ten thousand dollars. Look at this apartment, equipped with vacuum cleaners, electric dishwashers, all sorts of gadgets—"

"Because my man has only one arm, and I'm trying to—"

"Exactly. Because of your sentiment for this sodden hulk of the streets, you have dissipated your cash inheritance. Young man, the bank advises me you are overdrawn. Now then, I'm going to give it to you straight. Get out of this apartment. Go to a rooming-house somewhere and start living within your means. Strip off those tailored clothes, get into overalls, start doing hard manual labor. At the end of six months I will again discuss the matter with you ... Do you know how much you have spent in the last three months?"

"I never was much good at addition," Jerry confessed.

"Try subtraction then!" Anson snapped.

Bane's face was reproachful. "Just when I was about

to steer a lawsuit to your office—a spectacular case you're bound to win."

Anson's shrewd eyes showed a brief flicker of interest. "What's the case?"

"I can't tell you now."

"Bosh. Probably something I wouldn't touch with a ten-foot pole. And in any event, my decision would remain unaltered."

"A beautiful case," Bane went on. "A case involving defamation of character. The young woman defendant is entirely innocent. You'll have an opportunity to walk into court and make one of those spectacular, last-minute exposés of the other side. A case that has everything."

"Who is this client?"

"A raving, roaring beauty."

"I don't want them to rave. I don't want them to roar. I want them to pay," Anson said, and then added, "And I don't care whether they're beautiful or not."

Bane grinned. "But think of it, Anson. All this, and beauty too."

"Don't think you can bribe me, young man. I have been an attorney too long to fall for these blandishments, these nebulous fees which never materialize, these mysterious clients with their marvelous cases who somehow never quite get to the office. You have my ultimatum. I'll thank you to advise me within forty-eight hours that you have gone to work. Hard manual labor. At the end of what I consider a proper period I will then give you a chance to get a so-called white-collar job. Good day, sir."

"And you won't have a cup of coffee?"

"Definitely not. I never eat between meals."

Arthur Arman Anson slammed the door behind him.

Mugs Magoo found Jerry Bane sprawled out in the big easy chair, his mind completely absorbed in a book entitled *The Mathematics of Business Management*. Beside him on the smoking stand was a slide rule with which Bane had been checking the conclusions of the author.

Magoo stood by the chair for some two or three minutes before Bane, feeling his presence, fidgeted uneasily for a moment, then looked up. "I didn't want to interrupt you," Mugs said, "but I have a very interesting story."

"You talked with her?"

"Yes."

"Is she really as good-looking as the newspaper picture made her out to be?"

Mugs took a photograph from an envelope. "Better. This was taken last summer at a beach resort."

Jerry Bane carefully studied the picture, then gave a low whistle.

"Exactly," Mugs Magoo said dryly.

"Now how the devil did you get this, Mugs?"

"Well, I found that the store's about all she has in the world and she's pretty hard up for cash. I told her some of the big wholesalers were going to put on a campaign to feature neighborhood grocery stores and they wanted to get pictures that would catch the eye. I told her that if she had an attractive picture of herself, one that would look well in print, she might win a prize, and that if she did, a man would come to photograph the store and pay her a hundred and fifty dollars for the right to publish her picture; that if the picture wasn't used, she'd get it back and wouldn't be out anything."

Jerry Bane studied the picture. "Plenty of this and that and these and those. Lots of oomphs, Mugs."

"Plenty, sir."

"And she's hard up for cash?"

"Apparently so. She wants to sell the store, but she's worried about what may happen on this defamation-of-character suit."

"What's new in that case, Mugs?"

"Well, she's beginning to think she may have acted a little hastily. She isn't *certain* she saw the gun. She saw the man throw something over the fence, but the police haven't been able to find anything. Frankly, sir, I think she's beginning to feel she was mistaken ... But she wasn't."

"She wasn't?"

Mugs Magoo shook his head. "I got a look at this man, Haggard, who runs that jewelry store. I know some stuff about him the police don't."

"What?"

"He's a fence, and he's clever as hell. He buys stuff here and ships it by air express to retail outlets all over the country.

"An association of fences?"

Mugs nodded and said, "You can figure out what happened. This man Gordon had probably had some dealings with Haggard and had been given a double-cross. He decided to get even in his own way."

Bane nodded thoughtfully. "So, naturally, Haggard can't admit anything was taken because he doesn't dare describe the loot ... Let me take a look at that picture again, Mugs."

Mugs handed him the photograph of the girl in the bathing suit.

"Not that one," Jerry Bane said. "The one that shows her accusing Gopher Gordon, and Gopher Gordon accusing her. Do you know, Mugs, I'm beginning to get a very definite idea that may pay off."

"I thought you might," Magoo said. "A man can look at a picture of a jane like that and get ideas pretty fast."

The girl looked up from the cash register as Jerry entered the store.

Jerry noticed that she had a nice complexion and good lines, because he was something of an expert in such matters. Her long slender legs had just the right curves in keeping with her streamlined figure. Moreover, there was a certain alertness in her eyes, a mischievous, provocative something which held a definite challenge.

Jerry Bane, apparently completely preoccupied with his errand, picked up a market basket and walked around looking at the canned goods.

The girl tossed her head and returned to an inspection of the accounts on which she had been working when Jerry entered. This slack time of the afternoon was a period which she apparently set aside for her bookkeeping.

Left to his own devices, Jerry carefully selected a can of grapefruit and a package of rolled oats. He glanced back toward the cans of dog food on the counter where the girl bent over her work beside the cash register—the cans which had shown up so plainly in the news photo. Then he looked at his watch. Very soon—almost at once, in fact, if Mugs Magoo was on the beam—the telephone would ring and Bernice Calhoun would leave the counter to answer it. If Mugs could keep her there for a minute or two, there would be time enough for . . .

The phone shrilled. The girl looked up. Her eyes rested briefly on Jerry, then she shut the cash-register drawer and walked swiftly to the back of the store, where the telephone hung on the wall in a corner.

Jerry stepped in front of the pyramided cans of dog food. They were arranged so that the labels were toward the front—except for one can. He deftly extracted this can from the pile.

The lid had been entirely removed by a can opener which had made a smooth job of cutting around the top of the can. The interior contained bits of dried dog food still adhering to the tin, but, in addition to that, there was a flash of scintillating brilliance, light shafts from sparkling gems which showed ruby red, emerald green, and the indescribable glitter of diamonds.

Jerry's body shielded what he was doing from the girl. His hand, moving swiftly, dumped the contents of the can into an inside coat pocket, a coruscating cascade of unset jewels which rattled reassuringly.

From another pocket in his coat he took some cheap imitation jewels which he had removed from costume jewelry. When he had the can two-thirds full, he took some of the genuine stones and placed them on top in a layer of brilliant temptation.

He replaced the can, being careful to leave it just as he had found it, then wandered over to the shelf where the jams were displayed. As he picked up a jar of marmalade, he heard the girl's footsteps clicking back to the counter. He took his basket of groceries to her.

She seemed now to have definitely decided on an impersonal course of conduct.

"Good afternoon," she said politely, and jabbed at the keys of the cash register. "Two dollars and sixteen cents," she announced.

Jerry gravely handed her a five-dollar bill. She rang up the sale on the cash register.

"Too bad about your lawsuit," Jerry said. "I have an idea I can help you."

She was engaged in making change, but stopped and glanced up at him swiftly. "What's *your* game?" she asked.

"No game. I only thought I might be of some assistance."

"In what way?"

"I have a friend who is a very able lawyer."

"Oh, *that!*" She shrugged contemptuously.

"And, if I spoke to him, I'm quite sure he'd handle your case for a nominal fee."

She laughed scornfully. "I know, just because I have an honest face—or is it the figure?"

Jerry Bane said, "Perhaps I'd better explain myself. I have reason to believe you're being victimized."

"Indeed," she said, her voice as cutting as a cold wind on a wintry evening. "Your perspicacity surprises me, Mr.—er—"

"Mr. Bane," he said. "Jerry to my friends."

"Oh, yes, *Mister* Bane!"

"While you probably don't realize it," Jerry went on, "the man whom you identified as the stickup artist is known to the police of the northern cities. He doesn't have a criminal record in the sense that his fingerprints have ever been taken, and no one knows him here, but the police in the north know a little about him."

"Wouldn't that be valuable in—well, you know, in the event he sues me for defamation of character?" she asked, her voice suddenly friendly.

"It would be more than valuable. It would be priceless."

"You have proof?"

"I think I can get proof."

She slowly closed the drawer of the cash register. "Exactly what is it you want?" she asked.

Jerry made a little gesture of dismissal. "Merely an opportunity to be of service. Try me out."

"If I do, I'll hold you to your promise."

"I'd expect you to."

"What do you want me to do?"

"First, tell me exactly what happened—everything."

She studied him thoughtfully, then said abruptly, "Ever since my father died, I've been trying to make a go of this place. It won't warrant paying the salary of a clerk. It's a small place. I have to do the work myself.

"I keep track of the stock. I make up orders. I keep books. I open shipments, arrange the stock on the shelves, and do all sorts of odd jobs. I work here at night and early in the morning. During the daytime I fill in the time between customers with clerical work on the books.

"Day before yesterday I happened to be looking out of that window. From this position you can look right across to that little jewelry shop known as the Jewel Casket.

"I don't know much about that place. Now that I think of it, I don't know how a person could expect to make a living with a jewelry store in that location, but Mr. Haggard evidently does all right. Of course, he doesn't have a high rent to pay.

"Well, anyway, as I was looking out of the window, I saw this man's back and I felt certain he was holding a gun. I thought I could see someone in the store holding his hands up. Then this man, Gordon, came out into the street, and I'm almost positive he tossed something over the board fence into that vacant lot.

"Then I saw him stiffen with apprehension and he seemed to be ready to run. I couldn't see what had frightened him at the moment, but I could see he was looking over his left shoulder, up the street."

"Go on," Jerry said.

"Well, he didn't run. He hurried across the street over here. Just as he came in the door, I saw what it was that had frightened him."

"What was it?"

"A police prowl car. It came cruising by, going slowly, the red spotlight on the windshield and the radio antennae showing plainly it was a police car. I was frightened, simply scared stiff."

"You have a dog here?" Banc asked.

"Yes, but he's a good-natured, friendly dog. He would be no protection unless, perhaps, someone should attack me."

"What did this man do after he got inside here?"

"Walked around the store and tried to act like a customer, picking out canned goods to put in a basket, but picking them out carefully and with such attention to the labels that I knew he was simply stalling.

"I guess I was in such a panic that I didn't stop to think—I just don't know. At the time I really felt he was a stickup man. Now I'm not so sure. Anyhow, I went to the phone and got police headquarters. The phone's so far back in the store," she explained, "that he couldn't hear me from where he was."

Jerry nodded. "Not very convenient to have it so far

away. Usually, I mean—for orders and that sort of thing."

"I don't take phone orders," she said. "That's what I kept trying to tell that guy that called just now. But he couldn't seem to understand. Maybe because he was English. You know, very lah-de-dah kind of voice."

Jerry grinned. Mugs and his imitation of Jeeves! He'd do it at the drop of a hat.

"So you called the police," he prompted the girl.

"Yes. I told them who I was, explained that a man had just held up the jewelry store across the street, had been frightened by a police radio car, and had taken refuge in my store. I knew that the police department could get in touch with the radio car right away and I suggested they have the driver turn around and come back here."

"And that was done?"

"Yes. It took them about—oh, I'd say a few minutes."

"And what happened when the police arrived?"

"The car pulled up in front of the store. The officers jumped out with drawn guns, and I pointed out this man to them and accused him of having held up the store across the street.

"At that time the man had finished buying his groceries and was standing here at the cash register. I'd been fumbling around a bit making his change, so that the radio car would have time to get back.

"This man said his name was Gordon and that I was crazy, that he'd stopped to look in the window of the Jewel Casket, had started to go in to buy a present for his girl friend, and then changed his mind and decided to buy some groceries instead. He said that he'd never carried a gun in his life. The police searched him nd found nothing. I told them to go over to the Jewel Casket. I thought perhaps they'd find Mr. Haggard dead."

"What happened."

"That's the part I simply can't understand. Mr. Haggard was there in the store and he said that no one had been in during the last fifteen minutes and that he hadn't been held up. I—I felt like a complete ninny."

"Would you gamble a little of your time and do *exactly* what I say if it would get you out of this mess?" Bane asked.

"What do you want?"

"I want you to close up the store and come with me to see my lawyer, Arthur Anson. I want you to tell him your story. After that I want you to promise me that, in case he should return to the store with you, you'll stay right beside him all the time he's here."

"Why that?" she asked.

Jerry grinned. "It's just a hunch. Do *just* as I tell you and you may get this cleaned up."

She thought that over for several seconds, then said, "Oh, well, what have I got to lose?"

"Exactly," Jerry said, and his smile was like spring sunshine.

Arthur Arman Anson was cold as a wet towel.

"Jerry, I'm a busy man. I have no time to listen to your wheedling. I will not give you—"

"I told your secretary that I have a client waiting," Jerry Bane interrupted.

"I recognize the typical approach," Anson said. "I not only fear the Greeks when they bear gifts, but I shall not change my decision in your case by so much as a single, solitary penny! Kindly remember that."

Jerry Bane whipped the bathing-suit photograph out of his briefcase. "This is a picture of the client."

Arthur Anson adjusted his glasses and peered through the lower segments of his bifocals. He *harrumphed* importantly.

Jerry Bane whipped out the other photograph, the one taken by the Shooting Star photographer, and said, "Take a look at *that* picture. Study the caption."

Arthur Anson looked at the photograph, read the caption, and once more cleared his throat.

"Interesting," he said noncommittally, then added after a moment, "Very."

"Now then," Jerry Bane went on, "this man, Mugs Magoo, who works for me—"

"A thoroughly disreputable character," Anson interrupted.

"—has a camera eye and a great memory," Bane went on as though the interruption had not been made. "As soon as he looked at this picture he recognized this man as a crook."

"Indeed!"

"He's known as Gopher Gordon because he works underground and by such devious methods the police have never been able to get anything on him. This is the first time he's actually been held for anything and the first time he's ever been fingerprinted. That's why he's so furious at Bernice, and so determined to sue her."

Anson stroked the long angle of his jaw with the tips of bony fingers. "A bad reputation is a very difficult thing to prove. People don't want to get on the witness stand and testify. However, of course, if this young woman insists on consulting me, and if she has sufficient funds to pay me an ample retainer as well as to hire competent detectives—"

"She isn't going to pay you a cent," Jerry Bane said.

Sheer surprise jerked Arthur Anson out of his professional calm. "What's that?"

"She isn't going to pay you a cent."

Anson pushed back the photographs. "Then get her out of my office," he stormed. "Damn it, Bane, I—"

"But," Jerry interrupted, "you're going to make a lot of money out of the case just the same, because you're going to get such a spectacular courtroom victory it'll give you an enormous amount of advertising."

"I don't need advertising."

"A man can't get too much of it," Jerry said, talking rapidly. "Now, look what happened. This man Haggard says he *wasn't* held up. Bernice knows that he was.

He's lying. You can tear into him on cross-examination and—"

"And prove my client is a liar."

"I tell you she isn't a liar. She's a sweet young girl who is being victimized."

Anson shook his head decisively, "If this jewelry store man says he wasn't held up, that finishes it. This young woman is a blackmailer and a liar. Get her out of my office."

Jerry Bane said desperately, "I wish you'd listen to me. These men are both crooks.

"Both?"

"Yes, both. They have to be."

"Indeed," Anson said with elaborate irony. "Simply because these men tell a story which fails to coincide with that told by a young woman with whom you have apparently become infatuated—"

"Don't you see?" Jerry interrupted once more. "Haggard is running a jewelry store out there in a neighborhood where the volume would be too small to support his overhead unless the store were a mask for some illegitimate activity. Out there he poses as a small operator, selling cheap jewelry to a family trade, costume jewelry to schoolgirls, fountain pens, cigarette lighters, various knick-knacks. Actually he has a more profitable activity. He's a fence."

"Being out in that district of small neighborhood stores, he's in a position to keep irregular hours. No one thinks anything of it when he comes down at night and putters around in his store, because many of the storekeepers who can't afford help do the same thing. So Haggard uses this fact as a shield for an illicit business.

"This man Gordon is a crook. Gordon knew what Haggard's business was. He undoubtedly knew that some very large haul of stones had been purchased by Haggard, and Gordon saw a chance to step in and clean up. He knew that Haggard wouldn't be in a position to report his loss to the police. Gordon was personally unknown to Haggard, just as he is unknown to the police here. He hoped that no one who had known him in the north would catch up with him and identify him.

"An ordinary crook, established here in this city, wouldn't have dared to hold up a fence. The underworld has its own way of meting out punishment. But Gordon was an outsider, a slick worker, a man who could step in, make a stickup, and then get out. He's noted for that."

"And what did he do with the loot?" Anson asked sarcastically. "Remember, the police searched him."

"Sure, the police searched him. But he'd been in that grocery store for some five minutes before they searched him, and he saw the young woman go over to the telephone and start talking in a low tone of voice. He wasn't so dumb but what he knew that he was trapped. His only chance was to get rid of the jewelry."

"Where did he put it?"

"It's concealed in various places around the store . . . Why, look here!" Jerry said in a sudden excitement, as though the idea had just occurred to him. "What would have prevented him from opening a can, dumping out the contents, and putting the jewelry in the empty can?"

"Ah, yes," Anson said, his voice a cold sneer. "The typical reasoning of a fat-brained, young spendthrift. I suppose he opened a can of peaches, dumped the peaches on the floor, and then put the jewelry in the can. The police searched the place and couldn't find anything wrong. They never noticed the dripping can or the peaches on the floor. Oh, no!"

"Well," Bane said, "It wouldn't have to be a can of peaches. And he could have opened a can so neatly that . . . Why, suppose he'd opened a can of dog food and put *that* on the floor! The dog would promptly have gulped it up and . . . Say, wait a minute—"

Jerry broke off to look at the photograph with eyes that were suddenly wide with surprise, as though he were just noticing something he hadn't seen before. "Look right here!" he said. "There's canned dog food piled on the counter. And—yes—here's one can that's turned around, turned the wrong way so the brand name doesn't show."

Anson was now studying the photograph too. Jerry pointed to the pile of groceries on the counter. "And look at what he has there—a can opener! That settles it. He picked up the can opener—I saw a box of them by the canned-fruit shelves when I was there—and he used it on the can of dog food. Probably while the girl was at the back of the store phoning the police. It—"

Anson snatched the photographs out of Jerry Bane's hand and propped them into a drawer in his desk. "Young man," he said, "your reasoning is asinine, puerile, sophomoric, and absurd. However, you have brought a young woman to my office, a young woman who is in a legal predicament. I will, at least, talk with her. I will not judge her entirely on the strength of what you say."

"Very well, I'll call her in," Jerry said, his voice without expression.

"You'll do nothing of the sort, young man. I do not discuss business with clients in the presence of an outsider. You have brought this woman to my office. I will talk with her and I will talk with her privately. I'll excuse you now, Mr. Bane—and naturally I'll expect you to keep this entire matter entirely confidential."

"Any need for secrecy?"

"It's *not* secrecy. It's merely preserving the legal integrity of my office. Good afternoon, young man."

"Good afternoon," Jerry said.

Jerry Bane found Stella Darling waiting impatiently.

"Your phone call said you had a modeling job," she said. "I've been waiting here for over an hour."

"Sorry, I was a little late," Jerry said. "I was making arrangements with my clients."

"What sort of a modeling job is it?"

"Well," Jerry said, "to be frank with you, Miss Darling, it's just a bit out of the ordinary. It's—"

Her voice cut across his like a knife. "Nude?" she asked.

"No, no. Nothing like that."

"How did you find out about me?" she asked.

"I saw the photograph of you modeling the bathing suit in court."

"I see." Her voice indicated that she saw a great deal. Her appraisal of Jerry Bane was personal and, after a moment, approving.

Jerry said, "This job is one I'd like to have you carry out to the letter. I have here a sheet of typewritten instructions, telling you just what to do."

She said, "Look, Mr. Bane, I have a lot of things put up to me. I'm trying to make a living. I have a beautiful body. I'm trying to capitalize on it while it lasts. I made the mistake of winning a beauty contest once and thought I was going to become a movie star overnight. I quit school and started signing up with this and that ... Lord, what I wouldn't give to turn back the hands of the clock and be back in school once more!"

"Perhaps," Jerry said. "if you do *exactly* as I say, you'll have an opportunity to do that. I'm trying a unique exploitation of a brand-new dog food. If things go the way I want, I may be able to sell out the brand and the good will, lock, stock, and barrel.

"However, I haven't time to discuss details now. Here's some money to cover your regular hourly rate. If you do a good job, you'll receive a substantial bonus tomorrow. Now then, get busy."

"And I wear street clothes?"

"Street clothes," Jerry Bane said. "Just what you have on."

She sized him up, then said, "The modeling I have been doing has been—well, it's been a little bit of everything. You don't need to be afraid to tell me what it is. You don't need to write it out for me. Just go ahead and tell me."

Jerry Bane smiled and shook his head. "Read these typewritten instructions," he said. "Follow them to the letter and get started."

She took the typewritten sheet from him, once more gave him a glance from under long-lashed eyelids. "Okay," she said, "I'll do it your way."

"You'll have to go out on Sunset Way," he said. "You can read your instructions on the way out."

Jerry Bane found Mugs Magoo seated in the kitchen of the apartment, holding a newspaper propped up with one arm.

"Mugs," he said, "what would you do if you suddenly found yourself in possession of a lot of stolen jewelry?"

"That depends," Mugs said, looking up from the paper and regarding Jerry Bane with expressionless eyes.

"Depends on what?"

"On whether you wanted to be real smart or only half smart."

"I'd want to be *real* smart, Mugs."

"The point is," Mugs went on, "that if the jewelry is real hot, you'd have to fence it to sell it. If it was stuff that had cooled off a bit, it would be a great temptation to try passing off a little here and there. Either way would be half smart."

"And to be *real* smart, Mugs?"

"You'd get in touch with the insurance companies. You'd suggest to them that you *might* be able to help them make restorations here and there but you'd want it handled in such a way that you collected a reward."

"Would they pay?"

"If you make the right approach."

"How much?"

"If they thought they were dealing with a crook who was a squealer, they wouldn't pay very much. If they thought they were dealing with a reputable detective who had made a recovery, they'd come through handsomely."

Bane reached in his pocket, took out a knotted handkerchief, untied the knots, and let Magoo's eyes feast on the assorted collection of sparklers.

"Gosh!" Mugs Magoo said.

"I want to be *real* smart, Mugs."

"Okay," Mugs said, scooping up the handkerchief in his big hand. "I guess I know the angles . . . Somebody going to miss this stuff?"

"I'm afraid so," Jerry Bane said, "but I think I juggled the inventory. Someone else may get part of it, Mugs. A selfish, greedy someone who may be only *half* smart."

Magoo regarded his friend with eyes that were cold with cynicism. "If this is what I think it is, this other guy will find the underworld can stick together like two pieces of flypaper. If he tries to chisel, he might even wind up pushing up daisies."

Jerry said, "Of course, if he's *really* honest, he'll report to the cops."

"Do you think he will be?"

"No."

"Okay," Mugs said. "Let him lead with *his* chin. We'll work undercover."

Jerry Bane was stretched out in the easy chair, a highball glass at his elbow, when timid knuckles tapped on the door of the apartment.

Mugs Magoo opened the door.

Bernice Calhoun said, "Oh, good evening. I *do* hope Mr. Bane is home. I have to see him. I—why, you're the man who—"

"He's home," Mugs Magoo said. "Come in."

Jerry Bane was getting to his feet as she entered the room. She ran to him and gave him both her hands. "Mr. Bane," she said, "the most *wonderful* thing has happened! I simply can't understand it."

"Sit down and tell me about it," Jerry said. "What do you want—Scotch or bourbon?"

"Scotch and soda."

Jerry nodded to Mugs Magoo, then said, "All right, Bernice, what happened?"

She said, "I didn't like the lawyer you took me to. He was very gruff. He asked a lot of questions and then said he'd go down to the grocery store and look the place over, but he didn't think he'd be particularly interested in the case. He didn't seem at all eager, not even cordial."

"And what happened?"

She said, "Well, after he'd asked a lot of questions, he went down to the store with me. I opened up and showed him just where I had been standing and all that. Then he looked around and asked a few questions and looked the shelves over, and I remembered what you'd told me and I tagged right along with him, and that seemed to irritate him. He made several attempts to get rid of me, but I stayed right beside him."

"Then what?" Jerry asked.

"Then a young woman came in. She was a very theatrical young woman with lots of makeup. She said rather loudly that she had been having a hard time getting the brand of dog food her dog wanted and that she noticed I had a stock of that brand. She asked me if she could buy my entire stock and if I'd take her check. She said her name was Stella Darling."

"Then what happened?" Jerry asked.

"The *strangest* thing," she said. "This lawyer advised me to take no one's personal check, and he went back to the telephone and called his office."

"Go on," Jerry said.

"Well, it seemed that while he was telephoning, a client was in his office. This client had been looking for some small business that he could go into, something that he could operate on a one-man basis. I'd been telling Mr. Anson that I'd really like to sell out that grocery-store business, and—well, one thing led to another, and Mr. Anson negotiated over the telephone, and I sold the business right there."

"What did you do about an inventory?" Jerry flashed a glance at Mugs Magoo.

"Mr. Anson gave me his check, based on my own figures, and took immediate possession."

"And this Miss Darling who wanted to buy the dog food? Did the lawyer sell it to her?"

"Indeed, he did not. He literally put her out of the store, took the keys, and locked up." There was a moment of silence.

"And so," she said, "I—I wanted to thank you—personally."

The telephone rang and Jerry picked it up.

Arthur Arman Anson's voice came over the wire. "Jerry, my boy, I've been doing a little thinking. After all, you're young, and I suppose the war rather upset your whole life. I think a man must make allowances for youth."

"Thank you."

"I've covered the overdraft at your bank and deposited a few hundred dollars, Jerry, my boy. But try to be a little more careful with money."

"Yes, sir. Thank you, I will."

"And, Jerry, in case you should see Miss Calhoun, the young woman who had the grocery store, be very careful not to mention anything about that perfectly cockeyed theory you had. There was absolutely nothing to it."

"There wasn't?"

"No, my boy. I went down there and looked the place over. I inspected the can which the photograph shows was partially turned. It was just the same as any other can—nothing in it but dog food. However, it happened a client of mine was interested in a property such as Miss Calhoun has there and I was able to arrange a sale for her."

"Oh, that's splendid!" Jerry said.

"Purely a matter of business," Anson observed. "I was glad it worked out the way it did, because this young woman is very vulnerable to a lawsuit. She'd better get out of the state before papers can be served. As an ethical lawyer, I didn't want to tell her to do that, but in case you should see her, *you* can tell her to get out of the state at once. Get me?"

"Meaning I haven't your high ethics to handicap me?" Jerry asked.

"Very few men could live up to my ethics," Anson declared.

"Yes I presume so. Very well, I'll tell her."

"Well, I won't keep you up any longer," Anson said.

"Keep me up!" Jerry laughed. "Is it by any chance bedtime?"

"Well, it's after ten o'clock," Arthur Anson said. "Good night, Jerry."

"Good night."

Jerry hung up the phone and turned to Bernice Calhoun. "Under the circumstances," he said, "don't you think we should do some dinner dancing?"

"Well," she told him demurely, "I came to thank you—"

Mugs said, "Did you by any chance hear the news on the radio?"

Jerry Bane looked up quickly. "Should I?"

"I think you should have."

"What was it?"

Mugs glanced at Bernice Calhoun.

"Go ahead," Jerry said. "She'll learn about it sooner or later."

"This man Gordon she had arrested," Mugs said, "was released from jail. He was being held on investigation and he dug up some bail. He was released about an hour ago.

"Indeed," Jerry said.

"And," Mugs went on, "the police are somewhat mystified. A witness told them that as Gordon walked down the jail steps, a car was waiting for him and a man said, 'Get in.' Gordon acted as though he didn't want to get in. He hesitated, but finally got in the car. The witness felt certain a man in the back seat was holding a gun on Gordon. He was so certain of it that he went to the police to report, but there wasn't much the police could do about it. The license number on the automobile was spotted with mud and the man hadn't been able to get it."

"Oh," Bernice said, "then that man must have been connected with the underworld after all! Why do you suppose they wanted him to—to go for a ride?"

"Probably," Mugs Magoo said, "they wanted to get some information out of him. And with all night at their disposal, they'll quite probably get the information they want."

His eyes were significant as he looked steadily at Jerry Bane.

Bane stretched his arms and yawned. "Oh, well," he said, "tomorrow's a new day for all of us, and my friend, Arthur Anson, has bought Bernice's grocery store."

Bernice said, "I'm *so* relieved. The lawyer promised me that, as part of the deal on the store, he'd see that I was indemnified in case this man started a suit against me. Now that I've sold the store, I feel I haven't any responsibilities."

"That's just the way with me," Jerry Bane said. "Not a care in the world! Let's go dance, Bernice."

Hung Jury

by Jack Ritchie

I had just returned from my vacation and Ralph began filling me in on the case assigned to us.

"Three members of the jury were murdered," he said.

I nodded wisely. "Ah, yes. I see it all. The jury convicted a felon and he swore he would get his revenge."

"Not quite," Ralph said. "Actually it was a hung jury. Four for acquittal and eight for conviction."

"But of course," I said. "So the criminal promptly proceeded to kill three of the jurors who had voted for his conviction."

"Not that either, Henry. All three of the jurors murdered had voted for his acquittal."

"Why the devil would he want to murder three jurors who voted for his acquittal?"

"He didn't really murder anybody, Henry. He couldn't because he was dead."

"Ralph," I said patiently, "if you keep interrupting, I never will get to the nubbin of this case. Start at the beginning."

"Last year," Ralph said, "one Mike Winkler was arrested for the murder of a Jim Hurley. Both of them had long records for breaking-and-entering. They had just finished a job and they got into an argument about how they should divide the loot. Winkler pulled a gun and shot Hurley four times, which was enough to kill him. Somebody in a neighboring apartment heard the shots and called the police. They arrived to find Winkler sitting on his couch trying to figure out what to do with Hurley's body. Winkler confessed on the spot that he had killed Hurley and why."

"That should have wrapped it all up."

"Unfortunately, as soon as Winkler got hold of a lawyer, or vice versa, he withdrew the confession. Said he'd been beaten into making it by the arresting officers."

"Was he?"

"No. You know how it is in the department. If one of us does any roughing up, everybody learns about it in time. That doesn't mean that we fall all over ourselves to let the public know. But it's no big secret among ourselves, and nobody laid a finger on Winkler. Anyway, his story was that he went out for a newspaper and when he came back he found Hurley dead and the gun on the floor. But even without the confession, the case against him was still solid as a rock—powder grains on his hands, fingerprints on the murder gun, and so forth."

"But still the jury refused to convict him?"

"It was just one of those things that happen every now and then. You get a balky jury that believes what it wants to believe no matter what the evidence. Maybe it has something to do with the phases of the moon. The jury deliberated for five days without reaching a verdict and the judge finally dismissed it."

"Winkler went free?"

"No. He was taken right back to the county jail while the gears of justice meshed to try him for a second time with a new jury. But there never was a second trial. While Winkler waited, he managed to saw his way out of his cell and steal a car on the street. A squad car spotted him and the chase began. It finally ended when Winkler crashed into another car on a freeway ramp. Both Winkler and the driver of the other car were killed outright."

Faintly I remembered reading about it in the newspapers.

"It happened on the twenty-second of January, this

year," Ralph went on. "And now we move on to the twenty-second of the next month, February. One Amos Albee, a bachelor, age thirty-six, accountant, was found hanging by the neck from a rafter in his garage. It was assumed he got onto a chair, slipped the noose around his neck, and then stepped off."

"He didn't leave a suicide note?"

"No. But then many suicides don't. Albee's background indicated that he was a loner, melancholy by nature, and so it looked like he'd gotten a little more melancholy than usual and decided to end it all. And then exactly one month later, on the twenty-second of March, a Cora Anderson was found dead, also by hanging, in the laundry room of her apartment building. Cora was in her sixties, a widow in bad health, and it appeared that the loneliness of her life and her sickness had gotten too much for her and she decided to end her life."

"I gather that both Cora and Amos were members of the hung jury and that they had voted for Winkler's acquittal?"

"Yes, but at the time nobody connected them in any way. Who's to remember the names of the jurors in any of the dozens of trials going on in the courthouse every month? Besides, we get an average of ten suicides a month."

I alertly grasped the situation. "And then a third juror committed suicide, so to speak, and it took place on the twenty-second of the month following? April?"

"Exactly. Gerald Hawkins, a widower, retired, aged sixty-six, was found hanged in his basement. No suicide note either."

"But now somebody finally got suspicious?"

Ralph nodded. "Jurors get paid for their jury duty, but paperwork being what it is, it wasn't until July that the checks went out in the mail. Nine of them were delivered and accepted, but three of the envelopes were returned, addresses unknown. The City Clerk's office sent a man out to the last-known addresses to talk to neighbors and try to come up with some forwarding addresses. He discovered that all three of the jurors had hanged themselves. It seemed like just too much coincidence, so the City Clerk took the whole thing to the police. That was last week, while you were still on your vacation. By the way, where did you go?"

"Noplace. I stayed home and read and watched the educational channel on television. Also I did some Double-Crostics. Very refreshing and relaxing."

Ralph studied me for a moment and then continued. "We went back to the scenes of the deaths and were able to recover the ropes used on the three jurors—neighbors keep the damnedest things for souvenirs. In our lab we matched the rope ends. In other words, all three of the ropes had come from the same length or coil." He paused a moment. "You stayed in your apartment the entire two weeks?"

I nodded. "Most people travel on their vacations because they feel guilty about having all that free time and doing nothing. But I never feel guilty about having time off." I pondered the case for a moment. "You said that during his escape attempt, Winkler ran into another car and killed the driver."

"James Bellington. Age twenty-eight. A steam fitter and plumber. Married. No children. He was the only one in the car."

I smiled. "Ralph, if you search Bellington's garage, or basement, I'll wager you will find a coil of rope whose end exactly matches one end of the rope used on the third juror. My theory is that his wife was so traumatically affected by his death that she systematically hunted down every one of the jurors responsible for the—"

"We searched," Ralph said. "No rope. Besides, Bellington and his wife were separated and in the process of getting a divorce. She was minimum sad about his death, especially since she was still his life-insurance beneficiary."

"What about grieving relatives? Brother, sister, parents? Girl friend?"

"None. Bellington's parents are dead and he had no brother or sister. Also no girl friend."

I tried again. "What about the man Winkler shot? Who was unduly affected by his death?"

"Nobody. Hurley ran away from an orphan asylum at the age of fifteen. No relatives and no friends, except for the man who shot him."

I stroked my chin thoughtfully. "And yet it appears that someone has been commemorating the date of Bellington's death by executing a juror on the same day of succeeding months. Clearly someone is saying that if it weren't for the hung jury, Winkler would have been safely stowed in a maximum-security state prison rather than in our flimsy county jail where he had the opportunity to escape and subsequently cause the death of Bellington." I frowned. "Since we cannot find anyone personally devastated by Bellington's death, we must assume that somewhere out there in this city there is a dedicated nut who has taken it upon himself to balance the scales of justice. He could be any one of a million people."

"Possibly," Ralph said. "But on the other hand, looking closer to home, we find that the Winkler jury members were practically at each other's throats after five days of deliberation. The eight who voted for Winkler's conviction felt quite strongly that it was a miscarriage of justice not to find Winkler guilty of murder."

I nodded judiciously. "One of those eight jurors must be our murderer."

"We were able to establish that each of the murders must have occurred between ten and twelve in the evening. And if we assume that one person committed all three of the murders, we can eliminate six of the jurors for one reason or another. They have solid alibis for one, two, or all three of the murders."

I rapidly subtracted six from eight. "Ralph, I believe we've narrowed it down to two persons."

Ralph agreed. "One of them is an Elmer Poulos. Age twenty-eight. Physical culture enthusiast. Works in a florist shop at the Mayfair shopping center. The other is Deirdre O'Hennessey. She's twenty-five and has a job as a secretary in a construction firm."

"Ralph," I said, "when we have a chain of murders like this, the murderer's insufferable ego usually impels him to leave something in the nature of a signature at the scene of each crime. Something more personal than just matching rope ends."

Ralph nodded. "Good for you, Henry. After we decided it was murder, we went over everything again with a fine-tooth comb. We found a small cross, about half an inch in size, scratched on the underside of each of the chairs supposedly used by the suicides."

"Hmm," I said. "What kind of cross was it, Ralph? Latin? Lorraine? Celtic? Maltese?"

"Just a plain ordinary cross." He drew one on a sheet of paper.

"Ah," I said. "The Greek cross. Unless, of course, you tilt it forty-five degrees to either the left or the right. In which case, it becomes a Cross of St. Andrew's."

Ralph and I went downstairs to the police garage where we picked up our car and drove it to the Mayfair shopping center. At the florist shop we talked to the owner who directed us to a room at the rear of the store.

We found Elmer Poulos, a muscular young man in a T-shirt, making a funeral wreath.

Ralph introduced me. "This is Sergeant Henry Turnbuckle. My regular partner. He'd like to ask you a few questions."

I nodded. "I will get directly to the point. I understand that you have no alibi for any of the nights of the murders."

He smiled happily. "Absolutely none. I always go to

sleep at nine thirty and alone. I have to get a good
night's rest so that I can lift the weights."

Ralph studied him. "We think that the murderer first
subdued his victims, possibly with chloroform, then
put a noose around their necks and hoisted them to the
ceiling. Which means that our murderer must be quite
a strong man."

"Not necessarily, Ralph," I said. "The murderer
could have simply pointed a gun at his victims and ordered them to get on the chair and slip the noose
around their necks. Then the murderer kicked the chair
away."

"Now, Henry," Ralph said, "I find it hard to believe
that his victims would cooperate with him to that ex-
tent."

Poulos agreed. "I'll bet that ninety-nine percent of
the people on this earth would rather be shot than
hanged."

"True enough," I said, "*if* the victims were absolutely certain they were really about to be hanged. But
I suspect that being human and hopeful, they thought
that it might just be some kind of bad practical joke
and that the best thing to do was to humor the
gunholder by cooperating to a point. They would get
on the chairs and put the nooses around their necks.
Having the chairs kicked out from under them would
come as somewhat of a surprise."

Poulos dissented. "Personally I go with the chloro-
forming and the hoisting."

I regarded him pointedly. "If that was indeed the
method used, then you are certainly our most logical
suspect."

Poulos beamed. "I don't mind being a logical suspect. Just as long as you can't prove anything. I'm getting a lot of respect around here now. They think
maybe I did it. I mean working in a flower shop isn't
all that macho and you need all the help you can get."

A thought came to me. "Ralph, Bellington was
killed on the twenty-second of January and then on the

twenty-second of each succeeding month—February, March and April—another juror was hanged But why wasn't the *fourth* juror murdered on the twenty-second of May? It was certainly his turn. Why did the murderer stop killing? He still had one more juror to go. And yet the twenty-second of May passed and there was no dead fourth juror. Why? Did the murderer forget his name? His address? Who is the fourth juror who voted for acquittal?"

Ralph was about to give me the name, but then he eyed Poulos and changed his mind. "The fourth juror is a woman of thirty. Married, with four children, the oldest twelve."

I frowned in cogitation. "Every one of the murdered jurors was single. Alone. In other words their deaths affected no one but themselves. Is it really too much to postulate that the murderer stopped killing because his heart weakened at the prospect of murdering a woman with four minor children?" I turned to Poulos. "Do you like children?"

He thought about that. "Would it be un-American if I said not particularly?"

I cunningly questioned Poulos for another half hour, but gained nothing additional.

When we left Poulos, Ralph drove to an apartment building on the east side. We took the elevator up to the fourth floor.

I glanced at my watch. "Ralph, you said this Deirdre O'Hennessey is a secretary. However, since this is a weekday and therefore a workday, I predict you won't find her home."

"She'll be home," Ralph said. "She's still on her vacation."

Deirdre O'Hennessey had raven hair and extremely violet eyes. She regarded Ralph. "Oh, it's you again."

She let us into her apartment.

I glanced about the room, noticing that she had evidently been working on a Double-Crostic when we rang. I recognized it as one I'd completed several days before.

"Miss O'Hennessey," I said, "I understand you have absolutely no alibi for the nights on which the three jurors were murdered."

She agreed. "None. On the other hand, I doubt very much if I would have had the strength to tie a rope around anybody's neck and hoist him to the ceiling."

I smiled wisely. "We in the department have the suspicion that the hangings might have been accomplished without the need of any strength at all. Do you have a revolver? A threatening weapon of any kind?"

She nodded. "I have a crossbow in the closet. I really don't know what to do with it, but it was on sale and I just couldn't resist it."

I considered the picture. Did she point a crossbow at the quailing? . . .

Deirdre O'Hennessey sat down beside the Double-Crostic. "What is a six-letter word for any of a group of isomeric hydrocarbons of the paraffin series? The second letter has to be a 'c.' "

"Octane," I said.

She stared at me for a second and then lettered in the word. She looked up. "I have a question. Three of the four jurors who voted for Winkler's acquittal were murdered. Why not the fourth?"

"We don't know," Ralph said.

I found myself chortling.

They looked at me and Ralph said, "Henry, why are you chortling?"

"Ralph, I know who the killer is."

Ralph studied me and then nodded. "All right, Henry, who is the murderer?"

"Well, I don't actually know his name. But it all reminds me of Jack the Ripper."

Clearly I had their undivided attention.

"Why does it all remind you of Jack the Ripper?" Ralph asked.

I smiled. "Well, Jack the Ripper had a pattern too.

He murdered a number of women and then as suddenly as the killings began, they stopped. Why?"

"I give up, Henry," Ralph said. "Why?"

"No one knows for certain, Ralph. But there are a number of theories advanced—that he decided the risk was becoming too great, that he finally saw the error of his ways, that he lost interest, and so on. Anyway, to my mind, the theory which holds the most water is that the killings stopped simply because Jack the Ripper died—by natural causes, disease, accident, or whatever.

"What I am saying, Ralph, is that our killer is dead. That is why he did not murder the fourth juror. You said that six of our jurors had alibis of 'one sort or another.' " I smiled broadly. "All right, Ralph, which one of our jurors is dead?"

"None," Ralph said.

I stared out of the window for a few moments. "On the other hand, it is entirely possible that Jack the Ripper emigrated. People did a lot of emigrating in those days. Perhaps his ship was even lost at sea, which may account for the fact that there were no more Jack-the-Ripper-style murders in America, Canada, Australia, or New Zealand."

Deirdre O'Hennessey had been listening to me, obviously impressed. "Why did the murderer go through the bother of making the deaths look like suicide? Why couldn't he just kill his people and leave it at that?"

I had the answer, of course. "Because he didn't want the police interfering before his mission was completed."

I lapsed into thought for a few moments and then chortled again.

Deirdre O'Hennessey tilted her head. "Why are you chortling now?"

"It is my theory that the murderer is off his rocker. Ralph, have head X-rays been taken of our suspects?"

"No, Henry."

"Ralph, you must agree that it is a bit unusual for a

man to commit three murders for what is basically an abstract, rather than a personal, motive—that is, the desire to achieve justice. Therefore I deduce that the murderer has something wrong with his head and that this accounts for his actions. I believe X-rays are in order."

"I don't know about the legal aspects of that, Henry," Ralph said, staring at the ceiling. "It might be considered an invasion of privacy. At the very least, I think we'd have to get warrants. Why couldn't our murderer be just an ordinary run-of-the-mill psychotic?"

"You have a point there, of course," I conceded. "Or perhaps the murderer has a basal metabolism problem. Or low blood sugar. I rather think that if we X-rayed our suspects, or at least gave them a thorough physical examination, it might prove fruitful."

"What is a five-letter word for unearthly, uncanny, wild?" Deirdre asked.

I pondered. "Weird?"

She nodded. "That's it exactly."

I frowned thoughtfully. Strange. I didn't remember that particular word in the Double-Crostic.

I continued my incisive questioning of Deirdre O'Hennessey for another hour and then Ralph and I returned to headquarters.

Assistant District Attorney Orville Jepson came to our desk. "Well, did you come up with anything new on the dead jurors?"

"Nothing yet," Ralph said.

Jepson is considered to be a brilliant dedicated worker and no one has ever failed to notice his Phi Beta Kappa key.

Ralph spoke to me. "Orville handled the Winkler trial."

The memory of it darkened Jepson's brow. "The only case I ever lost. It made no sense at all. He was guilty as hell and I proved it beyond a doubt."

Ralph tried to be consoling. "Maybe Winkler managed to bribe those jurors."

Jepson shook his head. "No. Winkler was broke. The court had to appoint an attorney for him. Besides, even if he managed to get to the jury, all he needed was to bribe one person. Not four." Jepson glowered. "I just had a stinking jury. No wonder people have no respect for our judicial system. As far as I'm concerned, letting a murderer off is tantamount to being an accessory to the act—or anything that follows."

I nodded. "You mean Benninger's death?"

He corrected me. "Bellinger. Edward Slocum Bellinger."

Something clicked in my mind. "You remember his middle name?"

"Of course," Jepson said. "I have a good memory for names."

I studied Jepson and then smiled thinly. "Let me paint a portrait of our murderer. First of all, he is a perfectionist. He is also extremely brilliant. He must be perfect in everything he undertakes. He cannot endure defeat—even one defeat. And what is more, he believes fiercely in justice. The guilty must be punished. And if this can't be done legally, it must be done extra-legally."

Jepson cocked his head. "Brilliant, you say?"

"Of course. A twisted brilliant mind. He feels that if the guilty are not punished, it is a failure on his part and he must make amends. Now, sir, where were you on the night of—"

Ralph sat up quickly. "How did you like Hong Kong, Orville?"

Jepson brightened. "It was great. We all had a swell time."

Ralph turned to me. "Henry, you *do* remember that Orville took a vacation trip to the Orient with his wife and family. Hong Kong, Honolulu, Manila. The works. And they were gone *all* of April."

By George, he was right.

Jepson nodded. "We didn't get back until the beginning of May. Just in time for the funeral."

"Funeral?" I said. "What funeral?"

"Judge Remsford's funeral. He presided at the Winkler trial. Took the hung jury rather hard too, as I remember. His face got quite livid and he had a few choice words for the jury before he dismissed it." Jepson sighed. "The judge was a fine man. Cut down in the prime of his life, you might say."

"Cut down?"

"Yes. Terminal disease. Began acting a bit erratic. His wife finally took him to a doctor. X-rays showed that it was inoperable. Died on the first or second of May." Jepson reflected on the death. "Yes, a fine man. Wilbur Cross Remsford."

Wilbur *Cross* Remsford?

"Left a wife and three children," Jepson said. He patted Ralph on the shoulder. "Well, keep at it. Let me know if you come up with anything new."

Ralph and I were silent after he left.

Finally Ralph cleared his throat. "Henry, I have the feeling that if we looked in Remsford's garage or basement we'd find a certain coil of rope."

I agreed.

Neither one of us made a move to rise.

"On the other hand," I said, "what would be the point of it all? Remsford is dead. He can't be punished. The only ones to suffer if this came out into the open would be his family."

Ralph and I came to an agreement. The case was officially closed.

Our phone rang and Ralph picked it up. He listened and then turned to me. "She wants to know what's a South African eleven-letter word for a tall acacia on which the giraffe often browses."

That *had* been a difficult one. I smiled. "Kameeldoorn. Literally meaning camel thorn."

Ralph turned back to the phone. "He can't think of the word right now, but he'll have it tonight when he drops in at about seven thirty. By the way, the only thing he drinks is sherry." Ralph hung up.

"Now, Ralph," I said, "why did you tell her I'd be over?"

"Henry," Ralph said, "she didn't go through the jungle of our headquarters switchboard just so that she could find out what some giraffe—" He stopped and smiled. "Henry, we just can't have her calling day and night and disrupting the department. You go over there tonight and give her all the words you've got."

Deirdre had a bottle of sherry waiting when I arrived that evening.

The Ehrengraf Presumption

Lawrence Block

"Now let me get this straight," Alvin Gort said. "You actually accept criminal cases on a contingency basis. Even homicide cases."

"Especially homicide cases."

"If your client is acquitted he pays your fee. If he's found guilty, then your efforts on his behalf cost him nothing whatsoever. Except expenses, I assume."

"That's very nearly true," Martin Ehrengraf said. The little lawyer supplied a smile which blossomed briefly on his thin lips while leaving his eyes quite uninvolved. "Shall I explain in detail?"

"By all means."

"To take your last point first, I pay my own expenses and furnish no accounting of them to my client. My fees are thus all-inclusive. By the same token, should a client of mine be convicted he would owe me nothing. I would absorb such expenses as might incur acting on his behalf."

"That's remarkable."

"It's surely unusual, if not unique. Now the rest of what you've said is essentially true. It's not uncommon for attorneys to take on negligence cases on a contingency basis, participating handsomely in the settlement when they win, sharing their clients' losses when they do not. The principle has always made eminent good sense to me. Why shouldn't a client give substantial value for value received? Why should he be simply charged for service whether or not the service does him any good? When I pay out money, Mr. Gort, I like to get what I pay for. And I don't mind paying for what I get."

"It certainly makes sense to me," Alvin Gort said. He dug a cigarette from the pack in his shirt pocket, scratched a match, drew smoke into his lungs. This was his first experience in a jail cell and he'd been quite surprised to learn that he was allowed to have matches on his person, to wear his own clothes rather than prison garb, to keep money in his pocket and a watch on his wrist.

No doubt all this would change if he were convicted of murdering his wife. Then he'd be in an actual prison and the rules would most likely be more severe. Here they had taken his belt as a precaution against suicide, and they would have taken the laces from his shoes had he not been wearing loafers at the time of his arrest. But it could have been worse.

And unless Martin Ehrengraf pulled off a small miracle, it would be worse.

"Sometimes my clients never see the inside of a courtroom," Ehrengraf was saying now. "I'm always happiest when I can save my clients not merely from prison but from going to trial in the first place. So you should understand that whether or not I collect my fee hinges on your fate, on the disposition of your case—and not on how much work I put in or how much time it takes me to liberate you. In other words, from the moment you retain me I have an interest in your future, and the moment you are released and all charges dropped, my fee becomes due and payable in full."

"And your fee will be—?"

"One hundred thousand dollars," Ehrengraf said crisply.

Alvin Gort considered the sum, then nodded thoughtfully. It was not difficult to believe that the diminutive attorney commanded and received large fees. Alvin Gort recognized good clothing when he saw it, and the clothing Martin Ehrengraf wore was good indeed. The man was well turned out. His suit, a bronze sharkskin number with a nipped-in waist, was clearly not off the rack. His brown wing-tip shoes had been polished to a high gloss. His tie, a rich teak in hue with an unobtrusive below-the-knot design, bore the reasonably discreet trademark of a genuine countess. And his hair had received the attention of a good barber while his neatly trimmed mustache served as a focal point for a face otherwise devoid of any single dominating feature. The overall impression thus created was one of a man who could announce a six-figure fee and make you feel that such a sum was altogether fitting and proper.

"I'm reasonably well off," Gort said.

"I know. It's a commendable quality in clients."

"And I'd certainly be glad to pay one hundred thousand dollars for my freedom. On the other hand, if you don't get me off then I don't owe you a dime. Is that right?"

"Quite right."

Gort considered again, nodded again. "Then I've got no reservations," he said. "But—"

"Yes?"

Alvin Gort's eyes measured the lawyer. Gort was accustomed to making rapid decisions. He made one now.

"*You* might have reservations," he said. "There's one problem."

"Oh?"

"I did it," Gort said. "I killed her."

"I can see how you would think that," Martin Ehrengraf said. "The weight of circumstantial evidence piled up against you. Long-suppressed unconscious resentment of your wife, perhaps even a hidden desire to see her dead. All manner of guilt feelings stored up since early childhood. Plus, of course, the natural idea that things do not happen without a good reason for their occurrence. You are in prison, charged with murder; therefore it stands to reason that you did something to deserve all this, that you did in fact murder your wife."

"But I did," Gort said.

"Nonsense. Palpable nonsense."

"But I was there," Gort said. "I'm not making this up. For God's sake, man, I'm not a psychiatric basket case. Unless you're thinking about an insanity defense? I suppose I could go along with that, scream out hysterically in the middle of the night, strip naked and sit gibbering in the corner of my cell. I can't say I'd enjoy it but I'll go along with it if you think that's the answer. But—"

"Don't be ridiculous," Ehrengraf said, wrinkling his nose with distaste. "I mean to get you acquitted, Mr. Gort. Not committed to an asylum."

"I don't understand," Gort said. He frowned, looked around craftily. "You think the place is bugged," he whispered. "That's it, eh?"

"You can use your normal tone of voice. No, they don't employ hidden microphones in this jail. It's not only illegal but against policy as well."

"Then I don't understand. Look, I'm the guy who fastened the dynamite under the hood of Ginnie's Pontiac. I hooked up a cable to the starter. I set things up so that she would be blown into the next world. Now how do you propose to—"

"Mr. Gort." Ehrengraf held up a hand like a stop sign. "Please, Mr. Gort."

Alvin Gort subsided.

"Mr. Gort," Ehrengraf continued, "I defend the innocent and leave it to more clever men than myself to employ trickery in the cause of the guilty. And I find this very easy to do because all my clients are innocent. There is, you know, a legal principle involved."

"A legal principle?"

"The presumption of innocence."

"The presumption of—? Oh, you mean a man is presumed innocent until proven guilty."

"A tenet of Anglo-Saxon jurisprudence," Ehrengraf

said. "The French presume guilt until innocence is proven. And the totalitarian countries, of course, presume guilt and do not *allow* innocence to be proved, taking it for granted that their police would not dream of wasting their time arresting the innocent in the first place. But I refer, Mr. Gort, to something more far-reaching than the legal presumption of innocence." Ehrengraf drew himself up to his full height, such as it was, and his back went ramrod-straight. "I refer," he said, "to the Ehrengraf Presumption."

"The Ehrengraf Presumption?"

"Any client of Martin H. Ehrengraf," said Martin Ehrengraf, "is presumed by Ehrengraf to be innocent, which presumption is invariably confirmed in due course, the preconceptions of the client himself notwithstanding." The little lawyer smiled with his lips. "Now," he said, "shall we get down to business?"

Half an hour later Alvin Gort was still sitting on the edge of his cot. Martin Ehrengraf, however, was pacing briskly in the manner of a caged lion. With the thumb and forefinger of his right hand he smoothed the ends of his neat mustache. His left hand was at his side, its thumb hooked into his trouser pocket. He continued to pace while Gort smoked a cigarette almost to the filter. Then, as Gort ground the butt under his heel, Ehrengraf turned on his own heel and fixed his eyes on his client.

"The evidence is damning," he conceded. "A man of your description purchased dynamite and blasting caps from Tattersall Demolition Supply just ten days before your wife's death. Your signature is on the purchase order. A clerk remembers waiting on you and reports that you were nervous."

"Damn right I was nervous," Gort said. "I never killed anyone before."

"Please, Mr. Gort. If you must maintain the facade of having committed murder, at least keep your illusion to yourself. Don't share it with me. At the mo-

ment I'm concerned with evidence. We have your
signature on the purchase order and we have you identified by the clerk. The man even remembers what you
were wearing. Most customers come to Tattersall in
work clothes, it would seem, while you wore a rather
distinctive burgundy blazer and white flannel slacks.
And tasseled loafers," he added, clearly not approving
of them.

"It's hard to find casual loafers without tassels or
braid these days."

"Hard, yes. But scarcely impossible. Now you say
your wife had a lover—a Mr. Barry Lattimore."

"That toad Lattimore!"

"You knew of this affair and disapproved."

"Disapproved! I hated them. I wanted to strangle
both of them. I wanted—"

"*Please,* Mr. Gort."

"I'm sorry."

Ehrengraf sighed. "Now your wife seems to have
written a letter to her sister in New Mexico. She did in
fact have a sister in New Mexico?"

"Her sister Grace. In Socorro."

"She posted the letter four days before her death. In
it she stated that you knew about her affair with
Lattimore."

"I'd known for weeks."

"She went on to say that she feared for her life. 'The
situation is deteriorating and I don't know what to do.
You know what a temper he has. I'm afraid he might
be capable of anything, anything at all. I'm defenseless
and I don't know what to do.' "

"Defenseless as a cobra," Gort muttered.

"No doubt. That was from memory but it's a fair
approximation. Of course I'll have to examine the original. And I'll want specimens of your wife's handwriting."

"You can't think the letter's a forgery?"

"We never know, do we? But I'm sure you can tell
me where I can get hold of samples. Now what other

evidence do we have to contend with? There was a neighbor who saw you doing something under the hood of your wife's car some four or five hours before her death."

"Mrs. Boerland. Damned old crone. Vicious gossiping busybody."

"You seem to have been in the garage shortly before dawn. You had a light on and the garage door was open, and you had the hood of the car up and were doing something."

"Damned right I was doing something. I was—"

"Please, Mr. Gort. Between tasseled loafers and these constant interjections—"

"Won't happen again, Mr. Ehrengraf."

"Yes. Now just let me see. There were two cars in the garage, were there not? Your Buick and your wife's Pontiac. Your car was parked on the left-hand side, your wife's on the right."

"That was so that she could back straight out. When you're parked on the left side you have to back out in a sort of squiggly way. When Ginnie tried to do that she always ran over a corner of the lawn."

"Ah."

"Some people just don't give a damn about a lawn," Gort said, "and some people do."

"As with so many aspects of human endeavor, Mr. Gort. Now Mrs. Boerland observed you in the garage shortly before dawn, and the actual explosion which claimed your wife's life took place a few hours later while you were having breakfast."

"Toasted English muffin and coffee. Years ago Ginnie made scrambled eggs and squeezed fresh orange juice for me. But with the passage of time—"

"Did she normally start her car at that hour?"

"No," Gort said. He sat up straight, frowned. "No, of course not. Dammit, why didn't *I* think of that? I figured she'd sit around the house until noon. I wanted to be well away from the place when it happened—"

"Mr. Gort."

"Well, I did. And all of a sudden there was this shock wave and a thunderclap right on top of it and I'll tell you, Mr. Ehrengraf, I didn't even know what it was."

"Of course you didn't."

"I mean—"

"I wonder why your wife left the house at that hour. She said nothing to you?"

"No. There was a phone call and—"

"From whom?"

Gort frowned again. "Damned if I know. But she got the call just before she left. I wonder if there's a connection."

"I shouldn't doubt it." Ehrengraf continued to probe, then he asked who inherited Virginia Gort's money.

"Money?" Gort grinned. "Ginnie didn't have a dime. I was her legal heir just as she was mine, but I was the one who had the money. All she left was the jewelry and clothing that my money paid for."

"Any insurance?"

"Exactly enough to pay your fee," Gort said, and grinned this time rather like a shark. "Except that I won't see a penny of it. Fifty thousand dollars, double indemnity for accidental death, and I think the insurance companies call murder an accident, although it's always struck me as rather purposeful. That makes one hundred thousand dollars, your fee to the penny, but none of it'll come my way."

"It's true that one cannot profit financially from a crime," Ehrengraf said. "But if you're found innocent—"

Gort shook his head. "Doesn't make any difference," he said. "I just learned this the other day. About the same time I was buying the dynamite, she was changing her beneficiary. The change went through in plenty of time. The whole hundred thousand goes to that rotter Lattimore."

"Now that," said Martin Ehrengraf, "is very interesting. . . ."

* * *

Two weeks and three days later Alvin Gort sat in a surprisingly comfortable straight-backed chair in Martin Ehrengraf's exceptionally cluttered office. He balanced a checkbook on his knee and carefully made out a check. The fountain pen he used had cost him $65. The lawyer's services, for which the check he was writing represented payment in full, had cost him considerably more, yet Gort, a good judge of value, thought Ehrengraf's fee a bargain and the pen overpriced.

"One hundred thousand dollars," he said, waving the check in the air to dry its ink. "I've put today's date on it but I'll ask you to hold it until Monday morning before depositing it. I've instructed my broker to sell securities and transfer funds to my checking account. I don't normally maintain a balance sufficient to cover a check of this size."

"That's understandable."

"I'm glad something is. Because I'm damned if I can understand how you got me off the hook."

Ehrengraf allowed himself a smile. "My greatest obstacle was your own mental attitude," he said. "You honestly believed yourself to be guilty of your wife's death, didn't you?"

"But—"

"Ah, my dear Mr. Gort. You see, I knew you were innocent. The Ehrengraf Presumption assured me of that. I merely had to look for someone with the right sort of motive, and who should emerge but Mr. Barry Lattimore, your wife's lover and beneficiary, a man with a need for money and a man whose affair with your wife was reaching crisis proportions.

"It was clear to me that you were not the sort of man to commit murder in such an obvious fashion. Buying the dynamite openly, signing the purchase order with your own name—my dear Mr. Gort, you would never behave so foolishly! No, you had to have been framed, and clearly Lattimore was the man who had reason to frame you."

"And then they found things," Gort said.

"Indeed they did, once I was able to tell them where to look. Extraordinary what turned up! You would think Lattimore would have had the sense to get rid of all that, wouldn't you? But no, a burgundy blazer and a pair of white slacks, a costume identical to your own but tailored to Mr. Lattimore's frame, hung in the very back of his clothes closet. And in a drawer of his desk the police found a half a dozen sheets of paper on which he'd practised your signature until he was able to do quite a creditable job of writing it. By dressing like you and signing your name to the purchase order, he quite neatly put your neck in the noose."

"Incredible."

"He even copied your tasseled loafers. The police found a pair in his closet, and of course the man never habitually wore loafers of any sort. Of course he denied ever having seen the shoes before. Or the jacket, or the slacks, and of course he denied having practised your signature."

Gort's eyes went involuntarily to Ehrengraf's own shoes. This time the lawyer was wearing black wing tips. His suit was dove-gray and somewhat more sedately tailored than the brown one Gort had seen previously. His tie was maroon, his cuff links simple gold hexagons. The precision of Ehrengraf's dress and carriage contrasted sharply with the disarray of his office.

"And that letter from your wife to her sister Grace," Ehrengraf continued. "It turned out to be authentic, as it happens, but it also proved to be open to a second interpretation. The man of whom Virginia was afraid was never named, and a thoughtful reading showed he could as easily have been Lattimore as you. And then of course a second letter to Grace was found among your wife's effects. She evidently wrote it the night before her death and never had a chance to mail it. It's positively damning. She tells her sister how she changed the beneficiary of her insurance at Lattimore's insistence, how your knowledge of the affair was making Lattimore irrational and dangerous, and how she couldn't avoid the feeling that he planned to kill her. She goes on to say that she intended to change her insurance again, making Grace the beneficiary, and that she would so inform Lattimore in order to remove any financial motive for her murder.

"But even as she was writing those lines, he was preparing to put the dynamite in her car."

Ehrengraf went on explaining and Gort could only stare at him in wonder. Was it possible that his own memory could have departed so utterly from reality? Had the twin shocks of Ginnie's death and of arrest have caused him to fabricate a whole set of false memories?

Damn it, he *remembered* buying that dynamite! He *remembered* wiring it under the hood of her Pontiac! So how on earth—

The Ehrengraf Presumption, he thought. If Ehrengraf could presume Gort's innocence the way he did, why couldn't Gort presume his own innocence? Why not give himself the benefit of the doubt?

Because the alternative was terrifying. The letter, the practise sheets of his signature, the shoes and slacks and burgundy blazer—

"Mr. Gort? Are you all right?"

"I'm fine," Gort said.

"You looked pale for a moment. The strain, no doubt. Will you take a glass of water?"

"No, I don't think so." Gort lit a cigarette, inhaled deeply. "I'm fine," he said. "I feel good about everything. You know, not only am I in the clear but ultimately I don't think your fee will cost me anything."

"Oh?"

"Not if that rotter killed her. Lattimore can't profit from a murder he committed. And while she may have intended to make Grace her beneficiary, her unfulfilled intent has no legal weight. So her estate becomes the beneficiary of the insurance policy, and she never did get around to changing her will, so that means the money will wind up in my hands. Amazing, isn't it?"

"Amazing." The little lawyer rubbed his hands together more briskly. "But you do know what they say about unhatched chickens, Mr. Gort. Mr. Lattimore hasn't been convicted of anything yet."

"You think he's got a chance of getting off?"

"That would depend," said Martin Ehrengraf, "on his choice of attorney."

This time Ehrengraf's suit was navy blue with a barely perceptible stripe in a lighter blue. His shirt, as usual, was white. His shoes were black loafers—no tassels or braid—and his tie had a half-inch stripe of royal blue flanked by two narrower stripes, one of gold and the other of a rather bright green, all on a navy field. The necktie was that of the Caedmon Society of Oxford University, an organization of which Mr. Ehrengraf was not a member. The tie was a souvenir of another case and the lawyer wore it now and then on especially auspicious occasions.

Such as this visit to the cell of Barry Pierce Lattimore.

"I'm innocent," Lattimore said. "But it's gotten to the point where I don't expect anyone to believe me. There's so much evidence against me."

"Circumstantial evidence."

"Yes, but that's often enough to hang a man, isn't it?" Lattimore winced at the thought. "I loved Ginnie. I wanted to marry her. I never even thought of killing her."

"I believe you."

"You do?"

Ehrengraf nodded solemnly. "Indeed I do," he said. "Otherwise I wouldn't be here. I only collect fees when I get results, Mr. Lattimore. If I can't get you acquitted of all charges, then I won't take a penny for my trouble."

"That's unusual, isn't it?"

"It is."

"My own lawyer thinks I'm crazy to hire you. He had several criminal lawyers he was prepared to recommend. But I know a little about you. I know you get results. And since I *am* innocent, I feel I want to be represented by someone with a vested interest in getting me free."

"Of course my fees are high, Mr. Lattimore."

"Well, there's a problem, I'm not a rich man."

"You're the beneficiary of a hundred-thousand-dollar insurance policy."

"But I can't collect that money."

"You can if you're found innocent."

"Oh," Lattimore said. "Oh."

"And otherwise you'll owe me nothing."

"Then I can't lose, can I?"

"So it would seem," Ehrengraf said. "Now shall we begin? It's quite clear you were framed, Mr. Lattimore. That blazer and those trousers did not find their way to your closet on their own accord. Those shoes did not walk in by themselves. The two letters to Mrs. Gort's sister, one mailed and one unmailed, must have been part of the scheme. Someone constructed an elaborate frameup, Mr. Lattimore, with the object of implicating first Mr. Gort and then yourself. Now let's determine who would have a motive."

"Gort," said Lattimore.

"I think not."

"Who else? He had a reason to kill her. And he hated me, so who would have more reason to—"

"Mr. Lattimore, I'm afraid that's not a possibility. You see, Mr. Gort was a client of mine."

"Oh. Yes, I forgot."

"And I'm personally convinced of his innocence."

"I see."

"Just as I'm convinced of yours."

"I see."

"Now who else would have a motive? Was Mrs. Gort

emotionally involved with anyone else? Did she have another lover? Had she had any other lovers before you came into the picture? And how about Mr. Gort? A former mistress who might have had a grudge against both him and his wife? Hmmm?" Ehrengraf smoothed the ends of his mustache. "Or, perhaps, just perhaps, there was an elaborate plot hatched by *Mrs. Gort.*"

"Ginnie?"

"It's not impossible. I'm afraid I reject the possibility of suicide. It's always tempting but in this instance I fear it just won't wash. But let's suppose, let's merely suppose, that Mrs. Gort decided to murder her husband to implicate you."

"Why would she do that?"

"I've no idea. But suppose she did, and suppose she intended to get her husband to drive her car and arranged the dynamite accordingly, and then when she left the house so hurriedly she forgot what she'd done, and of course the moment she turned the key in the ignition it all came back to her in a rather dramatic way."

"But I can't believe—"

"Oh, Mr. Lattimore, we believe what it pleases us to believe, don't you agree? The important thing is to recognize that you are innocent and to act on that recognition."

"But how can you be absolutely certain of my innocence?"

Martin Ehrengraf permitted himself a smile. "Mr. Lattimore," he said, "let me tell you about a principle of mine. I call it the Ehrengraf Presumption."